'I believe I as... lord.'

For answer Salter... chair and looked in...

'Will you ask your servant to put me out?' he enquired.

In spite of her annoyance Aurelia found it hard to keep her countenance. The thought of frail old Jacob attempting to manhandle this provoking brute had its comic side. She strove for a severe expression, but her dancing eyes gave her away.

'Quite!' His Lordship murmured.

After living in southern Spain for many years, **Meg Alexander** now lives in Kent, although, having been born in Lancashire, she feels that her roots are in the north of England. Meg's career has encompassed a wide variety of roles, from professional cook to assistant director of a conference centre. She has always been a voracious reader, and loves to write. Other loves include history, cats, gardening, cooking and travel. She has a son and two grandchildren.

THE LAST ENCHANTMENT

Meg Alexander

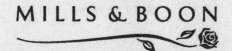

MILLS & BOON

MILLS & BOON LIMITED
ETON HOUSE, 18–24 PARADISE ROAD
RICHMOND, SURREY, TW9 1SR

*MILLS & BOON, the Rose Device and LEGACY OF LOVE
are trademarks of the publisher.*

*First published in Great Britain 1995
by Mills & Boon Limited*

© Meg Alexander 1995

*Australian copyright 1995   Philippine copyright 1995
This edition 1995*

ISBN 0 263 79026 6

*Set in 10 on 12 pt Linotron Times
04-9504-80981*

*Typeset in Great Britain by Centracet, Cambridge
Printed in Great Britain by
BPC Paperbacks Ltd*

CHAPTER ONE

AURELIA was about to ring for candles when she heard the sound of carriage wheels. She looked up in surprise. Only the most foolhardy of travellers would venture on to the marshes in growing darkness. Whoever it was must have an urgent reason for their visit.

An emergency in the village? No, it could not be that. The messenger would have come on horseback, or on foot. It was doubtless a case of lost direction. Jacob would deal with it. She hesitated for only a moment. Then, with a sigh, she replaced the stoppers on the bottles in the still-room. Courtesy dictated that she should offer hospitality in that isolated spot. The batch of simples must wait. She rinsed her hands, smoothed her hair, and made her way to the Great Hall.

Her eyes widened as a small figure hurried towards her.

'Caro. . .my dear! I had not expected you. . .of all people.' Aurelia looked into a pair of swimming eyes.

Caroline launched herself into her aunt's arms. 'I've run away,' she sobbed. 'Please let me stay. I've nowhere else to go.'

Aurelia laid a soothing hand on the blonde head.

'You are chilled to the bone, my love.' She led the trembling girl towards the fire. 'Now, Caro, do compose yourself. Tell me what has happened.'

'They shall not drag me back. I'd rather die.' The

dramatic announcement preceded a fresh outburst of tears.

'Few things are worth dying for,' Aurelia observed drily. 'Suppose you begin at the beginning. . .'

Caroline was beyond such reasonable advice.

'I won't marry him! I won't! I don't care how deep Frederick is in debt. They shall not make me. . .'

'And who is it that you have refused to marry?' Aurelia realised that she would come at the gist of it only by a series of questions.

'Salterne, of course. He's old, and ugly, and I cannot bear him.'

Aurelia tried to hide her surprise. The Duke of Salterne was well-known, at least by reputation. Since he was a friend of the Prince Regent, and one of the wealthiest peers in England, it seemed unlikely, to say the least, that he had offered for a penniless and unsophisticated child like Caroline.

'Perhaps you are mistaken,' she suggested cautiously. 'Has he made his intentions clear?'

'It's all arranged.' The girl's voice was bitter. 'Father was only too happy to agree.'

'And your mother?' Aurelia spoke without much hope. If Ransome had made the bargain her sister would not dispute his wishes.

'She says. . .she says that I have no choice. Father's pockets are to let, and Frederick is in the hands of the money-lenders. If I don't marry Salterne he'll go to a debtor's prison.'

Caroline sank into a chair and began to sob as if her heart would break.

Aurelia flushed with anger. She had never liked her nephew, or his worthless father. She had never understood why her brilliant elder sister had married such a wastrel. Ransome was as handsome as Lucifer, but his wife had paid a heavy price for her infatuation. Her fortune had disappeared before her son was ten.

Aurelia had come to the rescue on more than one occasion, but last time she'd vowed that it must stop before her own inheritance went the way of Cassie's.

She turned her attention to the wilting figure of her niece.

'How did you come here, Caro? You did not drive alone from Surrey?'

'Richard brought me.' Caroline turned as a young man moved out of the shadows. His bow was graceful, but he was obviously ill at ease.

'What is the meaning of this?' Aurelia said stiffly. 'Do you make a habit of escorting young ladies about the countryside without the knowledge of their parents?'

The young man coloured, but he stood his ground. Before he could speak Caroline rushed towards him and took his hand.

'Richard loves me,' she cried. 'We hoped to marry but Father won't hear of it. Richard is a younger son. . .and his people. . .'

'Hush, Caro!' The words were gentle, but Caroline was silent as her companion spoke. 'I had not intended to intrude, ma'am, but Caroline would have me stay in case you refused to help her.'

'And if I do. . .?'

'I won't go back!' Caroline was on the verge of hysteria. She threw her arms about Richard's neck. 'Why would you not listen to me? I begged you to take me to London. We might have been married there tonight.'

Richard disengaged her gently. Then he looked at

Aurelia. 'It is true, Miss Carrington. We do love each other, but I thought it best to bring Caroline to you. She would not stay at home, you see. It seemed to be the only solution.'

Aurelia eyed him with sudden respect. 'Possibly,' she observed quietly. 'Yet you have taken a serious risk, young man. You realise that you might well be charged with abduction?'

'I wasn't abducted.' Caroline's face grew sullen. 'I should have run away whether Richard came with me or not. I told him so.'

'That was ill done of you, my dear. You have placed your friend in a dangerous position, though he has shown good sense in bringing you to me.' Aurelia turned to Richard. 'I suggest, sir, that you return home at once, before your absence is remarked.'

'No, no! Richard, you cannot leave me!' It was a wail of despair, which died away at the sight of Aurelia's expression.

'Caroline, you impress neither of us with your grasp of the situation. Please try not to make matters worse. Would you prefer to see your friend in the hands of the magistrates. . .?'

'No one knows we are here,' came the sulky reply.

'Someone does. . .or so it would appear. . .' Aurelia's quick ear had caught the sound of a horseman riding at full gallop. She walked over to the window. 'Our visitor has been travelling hard.'

Caroline ran to her side and gave a shriek of terror.

'It is Salterne! Richard, we must leave at once!'

'You will do no such thing! I will see the Duke. Now quickly, go upstairs to my sitting-room. You must stay out of sight until the Duke has gone. . .both of you.'

'You will not—you will not make me speak to him?' Caroline quavered. 'I do not wish to see him; indeed I could not bear it.'

'There will be no need for you to do so. Now please obey me.' Aurelia walked swiftly across the hall. 'I will see His Lordship in the library, Jacob.'

Richard Collinge hesitated, a mutinous look upon his face.

'I should prefer to face him, Miss Carrington.'

'And I prefer that you should not. Where is your common sense, young man? Think of Caroline's reputation.' She paused only to watch them hurry up the stairs, then she entered the library and closed the door behind her.

A moment later it was thrown open with a crash. Jacob was thrust aside as a giant of a man strode into the room. He was bespattered to the thighs in mud, and his face was dark with rage.

Aurelia's courage almost failed her. As the Duke towered above her chair his presence seemed to fill the room. The well-cut riding coat and breeches served only to emphasise his massive chest and heavily muscled limbs, but it was his face which held her.

A long scar bisected his forehead, only partially hidden by a mass of black hair, trained in the fashionable 'Brutus' cut. It curved along his cheek, only faintly paler than the deeply tanned skin, and almost reached the corner of his mouth. As a pair of cold grey eyes stared into her own she made a conscious effort not to show her repugnance.

'A shock to you, ma'am? Don't trouble to deny it.' The full lips twisted in a sneer.

Aurelia coloured. 'I beg your pardon. I did not mean to. . .'

'To show your disgust? Spare me your apologies. I'm used to the effect of this pretty sight on impressionable females.'

Aurelia's temper flared. 'It might be less unpleasant, sir, if it were accompanied by good manners. I do not know you, yet you enter my home unannounced, treat my servant roughly, and use me with scant courtesy. You will try for some conduct, if you please.'

'Don't trifle with me, ma'am.' He took a step towards her. 'You know who I am. That chit must have left you in no doubt——'

'You cannot be referring to my niece.' Aurelia's tone was icy. 'I see now why your suit has prospered. Such charm, Your Grace! It cannot fail to win all hearts.'

He stared at her. The sharp set-down appeared to have robbed him of speech. His brows came together in a frown.

'Since you will have it, then, let us preserve the amenities. Allow me to introduce myself. My name is Salterne. I take it that I am addressing Miss Carrington?'

Aurelia inclined her head.

'Your servant, ma'am!'

'Now that I should never have guessed,' Aurelia murmured.

In spite of herself her lips twitched, and he looked at her suspiciously.

'You will not insult my intelligence by attempting to deny that your niece is here,' he continued. 'I must see her at once.'

Aurelia gave him her sweetest smile. 'That will not be possible, Your Grace. My niece is exhausted and has retired to her room.'

A muscle twitched in his jaw.

'Yet I will see her.' His voice was soft with menace. 'Together with her paramour.'

Aurelia stiffened. 'You will not attempt to browbeat me, if you please. You have had your answer, sir. I think you had best leave.'

'Really?' He bent down until his face was close to hers. 'Madam, I have been on the road all day. I have not come so far to find myself denied.'

Aurelia yawned and reached out for the bell. 'I find your energy fatiguing, my lord. Will you sit down? Some refreshment, perhaps?'

He laughed then, and it was not a pleasant sound

'This is not a social call, Miss Carrington.' He did, however, spare a glance for his muddy boots and breeches.

'Then we shall not stand on ceremony. Pray do not trouble yourself about the mud. My nephews were used to romp about with no care for the furniture.'

His eyes glinted. 'A set-down, ma'am? You would seem to be mistress of the art.' He strolled over to the fire and rested an arm on the mantelshelf. Aurelia raised an eyebrow in pointed disapproval of his lack of courtesy, but she did not speak until Jacob entered the room.

'Canary wine, Your Grace, or a glass of orgeat?' She ignored Jacob's startled glance as she waited for the reply.

'Nothing, I thank you.' The Duke was well aware that he had been offered refreshment more suitable to feminine tastes, but his face was impassive.

'You know my errand, Miss Carrington. Your niece disappeared early this morning. I undertook to come in search of her.'

'That surely must be her father's part.'

'Ransome was—er—not available, ma'am.' For the first time His Lordship appeared to be nonplussed. 'I understand him to be in London. As Lady Ransome was so distressed, I undertook to come in search of Caroline.'

'Very noble of you,' Aurelia murmured smoothly.

The Duke's face darkened with anger. 'Her Ladyship felt that time was of the essence. It was— ah—necessary that she be found before nightfall.'

'I agree.' Aurelia gave him a limpid look. 'So dangerous for a young girl to travel in the dark. Thieves. . .footpads. . .so many hazards. . .'

'And one above all, Miss Carrington.'

'What can you mean?'

He gave her a mirthless smile. 'A good try, ma'am, but it will not serve. Your niece was not alone. She was without the means to pay for a seat on the stage, or to find lodgings. She must have had help. Her mother suspects——'

'My sister had always a vivid imagination,' Aurelia assured him. 'You may set your mind at rest, Your Grace. Caroline is quite unharmed. She arrived here not an hour ago. It was wrong of her to run off in a pet, but her mother had promised that she should visit me, and the young are so hasty. . .you must recall. . .'

'In the distant past, naturally.' Salterne glared at her. He was quieter now, and infinitely more danger-ous. 'Would you care to explain how she found it possible to come so far alone?'

'Perhaps she is more resourceful than we suspected.'

'A family trait, no doubt.' He did not believe her for a moment, but he could hardly accuse her of lying. 'May I see her?'

'I think not. I prefer that she should rest.'

'Then I will wait.' Salterne had recovered his self-possession, but his face was grim.

'I believe I asked you to leave, my lord.'

For answer he threw himself into a chair and looked into her eyes.

'Will you ask your servant to put me out?' he enquired.

In spite of her annoyance Aurelia found it hard to keep her countenance. The thought of frail old Jacob attempting to manhandle this provoking brute had its comic side. She strove for a severe expression, but her dancing eyes gave her away.

'Quite!' His Lordship murmured. 'You know, of course, that I have asked Caroline's father for her hand, and that he has agreed to the match?'

'And Caroline herself? What has she to say?'

'She is young.' The lines on the sombre face might have been etched in stone. 'She has not yet had time to weigh the advantages. I can give her all that a woman could want.'

'Then she is fortunate indeed.' The sarcasm was unmistakable, and a dark flush stained the Duke's face.

'Forgive me, ma'am, if I am at pains to point out that the matter is no concern of yours. Caroline must be guided by her parents.'

'You are mistaken, Your Grace. The welfare of my niece concerns me deeply. I intend to speak to my sister and her husband. . .'

'I see. May I know your objections?'

'Need you ask?' Aurelia was incensed by his peremptory warning not to interfere. 'Your age, your reputation. . . Do you wish me to go on?'

His Grace swung a booted leg in contemplation. 'Your brother-in-law sees no obstacle to our marriage.'

'He would not!' The hot blood rushed to Aurelia's cheeks. 'His own reputation is such that. . .' She caught herself up and averted her head. A long silence fell between them.

'Then if you will summon your niece, ma'am,' he said at last, 'I will take her home.'

'I have already told you——'

'I know what you told me, Miss Carrington, but I must insist. I was charged by your sister to bring Caroline back. Please don't try to gammon me further. I was not born yesterday.'

Aurelia was tempted to retort that so much was evident, but she controlled her temper with an effort.

'I could not permit it,' she announced. 'I have only your word on this betrothal, and it would be quite unseemly for my niece to travel unchaperoned with a. . .*gentleman*.' She stressed the word deliberately and was happy to see his lips tighten. 'It is out of the question. You came on horseback, did you not? How do you propose to convey her back again?'

'Perhaps by the carriage in which she arrived?' The hard grey eyes held her own, and the Duke gave an ironic laugh. 'I followed them, you see. They were not difficult to trace.'

Aurelia eyed him with acute dislike. She opened her mouth to speak, but there seemed little point in arguing further. He had known her to be lying from the first. Her face flamed.

She was saved from further humiliation by a disturbance in the hall. Then the door opened and her sister swept into the room.

'Caro is here?' Cassandra Ransome's face was ashen, and her eyes were bright with unshed tears.

'Of course she's here, Cass. Where else would she go?' Aurelia vented her irritation sharply.

'Thank heavens!' Cassie sank into a chair. 'Then we've found her in time.' She looked at her prospective son-in-law. 'Salterne, what can I say?'

'The less said the better, I should think!' Aurelia's voice was tart. 'You seem to have some wild idea that Caro was eloping. If so, why would she come to me? You didn't really believe it, did you, Cass? Otherwise you would have made for London.'

Cassandra looked bewildered.

'This was the first place I thought of. . .'

'Of course it was. You had promised her a visit. I am surprised at you.' Aurelia was careful to avoid the Duke's penetrating glance.

'We appear to have drawn the wrong conclusions, madam.' His ironic tone caught Aurelia on the raw. 'I beg your pardon for this intrusion. Now that I know my bride-to-be is safe I will take my leave of you. Your servant, ladies.' He bowed and strode towards the door.

'Salterne, I beg of you. . .do not attempt the marshes in darkness. It is suicide. Aurelia will tell you. . .' Cassie's face puckered in dismay. 'You must stay. . .at least until morning.'

Aurelia gave her sister a speaking look. Of all things to suggest! She prayed he would refuse. The thought of dining in a country mansion with two women who were scarcely known to him would doubtless promise intolerable boredom. She gave him a limpid smile.

'Much as I should wish to offer hospitality, I fear

that it is not possible. It would not be correct. Three women alone in the house but for the servants. . .'

'Oh, Lia, what a goose you are! You could not believe that I travelled here alone. Frederick will act as host.'

Aurelia's spirits sank. Her nephew was no favourite of hers. On his last visit he had been ordered from the house after an unfortunate incident with one of the maids.

His Grace was enjoying her discomfiture.

'We. . .we are not prepared for guests,' she said with resolution. If she could suggest that the beds were damp, and that he must dine on bread and cheese, he might prefer to risk the marshes in favour of the local inn.

The grey eyes held her own, and in them she saw determination to repay her with interest for her folly in defying him. He was under no misapprehension. He knew as well as she that she longed to see him go.

'Your concern is touching, Miss Carrington, but as a soldier I assure you that I am no stranger to—er— trying conditions, and since your invitation is so pressing I must accept it.'

'Then as a soldier we must hope that you do not find the conditions impossible,' Aurelia said sweetly. If this overbearing creature intended to indulge in a bout of verbal sparring he would find that he had met his match. Behind her she heard Cassie gasp.

'My sister likes to tease, Your Grace.' The words were accompanied by a nervous laugh. 'She keeps Marram as it was when Father was alive. . .though why I cannot imagine.'

'I do not care for mouldering ruins.' The tart reply brought a glint to the Duke's eyes, but Aurelia was undismayed. If he chose to regard the remark as a personal gibe she had not the least objection.

'Present company not excepted?' he murmured.

Cassie had turned away and was searching for a handkerchief in her reticule, so she did not see the flush which rose to her sister's cheek. Aurelia was already ashamed of her lack of hospitality, and Cassie had said nothing which was not true. The marshes were dangerous at night for all but the local men, and not only because of the nature of the land. They were a favourite haunt of smugglers, carrying goods from the coast, and strangers were seen as enemies. They might be revenue men.

But tonight of all nights. . .with Richard still in the house? She had no wish for a confrontation between the two men. She must keep them apart at all costs.

'Jacob will show you to your rooms,' she said calmly. 'If you'll excuse me I must speak to Cook.'

Cassie gave her a troubled look, but Aurelia's face was impassive as she closed the door, leaving her guests to what she was sure would be an uncomfortable conversation.

There was no time to lose. She hurried upstairs to her sitting-room, to be greeted with a barrage of questions from Caroline. Aurelia held up a hand for silence.

'The Duke is still here,' she announced. 'At your mother's request he is to stay overnight.'

'Mother is here too?' Caroline's lips quivered. 'Oh. . .! She will make me speak to him, and I cannot—I shall not. . . Aunt Lia, you promised. . .'

'Do not distress yourself,' Aurelia soothed. 'You need not come downstairs tonight. Mr Collinge, it is much too late for you to leave the house now.' She smiled at the two young people. 'If you and Caroline will dine up here. . .?'

The young man's face flushed with a mixture of pleasure and embarrassment.

'That is most kind,' he said. 'But I do not wish to be a trouble to you.'

'Then you will serve me best by doing as I say, and keeping out of sight. Jacob will put you in the west wing for the night. It is far enough away from the other rooms. Tomorrow you must leave at first light. You may take the bay mare. I have no need of her at present.'

Richard Collinge took a step towards her and bowed his thanks.

'What can I say, Miss Carrington, except to apologise for causing you this worry? I can only thank you for your patience.'

Aurelia gave him a brilliant smile.

'It is I who should thank you for your excellent good sense. I wonder if my niece has any idea how lucky she is to have such a friend? Matters might have been very different.'

She glanced at Caroline, who had the grace to blush.

'I. . . I'm sorry, Aunt,' she said uncomfortably.

'Very well. Now do not leave this room until the coast is clear. I will see you a little later.' Leaving them together, Aurelia made her way down to the kitchens.

'But what can we give them, Miss Lia?' Cook asked. 'Five extra. . .and three of them men?'

'They must take us as they find us, Bessie. There is the cold pigeon pie, which we were to have tomorrow, and the remains of yesterday's beef. And did you not make some of your excellent broth for the villagers?'

'Aye, ma'am. 'Tis as well you're always so generous to the poor. . .but for His Grace? I doubt it's fitting.'

'The Duke may think himself fortunate to be fed at all,' Aurelia said sharply. The knowledge of her own grudging invitation and Salterne's clear determination to infuriate her still rankled. Common sense returned as she saw the scandalised expression on Bessie's face.

'Do your best,' she encouraged. 'Look out the preserved goose, and the vegetables which were salted down. There is a ham, I believe, and afterwards perhaps a syllabub?'

Having given Jacob instructions as to which wines to serve, she made her way to Cassie's room, closing the door firmly behind her.

'Cassie, how could you?' she reproached. 'That hateful creature! Caro cannot possibly marry him. She's right—he's a boor.'

'He's also very rich.'

'So you will sell her to the highest bidder?' Aurelia's eyes flashed. 'You disgust me! I wish now that I had not agreed. . .'

'To give her a season? That was generous of you, Lia. Ransome could not afford it.'

'What can he afford? If he would but stop gambling, and attempted to control Frederick. . .'

'Ransome will not change. Gambling is his life, and he takes a positive pride in Frederick's debts.' Cassie patted her blonde curls as she gazed into the mirror. 'In this world, Lia, men do as they choose. Had you ever married you would know the truth of it.'

'Whom should I have chosen from that crowd of popinjays at Almack's?' Aurelia demanded. 'Better to live alone than to submit to a life of misery.'

'Your season was not a success, I know. I could not

understand it. You were always a beauty, Sister, and even now, at twenty-five. . .well, it is not too late. You are thinner, which is not so becoming to you, but your eyes and your hair are still so fine. . .'

'My appearance is not the point at issue here,' Aurelia cried impatiently. 'What are you going to do about Caroline?'

'I shall take her home, naturally. Ransome must not learn of this escapade. He would thrash her soundly.'

'A bully too?' Aurelia raised her eyebrows. 'You have had more to suffer than I thought.'

Cassie flushed. 'It's easy for you to criticise. You have all the money you are ever like to need, but since Father died you have become so hard.'

Aurelia looked at her steadily and Cassie's eyes fell.

'I'm sorry, Lia. That was ill said.' She put out a placatory hand. 'You have been more than generous to us. If you could but see your way. . .?'

'Not another penny,' Aurelia said firmly. 'My fortune shall not go the way of yours.'

'Then Caroline must marry Salterne. His pockets are deep enough. The duns will hold off when the betrothal is announced.'

Aurelia shuddered. 'When I think of him. . .his manner. . .and that scarred face. . .'

'That is unfair. The scar is not the result of a duel. He was wounded at Talavera. You of all people should sympathise. Was not our own brother killed there, and that friend of yours, Tom Elliott?'

Aurelia turned away. The pain of Tom's death was with her always, though she knew that the living must go on. Even four years later she could not bear to speak of it.

'And Salterne is not so very old,' Cassie continued. 'He is but in his late thirties. . .'

'You do not consider a man of your own age too old for Caro? I am sorry to have spoken of the scar. He cannot help his appearance, but think of his reputation, Cass, and his manner is so arrogant.'

'You saw him at his worst. He was well out of temper, and who could blame him? Do try to understand. He has had a sad time of it in recent years. His son was stillborn, and the mother died in childbed. I believe he was devoted to her. There is an older child. . .a girl. . .who is about six. . .'

'That is sad, and I feel for him, but why Caroline, Sister? With his wealth he might have chosen anyone. . .and she is but eighteen.'

'She has the family looks,' Cassie said complacently. 'It puzzled me, though, I will admit, but I could scarce ask him outright. And Ransome was so pleased that she had caught his fancy. The truth of the matter is that Salterne needs an heir, and a mother for his child. She lives with the Dowager Duchess at present, but the old lady is failing. He may have thought that Caro would be biddable, and kind to both of them.'

'Possibly. But will she be happy with him?'

'He is no worse than many another.' Cassandra walked over to the mirror. 'What a wreck I look! This gown is crushed beyond anything.' She made an ineffectual attempt to smooth her skirt. 'Will you send Hannah to me? I cannot dine in this.'

'Hannah is too busy,' came the uncompromising reply. 'Cass, promise me that you won't force Caro into marriage.'

'What can I do? Caroline must marry him, and that is an end of it.'

'She doesn't love him,' Aurelia said in a low voice.

'What has that to say to anything? I married for love, and much good it has done me.' Her voice trembled. 'I have seen what poverty can do.'

On an impulse Aurelia kissed her sister's cheek.

'Forgive me,' she said. 'You'll stay, of course? Ransome can spare you for a few days, I'm sure.'

'I doubt if he'll know we're gone.' Cassie looked uncomfortable. 'I haven't seen him for weeks.' She sighed. 'I had best see Caro, I suppose, though how she is to explain her behaviour to Salterne I cannot imagine.'

'She is distraught,' Aurelia said quickly. 'Caro is in no fit state for company. Would you have Salterne see her as she is? I should not blame him if he had second thoughts. . . I have promised that she need not join us this evening. She may dine in my sitting-room.'

Cassie looked doubtful.

'The Duke will think it odd.'

'He may speak to her tomorrow,' Aurelia cried impatiently. 'And you may scold her later if you will. Now, Cass, we must make haste. Come help me change my gown. In any case you will wish to attend to your hair. It is sadly disarranged.'

The remark was enough to divert Cassie's attention, and by the time they joined the Duke and Frederick in the Great Hall she had recovered some of her composure.

CHAPTER TWO

With punctilious courtesy the Duke advanced towards them, briefly raising Cassandra's hand to his lips. Then he turned to Aurelia. She had perforce to allow him to do the same, though she felt a curious reluctance to submit to what was, after all, the merest civility.

She glanced down at the dark head bent low before her, realising, to her annoyance, that the gesture was prolonged far beyond common politeness. Unobtrusively, she tried to draw her hand away, resenting the disturbing sensation of his lips upon her skin, and at last he released her.

As he straightened she saw the mocking amusement in his eyes. She gave him an indignant look, and the look of amusement deepened. It was a deliberate attempt to discomfit her. Aurelia looked at him coldly.

'You are quite recovered from your journey, I trust?'

Salterne bowed. 'A trying experience for a man of my advancing years, Miss Carrington, but your kind offer of hospitality has done much to restore my spirits.'

Aurelia saw the gleam in his eye, and she stiffened. If he intended to amuse himself at her expense she would teach him that two could play at that game.

She turned to her nephew.

'Well, Frederick, how do you go on? It has been some time since your last visit.' It was as clear a warning as she could give that Frederick's previous

23

misdeeds were not forgotten, and that he was to behave himself.

'So unexpected, Aunty, dear.' The young man's smile was calculating. 'My sister is not to join us?'

'Caroline is resting. You will excuse her, Your Grace.'

It was a statement rather than a question, and Salterne was aware of it.

'We must trust to your judgement, for this evening at least,' he told her smoothly.

Aurelia's look would have frozen a lesser man, but the Duke appeared to be unaware of it.

It promised to be a difficult evening, but a quick glance at the serving tables assured Aurelia that, whatever else, her guests would dine well. She was prepared to find that Salterne, accustomed to the Regent's lavish fare, might find the meal beneath his attention. She had not allowed for the appetite of a large and hungry man who had spent the day in the saddle.

He ate heartily, and with evident relish, though he drank but sparingly of the vintage wines which Jacob had produced from the cellar.

The same could not be said of Frederick. His glass needed constant replenishment, and long before the meal was ended his speech was becoming slurred. Aurelia eyed him with distaste. Unusually subdued in the Duke's presence, he had added little to the general conversation.

His Grace had all the address of a man of breeding. With the ease of an accomplished raconteur he chatted throughout the meal, ignoring Cassie's anxious glances at her son.

Aurelia's anger was growing. She signalled to Jacob

with a barely perceptible shake of her head, but when he moved away from Frederick's chair the young man stayed him and seized the bottle.

Perhaps it was all for the best, she told herself. If Salterne saw this young puppy in his cups he might think twice about the proposed betrothal. Frederick as a relative was not a pleasant prospect.

It was as Cassie was speaking of a mutual acquaintance that he interrupted his mother's conversation.

'You've some fine horseflesh in your stables, Aunt.' He gave her a knowing look. 'I can get you an offer for the mare.'

'The mare is not for sale.'

'Only trying to do you a favour,' he muttered. 'I know a fellow. . .'

'I'm sure you do, but I repeat, the mare is not for sale.'

Frederick was an expert judge of horseflesh. It was his only talent. Aurelia repressed an acid comment.

'Lia. . .you can't be keeping bloodstock?' Cassie was appalled.

'I had considered breeding. It is profitable. . .as Frederick will assure you.'

'But for a woman to do so. . .?'

'Haven't you heard of Letty Lade?' Frederick sniggered.

'I have indeed.' Cassie looked down her nose, but she made no further comment. Her son had no such reservations.

'Did you hear of her latest wager, Aunty, dear? She offered five hundred guineas to any female who would drive a four-in-hand across Newmarket Heath.'

'She had no takers, so I understand,' the Duke murmured quietly.

'I should hope not. I wonder that she lays claim to the name of female,' Cassie asserted.

Frederick gave a shout of laughter.

'She's that all right. You know where Lade found her, I suppose?'

It was common knowledge that the redoubtable Letty had enjoyed the protection of the Regent's brother, the Duke of York. Earlier she had been the mistress of Sixteen-String Jack, the highwayman. Letty had seen him hanged at Tyburn. Sir John Lade, it was rumoured, had met his future bride at her place of business, a bordello.

Aurelia attempted to change the subject, but Frederick was not to be diverted.

'When the Prince wishes to describe a particularly foul-mouthed acquaintance he says that the man can swear like Letty Lade,' he announced. As the Duke's eye rested upon him he fell silent. Salterne turned to Aurelia.

'Sir John, you must know, is a close friend of the Regent,' he said carelessly. 'Not only is he the Prince's riding tutor, he is also Master of the Royal Stables.'

Cassie was scarlet with mortification. Sir John might be as uncouth as the lowest of his grooms, but it was not for Frederick to criticise the Prince's friends, especially before a member of his inner circle.

'Sir John, I am told, is the finest whip in the country,' Aurelia said quickly.

'Indeed, ma'am. That is beyond question.' To her relief the Duke accepted the proffered olive-branch. He went on to speak of the forthcoming races at Brighton.

'Shall you attend, Miss Carrington? I think I have not seen you in the town before.'

'I was there some years ago, but recently I have had no opportunity to go.'

'Nor the desire, Your Grace, I assure you.' Cassie frowned at her sister. 'Aurelia has elected to bury herself in the country in spite of all our efforts to persuade her otherwise. I cannot understand her.'

'I have my books. . .and the garden.' Even to herself the reason for her self-imposed isolation sounded thin, but Aurelia treasured her quiet life. She could not explain this to a member of the *haut ton*, for whom the pleasures of gambling and womanising were likely to be all. And why should she attempt to justify herself to him, or to Cassie either, for that matter?

Salterne gave her a strange look.

'You find it enough, Miss Carrington? You do not yearn for balls, cards, and the pleasures of society?'

Aurelia's answer was already on her lips when Cassie gave her a warning look. His Grace would find it difficult to appreciate Aurelia's views on what he regarded as the pleasures of society.

'Life here has its benefits,' she murmured quietly.

'Your cook would appear to be one of them, ma'am. Will you give him my compliments?'

'Bessie will be happy to have pleased you, sir.' She gave him a demure look, gratified by his evident surprise.

She signalled to her sister. 'We will leave you to your wine, Your Grace.'

'Unnecessary, ladies, I assure you. May I take a turn about the grounds, Miss Carrington? I am used to walk a little before I retire.'

Aurelia bowed her assent, and bade him goodnight. She saw Cassie to her room, looked in on the sleeping figure of her niece, and hurried back to the dining-room. As she had expected Frederick was slumped across the table, the remains of a bottle at his elbow. As she approached him he raised his head.

'This is damned fine claret, Aunt. You keep a good cellar, I'll say that for you.' His face was flushed and the slurred words came with difficulty. 'Now, about the mare. . .'

'How many times must I explain? The mare is not for sale.'

'The chestnut, then? You've some useful horseflesh there.'

'Not in any circumstances.'

'Only trying to do you a favour,' he muttered.

'Spare me your lies. The only favours you are like to do are for yourself.'

He shot her a venomous glance. 'Clever Aunty,' he jeered. 'You may have gulled Salterne with your story, but I am not so easily persuaded. I know what happened today. Father will give Caro the thrashing she deserves, and she won't have a shred of reputation left when I——'

'You will hold your tongue.' Her voice was like the crack of a whip.

Frederick staggered to his feet and stumbled towards her, but Aurelia stood her ground. She was almost as tall as he.

'I should advise you to be very careful,' she said softly. 'What will you gain by spreading rumours? I do not ask you to lie to your father, but you would do well not to indulge in speculation without proof.'

'And we don't have that, do we, thanks to you?'

'What a very unpleasant creature you are.' Aurelia's voice was chilling. 'Shall I make myself clear? Salterne may own to a tarnished reputation, but he will not have it in his bride.'

Frederick was breathing heavily. He shook his head as if to clear the fumes of wine.

Aurelia pressed home her advantage. 'What will happen to you then?' she asked.

Her nephew wavered, still befuddled.

'I. . . I wasn't thinking. Excuse me, Aunt. I am somewhat disguised tonight. It is the wine. I am not used to take so much.'

'When your head is clearer, think about my words.' Aurelia rang for Jacob. 'You will see the sense of keeping silent.' She looked at Frederick for a long moment. 'It is a pity that we cannot offer you in the marriage market,' she observed. 'That would solve all your problems.'

'I ain't unwilling, Aunt.' The sly smile reappeared. 'A warm little wife would suit me well enough, if she had plenty of blunt. . . But who would take me?'

'Your name is an ancient one.' For a moment Aurelia felt a pang of pity. 'And you are a handsome boy. If you would but try. . .'

'Don't preach at me,' he snarled. 'God knows I've chased wenches enough, but their families will have none of me. Money is all that counts. . .'

Aurelia gave up a further attempt at conversation. She signed to Jacob to assist her nephew. As they left the room she sank into a chair. Her mind was deeply troubled. In just a few hours her pleasantly ordered life had been thrown into chaos. More distressing were her worries about her own part in the affair. The Duke had made it clear that she was interfering in matters which were none of her concern and there was some truth in his words, yet she had acted in good faith.

Her few evasions and straight words to Frederick might prevent a scandal which would be of benefit to no one.

Absently, she filled her glass. The wine might help her to sleep.

'May I join you, Miss Carrington?'

To her horror the Duke uncoiled himself from a long settle by the window and moved towards her.

'Oh!' she cried. 'How could you? You should have discovered yourself, Your Grace. Eavesdropping is not the act of a gentleman.'

'But one learns so much,' he protested. 'Some of it may be a trifle mortifying, but it is doubtless good for the soul.'

Aurelia rose from the table and made as if to leave him.

'No!' A firm hand closed about her wrist. 'Allow me to explain. Your nephew promised to need assistance; that is why I stayed.'

'I see.' Aurelia felt wretched as she searched her mind to recall the gist of her conversation with Frederick. 'Then you. . .you must have heard everything.'

'Your words came as no surprise,' he shrugged. 'Did you imagine that they would?'

'No, I did not,' Aurelia admitted. 'Yet had I known you were in the room I might not have been so. . . so. . .'

'Forthright?' He smiled at her then, and the harsh planes of his face were transformed. She could see something of the man he used to be. 'You are direct, at least. I do not take it amiss. I should have handled the matter much the same myself.'

'If you understand, then why. . .?' She caught herself before she committed a further indiscretion. 'I beg your pardon,' she said stiffly. 'I have no right to question your motives.'

'That is true, but I doubt if it will stop you.' He was very close and Aurelia felt unaccountably breathless. A lean forefinger slid beneath her chin, and tilted her face to his. 'Beneath that cool exterior, ma'am, I fear you are a firebrand. Take care! You may get burned. . .'

Aurelia gave him what she hoped was a downing stare.

'Threats, my lord? May I remind you that you are a guest in my home. . .?'

'I am well aware of it, and I thank you. I have much enjoyed this evening. So—er—instructive to be drawn into the bosom of my family-to-be. I shall find it difficult to tear myself away.'

Aurelia was tempted to strike him. Her face paled, and her deep blue eyes flashed fury.

'That was unworthy of you,' she cried fiercely. 'No doubt your words are justified, but they might have been left unsaid.'

'Piqued, Miss Carrington?' He was much too close, and her heart gave a curious flutter as the dark eyes continued to gaze into her own. Impatiently she struck his hand away.

'I find your manner offensive,' she said coldly. 'Your rank does not give you the right to treat me as. . .as. . .'

'As a woman?' She heard the laughter in his voice. 'But you are a woman, my dear. . .beautiful, high-spirited, and altogether irresistible.'

Aurelia sat down suddenly. For a second his sheer effrontery robbed her of all speech. This. . .this roué

was to marry her niece? She began to tremble with
rage. No woman would be safe with him. With an
effort she forced herself to look up at him, but that
glance did nothing to reassure her. A trick of the light
had thrown the scarred side of his face into shadow
and for the first time she was aware of the clean lines
of his jaw, the strong column of his throat, and the
beautifully moulded lips.

Her eyes lingered on his mouth, and colour flooded
her cheeks as she recalled the warmth of those lips
against her hand. She could well believe the stories of
his sexual prowess. This was a man who would take
women and enjoy them as he willed.

She gave a small *moue* of distaste and rose to her
feet. He should not have Caroline if she could prevent
it.

'It is late, Your Grace. You must excuse me.' It was
said with all the dignity at her command.

'Running away, Miss Carrington? Surely a compliment cannot frighten you?'

'"Fright" is not the word which springs to mind, my
lord. "Disgust" would be more accurate.'

'Come now, you shall not be so hard on me. Am I
not to be allowed to express my admiration?'

She stood in front of him then, her blonde head
barely reaching to his shoulder. It was difficult to
retain her self-control before this powerful figure.
There was something about him. For a second she
wondered what it could be. Then she had it. It was
sheer physical grace. He moved like an athlete, perfectly in command of his body, and incapable of an
awkward gesture.

Impatiently she thrust the troubling thoughts aside.

'Let us understand each other,' she said quietly.

'You have been much provoked, but so have I. If we are to deal together at all you will forgo this childish nonsense. Pay court to my niece if you will, but pray do not insult me by treating me as a fool. You will not find me easy to intimidate, Your Grace.'

To her astonishment he gave her a smile of singular sweetness, totally devoid of mockery.

'Forgive me,' he said quietly. 'Shall we call a truce?'

Aurelia nodded, and gave him her hand. He raised it to his lips, but he did not prolong the courtesy, and Aurelia was quick to excuse herself.

As she climbed the stairs she wondered if she had done enough to disarm his suspicion of her. He would be a formidable adversary, and she was in no doubt as to his ruthlessness. Yet she would find a way to save her niece no matter what steps she might be forced to take.

For some hours sleep eluded her. She tossed uneasily throughout the hours of darkness, turning her pillow, and finding herself first too hot and then too cold.

From the hall below she heard the clock strike first the quarters, then the hours, and it was after two before she drifted into oblivion.

As the sky paled, heralding the dawn, she awakened with a start. Something had alerted her. Then she heard a creak as someone descended the staircase. Swiftly, she slid out of bed and opened her door the merest crack.

Below her she saw the massive figure of the Duke, fully dressed in riding coat and breeches. As he strode across the hall she hesitated. He might be a law unto himself, but even he would scarce leave Marram without making his farewells. She guessed that he intended to take an early morning stroll about the grounds. She shrugged, and then stood frozen to the spot as memory flooded back.

Had she not insisted that Richard Collinge should leave the house at first light? The Duke could not fail to see him. With a muttered exclamation of annoyance she snatched at the gown in which she had been making simples and dragged it over her head. Her house shoes were too thin and would at once be drenched with dew, but she dared not wait to button up her fine kid boots. She tied a scarf about her hair and ran downstairs.

To her relief the Duke had paused to examine the inscription over the entrance door. He looked up and smiled and she hurried towards him.

'Love conquers All,' he translated easily. 'That strikes a fitting note, Miss Carrington. Don't you agree?'

Aurelia nodded hastily. This was no time for argument. At any moment Richard might appear.

'If. . .if you are interested in Latin tags there is another in the study,' she said quickly. 'I have forgot its meaning. Perhaps you could help me.'

He gave her a long look and then he bowed.

'I had intended to take a stroll. Shall we strike a bargain? If I am able to translate your mysterious inscription you will show me about the grounds?'

'Of course,' Aurelia agreed. At all costs she must draw him back indoors, and the study was at the back of the house, with no view of the drive.

Crossing her fingers, she prayed that Richard would take his departure within the next few moments. Even as she closed the study door she heard the sound of a horseman, but if the Duke was aware of it he gave no sign.

Hastily she drew him to the window embrasure. High on the wall was a carving in the stone. The lettering was almost worn away.

'This part of the house was built from the ruins of a monastery,' she chattered nervously. Even to herself her voice sounded too loud.

'Fascinating! But I fear that the insciption is too worn for me to distinguish more than a word or two. May I take a guess at the meaning? Does it now warn against deception?'

'I. . . I have forgot. . .as I explained.' In her confusion Aurelia backed away, overturning a small table. The bowl of flowers on it fell to the ground with a crash, shattering into fragments.

'Allow me,' the Duke said smoothly.

Aurelia looked at the black-haired giant kneeling at her feet. At least he did not use pomade, she thought absently. The dark hair gleamed with vitality and a lock or two had fallen across his brow. Without thinking she put out a hand to touch it, and then drew back as if she had been stung. What was she thinking of?

'Please do not trouble yourself, Your Grace. I will do it.' With shaking fingers she began to gather up the pieces.

'You will hurt yourself.' Imperturbably he moved her aside, collected the shattered fragments, and reached down to draw her to her feet. He did not release her hands at once.

'May I give you a word of advice, Miss Carrington?' The fine grey eyes shone with mockery as they gazed into her own. 'You should not attempt to dissemble.

You have not the talent for it. Your face is the mirror of your thoughts.'

'You speak in riddles, my lord. I do not understand you. Do you care to look around the grounds before we breakfast?'

'Now that the coast is clear, you mean?'

Scarlet with mortification, Aurelia did not reply. She lifted her chin and marched ahead of him to the side-door of the house.

'You will find it chill outside,' the Duke observed smoothly. 'Is this yours?' He reached for a cloak which was hanging by the door and placed it about her shoulders. Then he looked at her thin slippers.

'I cannot allow you to put yourself at risk in those. The grass is still wet.'

'I will wear my pattens,' Aurelia announced through gritted teeth. He was treating her like a child. So much for his promise of a truce. With every look and word he was attempting to annoy her, and he seemed to have a supreme gift for putting her in the wrong.

'A sensible idea,' he approved. 'May I help you?'

'Certainly not.' Aurelia picked up her pattens and sat down on the staircase to the servants' quarters, praying that the awkward fastenings would give her no trouble.

She was to be disappointed. Though His Lordship averted his eyes with studied indifference and strolled to and fro with no appearance of impatience, in the end she was forced to admit defeat.

'They are too stiff,' she said at last. 'If you will excuse me I will change into my outdoor boots.'

'Nonsense! We are wasting time.' He seated himself by her on the stairs, reached down and gripped her

ankle. Next moment her foot was resting on his knee
and the patten was fixed in place.

'Give me the other one,' he ordered.

Aurelia was too bemused than to do other than
obey him. No man had ever presumed to take such
liberties with her. Stiff with annoyance, she raised her
other foot, glaring at him as she did so.

The Duke hummed softly to himself. He might have
been shoeing a horse, she thought in fury. The task
accomplished, he gazed down at her feet.

'A sure sign of a thoroughbred,' he announced.

'Pattens?' Aurelia gave him a freezing look.

'No, my dear. . .a pair of slender, well-shaped
ankles.'

Aurelia did not deign to answer him. She stalked
out through the open door and made her way to the
herb garden.

She had hoped to spend as little time as possible in
his company, but once out of doors his manner
changed. In spite of herself she was impressed by his
interest in local farming practices and his pertinent
questions.

The sun was high in the sky before she bethought
herself of the time.

'You will wish to breakfast before you leave, Your
Grace,' she said at last. 'Do you travel far today?'

'I have some acquaintances in the neighbourhood.'
He did not elaborate, and she dreaded to ask. If he
intended to stay within a mile or two of Marram he
could visit at will, and that she must make every effort
to avoid.

They found the dining-room deserted. Cassie was
not an early riser, and Caro, she knew, would stay out

of sight until the Duke had gone. As for Frederick, she guessed that he would be nursing an aching head.

The Duke made an excellent breakfast, and to Aurelia's relief he confined his remarks to the running of her estate. At length he rose to his feet.

'I must not trespass further on your hospitality, Miss Carrington, but, believe me, I am happy to make your acquaintance.'

'Will you. . .will you not wait to see my sister? She would wish. . . I mean, she would not care to think that you had left without bidding her farewell.'

'Will you make my apologies to her and also to Caro? I shall not be far away. With your permission I shall call within a day or so. They remain here for the present, I believe?'

'Yes—er—of course.' Aurelia was mystified to find that Salterne intended to leave without speaking to his betrothed. She did not trust him in the least, but she too had plans.

With a sigh of relief she stood in the doorway to watch him ride away.

CHAPTER THREE

'Cass, what do you say to a trip to Brighton. . .just the three of us?' Aurelia perched herself on the end of her sister's bed.

Cassie almost overset her cup of chocolate.

'You wish to go to Brighton? Why on earth. . .? You never go into society.'

'May I not change my mind? Life can be dull at Marram, as you are never tired of telling me.'

Cassie eyed her narrowly. 'Have you come to your senses at last? Or are you up to some mischief, Lia?'

'Possibly.' Aurelia gave her a demure look. 'I am no longer in my first youth. If I am to settle myself I cannot afford to waste more time.'

'Marriage at last? No. . .you are making game of me!'

'Cassie, I mean to go, but I shall need a chaperon. You have offered in the past. . .and Caro may come too. It may serve to divert her attention.'

'That's true.' Cassie frowned. Then she shook her head. 'No. . .it would be impossible. Ransome would not agree. He could not afford our lodgings, and we have no suitable clothes. . .'

'It need cost him nothing,' Aurelia said curtly.

'He would not allow it, even so.'

'Cassie, he knows that the Duke will come to Brighton in the Regent's company. In such a setting Caroline may be more amenable.'

'I thought you were against the match?'

39

'It was a shock at first. I had not time to think. Now I believe that if Caroline is not pressed too hard she will find happiness.'

That much, at least, was true, Aurelia thought wryly. Though that happiness might not be what Cassie had in mind. In Brighton Caroline might receive a more acceptable offer.

Aurelia looked up as her niece sidled nervously into the room. Cassie's face hardened.

'Well, miss! What is the meaning of this disgraceful escapade? I have half a mind to send you home at once and let your father deal with you.'

Aurelia saw the look of terror in the girl's eyes.

'Nonsense!' she said briskly. 'Cassie, pray do not scold. No harm has been done. Let us look on this as a visit which was long overdue. I am so happy to see you both, and to have you to myself.'

'Lia, you may make light of Caroline's behaviour, but what of Salterne? He was in a rare taking yesterday.'

'He seemed pleasant enough this morning,' Aurelia murmured mildy. 'He sent you his apologies when he left.'

'He has gone?' Caroline's face cleared at once.

'But I do not understand. He did not ask to see Caro, or myself? Now see what you have done, you wicked girl! Salterne has changed his mind. He will withdraw his offer.'

'Calm yourself, Cass. He did not give me that impression. The Duke appeared to accept my explanation.'

'Are you sure?' Cassie eyed her suspiciously. 'You must be cleverer than I thought.'

'Oh, Cassie, do not worry so! Now, what do you say to my idea?'

'To go to Brighton? Well, I cannot deny that I should enjoy it above anything, and it is high time that you found yourself a husband, if that is truly what you want.'

'Caro?'

'Do you mean it, Aunt? Am I to go as well?' Caroline's face shone with pleasure.

'Of course. Jacob may leave today, to take a house for us. Meantime I must make arrangements for my absence.'

'This is all very sudden,' Cassie demurred. 'I do not know. . . But then, Frederick is here. He may escort us.'

'You are mistaken. Frederick will not escort us. I draw the line at that.'

They were still arguing as they sat down to a light luncheon. Then Frederick lurched into the room, blue-jowled, and in the worst of humours.

'Taking my name in vain? I don't doubt that you were speaking kindly of me, Aunt.' He gave Aurelia an ugly look.

'Your mother and Caro are to accompany me to Brighton,' Aurelia said coldly. 'You will please to find your father and give him a letter explaining our intentions.'

'A sudden decision, ain't it? Mother did not mention it to me. I thought we came to fetch my stupid sister.'

'Don't be tiresome, Frederick. Caro has been under a strain, due largely to your own behaviour. It ill becomes you to criticise.'

Her nephew shrugged. 'Have it your way, Aunt.

I've no objection to a trip to Brighton. It's damned dull here, saving your presence.'

'You misunderstood me. You will not accompany us.'

'But you will need an escort, ma'am. You cannot travel without protection.'

'I shall take the servants.' Her eyes met his. He knew that look of old. Further argument would be useless. The last trace of his self-control vanished, and he swung round on his mother.

'Father ain't going to like this above half,' he snarled. 'You had best ask him first. . .'

'Be quiet, you insolent puppy! Since when do you advise your mother? You will do as you are bid.'

Frederick's face was flushed with rage, but as Aurelia faced him his eyes fell.

'You have not forgot my advice, I trust,' she said softly. 'You would do well to heed it. Do you understand me?'

He nodded a surly assent and flung out of the room.

'You are so hard on him,' Cassie reproached.

'Not nearly hard enough, my dear. Now, if you will write your letter Caro shall help pack my things.

As they turned out drawers and cupboards Aurelia affected not to notice her niece's swollen eyes, though it was clear that the girl had spent the night in tears.

'Come,' she said. 'We have not much time. . .'

A silence greeted her words, and then she heard a sob. Turning, she gathered the desolate figure in her arms.

'Do not distress yourself so,' she comforted. 'We may yet find a way. . .'

'You do not know Father,' Caroline choked out.

'But I cannot marry Salterne. He frightens me. Aunt, you have met him. Is he not hateful beyond anything?'

'We could scarce expect him to be in the best of moods.' Aurelia chose her words with care.

'But. . .but how did you explain to him? What did you say?'

'I assured him that you were safe. It was no more than the truth.'

'Did he believe that I came alone? I was so afraid. I thought he might call Richard out.'

'He showed great forbearance. He followed you, you see.'

'Then he will not wish to marry me now.' Caroline brightened.

'He did not give me that impression,' Aurelia told her grimly.

'Then what is to be done?' The girl's voice was little above a whisper.

'For the moment, nothing. We shall go to Brighton, and there perhaps——'

She stopped as Cassie entered the room with no pleasant expression on her face. Aurelia guessed correctly that her sister had been treated to the rough side of Frederick's tongue.

'Children!' Cassie slumped into a chair. 'Lia, do you not find it strange that Salterne did not request an interview with Caroline?'

'He did—er—suggest it yesterday, but I explained that she was resting. He wished to take her away at once, but I could not permit it.'

'Have you run mad? They are betrothed.'

'I am not aware of it. No announcement has been made. I had only his word for it, as I told him.'

'You questioned his word? Aurelia, how could you? He is a close friend of the Prince.'

'And that makes him perfect? I did not find him so.' Aurelia stopped, suddenly aware of the expression on her niece's face. 'Caro, my dear, will you ask Hannah for a dish of tea?' She waited until the door had closed, then, 'The Duke must learn that the world does not jump when he raises a finger,' she continued. 'I found him insolent in the extreme.'

'Oh, Lia, you did not get upon your high ropes with him?'

'No more than he did with me. But do not distress yourself. I have not ruined your plans. His Grace, I believe, has every intention of proceeding with his suit.'

She was surprised to see that Cassies lips began to tremble. Then her sister turned her face away.

'I am so unhappy,' she whispered. 'This betrothal is none of my doing, Lia. You are right about Salterne. I cannot sleep for thinking of Caro at his mercy. I know it is the way of the world. . .but it is like offering a lamb to some ravening beast.'

'Now, Cass, that is too dramatic. Did you not tell me that he loved his first wife dearly?'

'He is too old for Caro, and too. . .too experienced. There have been so many women, if the stories about him are to be believed.'

Aurelia did not doubt it. From her own experience she knew that the Duke had little regard for the proprieties. He appeared to believe that a compliment or two would bring women fawning at his feet, and she could not deny that he had a certain animal attraction.

Her cheeks grew warm as she remembered the way

he had kissed her hand for much too long. She had felt that his lips must burn her skin. . .and that caressing grasp upon her ankle as he'd fixed her pattens. . . The man richly deserved his reputation as a roué. To him, any woman was fair game.

'Gossip loses nothing in the telling,' she said carefully. 'The stories may not all be true.' There was no point in upsetting Cassie further.

Her sister would not be comforted.

'Caro is terrified of him,' she continued. 'It was pitiful to see her when Ransome forced her to listen to his suit.'

'That was brutal!'

'You see, she fancies herself in love with Richard Collinge. He, at least, was kind to her. It is more than I can say for myself.'

'He knew that he was with her?'

'Of course. That is why I followed Salterne. He is capable of violence. . .'

'I don't doubt it, but he did not see either of them. Now dry your eyes, my dearest. All will be well. We shall find some way to make things right.'

Aurelia spoke with a confidence she was far from feeling. She had no idea as to how she might achieve such a desirable state of affairs. For the moment her main objective must be to leave Marram before the Duke returned. She had not mentioned to Cassie that he might be staying in the neighbourhood, and for the next few days she prayed fervently that she might be spared the sight of that tall figure riding towards the house. He did not appear, but it was with some relief that she greeted Jacob on his return from Brighton. He had found suitable lodgings on the Steyne, the

servants had been engaged, and now there was
nothing to delay their departure.

They left on a perfect summer morning, and
Aurelia's spirits lifted as they bowled through the leafy
lanes of Sussex. Though the marshes had a beauty of
their own it was pleasant to find herself in rolling
countryside. A week ago she'd had no thought of
leaving Marram. Now she looked forward with keen
anticipation to a change of scene.

How green it was in this rich farmland. An overnight shower had cleared the air and freshened the
new growth on trees and hedgerows. Overhead the
branches curved to form a tunnel, their foliage blocking out the strong rays of the sun. The half-light had a
mysterious quality, as if they were travelling beneath
the sea.

Her reverie was broken when Jacob stopped the
coach.

She leaned out of the window. 'Something is
wrong?'

'Two horsemen behind us, Miss Lia. They have
been following for some time.'

'Footpads!' Cassie paled with fright.

'That is unlikely,' Aurelia told her. 'They are more
probably gentlemen riding about their business. The
lane is narrow. They could scarce pass us here.'

She signalled to Jacob to drive on, but she could
not repress a slight feeling of anxiety. She was carrying
jewels and a large amount of gold, but both Jacob and
Matthew were armed. She settled back in her seat.

It was some time before Cassie recovered from her
fright, but as Aurelia appeared to be untroubled she
slipped into a doze, lulled by the rocking of the coach.
Caroline had brightened at the mention of the horse-

men, but Aurelia dismissed the notion that Richard might be following them. Even on short acquaintance she had become convinced of his good sense. By now, she imagined, he would have returned home, anxious to protect Caroline's reputation.

Unwillingly her thoughts returned to Salterne. What an enigma he was. She would never understand him. half dreaming, she wondered what it would be like to be loved by such a man. There had been moments when the sardonic mask had slipped and his smile had been free of mockery. Then his face had been transformed as the fine lines at the corners of his eyes had crinkled. They too could change, from the forbidding grey of a winter sea to a disturbing warmth.

Sternly she took herself to task. The man exuded a powerful sexuality, and honesty demanded that she must admit it, but her own reaction troubled her. She frowned. It was high time that she got away from Marram and took her rightful place in society. If casual contact with a well-known rake could cause such turmoil in her mind. . . She was behaving like an embittered spinster who had been starved of affection for too long.

She pushed the unwelcome idea to the back of her mind and gazed once more upon the passing countryside. There were no further alarms and Jacob drove on steadily, making for Hailsham, where they would rest the horses and refresh themselves.

She was roused by a violent jolt. Then, to her horror, the coach began to tilt. She heard a shout of panic and then they were over, amid the sound of splintering wood and breaking glass.

As the vehicle came to rest Aurelia found herself on top of Cassie and Hannah, with Caroline beneath the three of them. She realised that the coach was on its side in a ditch.

There was a long silence. Then Cassie began to scream.

'Stop that,' Aurelia ordered briefly. 'Help me climb out.' She tucked up her skirts and secured them with her scarf. Then she reached for the door above her head.

'Lia, please!' Cassie stopped screaming and caught at her sister's arm.

'What is it? Are you hurt?'

'No. . .but you cannot climb out like that. Your. . . your limbs are visible.'

Aurelia gave a shout of laughter.

'Really, Cass! We are overturned and you must think of the proprieties?'

'But Matthew and Jacob are out there.'

'I do not hear them. They may be hurt.'

She gave another hitch to her skirts and resumed her climb. It was difficult to open the door from below, but by exerting all her strength she forced it aside at last.

'Hannah, will you give me a push? Brace yourself lest I slip.'

She had set herself no easy task, but eventually she managed to inch through the open doorway. She found herself high above the lane, and in imminent danger of sliding down the polished side of the coach. Before she could decide on her next move a strong arm closed about her waist.

'Keep perfectly still, Miss Carrington. You are quite safe.'

Aurelia turned her head to find that she was gazing into the Duke's eyes. She was plucked from her dangerous perch as if she weighed no more than a feather, and then was lifted easily on to the saddle of Salterne's horse.

For a moment she allowed herself to rest against his broad chest as a surge of relief swept over her. Then she attempted to struggle free of the comforting safety of his arms.

'My sister. . .and Caro. . .they are inside. Can you get them out?'

'You are unhurt?'

She nodded, and he allowed her to dismount. Then he rose in the stirrups and gripped the sill of the carriage door. With barely an effort he lifted himself clear of his horse and, spread-eagled against the side of the coach, he reached inside.

'Give me your hands, Lady Ransome,' he ordered.

Aurelia could only marvel at his strength as he drew her sister through the opening, and slid with her to the ground.

'Thrust her head between her knees,' he ordered. 'She is faint, but she appears to be unharmed. Then you had best see to your servants.'

Aurelia did as she was bidden. Then she hurried to where a groom, resplendent in the Duke's livery, stood at the horses' heads.

'Over there, ma'am.' He gestured to where Matthew bent over Jacob's unconscious form.

'Is he badly hurt?' Aurelia fell to her knees beside the old man.

'He's taken a nasty fall, Miss Lia. There's a lump the size of an egg on the back of his head.'

'And you?'

'Just winded, ma'am. It was the rut in the road. Jacob didn't see it.'

With shaking fingers Aurelia ripped off a length of petticoat and dipped it in the shallow stream which ran along the bottom of the ditch. As she laid it on Jacob's head he stirred.

'Lie still,' a stern voice ordered. 'You will serve your mistress best by resting until we right the carriage. John, mount up and fetch some help. Miss Carrington's man will hold the horses.'

The Duke knelt down, ignoring the effect of the muddy ground upon his immaculate buckskins. He examined Jacob's head with surprisingly gentle fingers.

'He is badly shocked,' he told Aurelia quietly. 'I will stay with him. Do you attend your sister.'

Aurelia did not argue. She rose to her feet at once and returned to the others.

'What happened? I thought we should all be killed. . .' Cassie was perilously close to hysteria.

Aurelia caught her by the shoulders.

'Pull yourself together,' she said sharply. 'Caro has need of you.'

'My poor child! Are you hurt, my dearest?' Cassie forgot her own distress as she turned to the slight figure of her daughter.

'Naught but a cut, Mama. It must have been the broken glass. I put out my hand, you see.' Caroline was pale and shaken but she managed a faint smile.

'Well done, Caro! Are you able to stand unaided?' The Duke loomed over the little group, and Caroline allowed him to draw her to her feet. 'We shall not have long to wait for help.'

He walked over to his horse and reached into the saddlebag for a flask of brandy, offering a measure of the spirit to each of the ladies in turn. Then he turned his attentions to Hannah, advising her to walk up and down with the others to avoid a chill. His manner to her was as courteous as it had been towards the other ladies, much to Aurelia's surprise. She had thought him too high in the instep to trouble himself about a servant. Her eyes rested on his powerful figure. He had lost no time in taking command of the situation, she thought ruefully. And help would most certainly arrive. She might be sure of it.

As Salterne had predicted John returned within minutes. With him was a group of farmhands. Under the Duke's direction the coach was swiftly righted, and other than a broken window and splintered panelling in the door it was found to be in reasonable order.

After a generous distribution of largesse the Duke turned to Aurelia.

'Your coachman must go inside,' he announced. 'Your other man, I take it, is able to handle the team?'

'My lord, I cannot. . . I am but a groom.' Matthew's face was pale with fright.

'Then I will drive, and John shall ride my horse. Think you that you can manage his?' A quelling glance dared Matthew to disagree. 'Miss Carrington, you will ride with me. You are more warmly clad than the other ladies.'

Aurelia admitted the truth of his remark. Her travelling dress might not be the height of fashion, but the cloth was proof against the elements.

'Lia!' Cassie tugged her arm and looked pointedly at the bronze redingote, now sadly muddied and torn.

'Oh, yes. I had forgot.' Unruffled, Aurelia began to untie the scarf which held her skirt above her ankles.

'Leave it,' the Duke commanded briefly. 'Now ladies, I suggest that we waste no more time.' A quick word to John ensured that Jacob was carried to the coach with Matthew's help.

'Now, Miss Carrington, up you go.' Before Aurelia knew what was happening she was seated beside him on the box and the Duke had whipped up the horses. It was clear at once that the management of a four-in-hand presented him with no problems. Aurelia could only admire the skill with which he guided the badly shaken team along the narrow country lanes.

'I must thank you for your help, my lord. Had you not come to our aid I am afraid. . .'

'That is your trouble, ma'am. You seem to be a stranger to fear. What in the name of heaven persuaded you to entrust a team of thoroughbreds to a feeble ancient?'

'Jacob has always driven for my family,' Aurelia said stiffly.

'That may be so, but the years take their toll. He no longer has the strength. . .'

'Please. . . I beg of you. . .do not go on. Nothing you might say can make me feel worse than I do at present. I blame myself entirely for this mishap.'

'Well, that is something,' he admitted grudgingly. 'At least you did not give way to a fit of the vapours.'

Aurelia was silent. With bent head she studied her hands. Then her eye fell on a long rent in her skirt. It reached almost to her waist and beneath it a shapely leg was fully visible to her companion. She made a stealthy effort to draw the edges of the cloth together, but to no avail.

'Keep still!' The Duke frowned down at her. 'You will not shock me, Miss Carrington. I have seen women's limbs before.'

'I do not doubt it.' Aurelia was stung into an incautious reply.

'Dear me!' The Duke kept his eyes on the road. 'Did I not know you better I might ascribe that remark to jealousy or pique.'

'Why, you. . .you egotist!'

Salterne ignored the insult.

'You need have no cause for concern,' he resumed in a conversational tone. 'Your—er—limbs compare favourably with the best.'

'And as a connoisseur you would know, of course?'

'Of course!' His lips twitched as he looked at her flushed face. Then, satisfied that the set white look had vanished from about her mouth, he flung the skirt of his riding coat across her knees.

'Thank you,' she said shortly.

'I do not care to be distracted,' came the cool reply.

'If you will take us to the nearest inn, Your Grace, we need trouble you no longer. Perhaps in a day or two we may resume our journey.'

'With Jacob at the reins? Don't be a fool, Miss Carrington. I will take you to your destination. It is Brighton, is it not?'

Aurelia stiffened. How could he know? Her plan had not been thought of when he'd left Marram. Now another question troubled her.

'Your appearance was most opportune,' she murmured. 'I had not thought to find you still in Sussex.'

'No?' His smile was ironic.

'Two horsemen followed us,' she persisted. 'Yourself and your groom, was it not?'

'It was.'

'What a coincidence!' she cried hotly. 'I understood you to be staying with your friends.'

'Circumstances made it necessary for me to take my leave of them.'

'To follow us? My lord, I do not care to be spied upon.'

'But you made it necessary,' he said in mock-bewilderment. 'I guess that it would not be too long before your fertile brain thought of some means to attain your ends.'

'And they are. . .?'

'Come, my dear lady, you are transparent. You will stop at nothing to prevent this marriage, is that not so?'

Aurelia did not trouble to reply. 'Yet you are in a difficult situation,' the Duke continued. 'Your adversary is in an almost impregnable position. It would appear that he holds the high ground. You may chance a few guerrilla skirmishes, but they can have no effect on the final outcome.'

'This is not a war, Your Grace.'

'No? I thought it was. I have seen eyes like yours above a loaded pistol.'

'And that is your excuse for setting your man to spy on us?' Aurelia had no doubt that the groom had been ordered to stay close to Marram, to learn what he could. 'What a very excellent Bow Street Runner you might have made, my lord.'

'I like to be appraised of the enemy's plans in advance,' he assured her. 'I put myself in your place when I considered your possible strategy.'

'Indeed!'

'You had not many options open to you. Either you stayed at Marram and awaited the arrival of Ransome, come to remove his wife and daughter from your care, or you left for an unknown destination.'

'A remarkable deduction!'

'In London or Brighton some reason might be found to sanction the visit. Brighton, I felt, was more likely to be your choice, but I had to be sure.'

Aurelia was too angry to reply. How well he had divined her intentions.

'The estimable Frederick will doubtless lose no time in informing his father of your whereabouts. His Lordship, I understand, is still in the stews of the capital.'

'You are well-informed by your network of spies.'

'Ransome makes no secret of his pursuits.'

'As you appear to think so highly of my family, sir, I wonder that you care to contemplate an alliance with my niece.' Two bright spots of colour appeared on Aurelia's cheeks.

'I have my reasons, Miss Carrington. Shall we leave it at that?'

CHAPTER FOUR

THE Duke drove on in silence, with an occasional look at the sky. A bank of cloud had obscured the sun, and the wind was chill. Aurelia began to shiver. For all the protection offered by her redingote she might have been naked.

Salterne stopped the horses and shrugged out of his riding coat. He threw it about her shoulders. Then he reached out and drew her close to his side.

'Put your arms about my waist,' he said. 'You are suffering from delayed shock.'

Thankful for the promise of warmth offered by his body, Aurelia did as he suggested. He might be the most obnoxious creature she had met in the course of her experience, but there was something of comfort in being able to rest her head against his shoulder, and to feel the steady pounding of his heart beneath the fine cambric shirt.

He was her enemy, that was true, but the rules of war allowed one to make use of an enemy. She smiled at the thought. Was he not playing into her hands?

Slowly she relaxed and nestled closer to him as her eyelids began to droop. The Duke looked down at her and a slight smile curved his lips.

'You must take care, my general. Even the great Napoleon is not at his best when he is weary.'

'You would compare me with that. . .that monster?'

'A genius, ma'am! I venture to think that he would not be too proud to take advantage of a little warmth as you are doing now. It would, after all, give him the chance to fight another day.'

He tightened his grip and Aurelia was tempted to pull away from him. Then her sense of humour came to her rescue. Her shoulders began to shake with laughter.

'You are still cold?' His voice held concern.

'N—no, my lord, but it occurred to me. . . I doubt if Napoleon has ever found himself in this position.'

Making light of the situation was the only way she could think of to drive away the disturbing sensations which possessed her. By turning her head only slightly she could see a small pulse beating in the base of his throat. She clenched her fingers into a fist, to prevent herself from touching the tanned skin.

How dark he was. . .almost gypsy-like in colouring. She could understand why Caroline found him such a threatening figure.

Great heavens! Caroline! And she, Aurelia, was the aunt of the bride-to-be. What could she have been thinking of to allow herself to get into this ridiculous position, embracing—actually embracing—the Duke of Salterne?

She stiffened, dropped her arms, and tried to pull away, but the Duke tightened his grip.

'I should advise you not to struggle, my dear. The horses are still nervous.'

Not only the horses, Aurelia thought uneasily. The rent in her skirt had opened wide, and her leg was pressed against the Duke's thigh. She was intensely aware of the sinewy strength of his muscles against her own soft flesh. The male scent of his body filled her nostrils, combined with the smell of newly washed linen, and her heart gave an odd little jump.

She could not but compare him with the perfumed dandies of her London season. However she might criticise Salterne's arrogance and regret his ugly reputation, this, at least, was a man. If only he did not have such an infuriating urge to put her at a disadvantage every time they met she might learn to tolerate his company, though she was determined that her niece should not be forced to marry him.

A small frown creased her brow. She would fight him, but he had pointed out her difficulties only too clearly.

'Something is troubling you?' The heavy-lidded grey eyes were regarding her intently.

'We had planned to rest the horses at Hailsham, Your Grace.'

'They will do well enough. I have not pushed them hard, and there is still some way to go. Your man will need attention. I had best send John ahead to find the surgeon. Will you give me your direction?'

Aurelia had hoped to keep their whereabouts a secret, but she did not hesitate. Jacob must be her first consideration. As the team continued to cover the miles she began to doze.

'Asleep on duty, General?' The teasing voice roused her with a start. 'You must remember that the enemy will always take advantage of a lack of vigilance.' The Duke bent towards her and Aurelia looked at him with startled eyes.

'No. . . . I did not intend to kiss you.' A large hand reached out and brushed a strand of hair from her cheek. 'Though the thought is tempting.'

Aurelia was tempted to strike him and he laughed.

'I should not advise it,' he warned. 'I have sparred with the professionals.'

'Then I wonder that you should care to spar with me, even verbally,' Aurelia answered coldly. 'Since our first meeting you have done your best to annoy me.'

'With compliments?'

'With a manner which I find over-familiar.'

He gave a shout of laughter.

'We cannot stand upon ceremony on this box,' he said drily. 'However, your trials are almost at an end. There is your destination.'

He pointed ahead and minutes later he turned off the Brighton road into a stable-yard. Along one side the lights of a small house gleamed softly in the dusk.

'A good choice,' he approved. 'Stabling is hard to come by in the town.' He dismounted from the box and held up his arms. Aurelia was tempted to announce that she would descend to the ground unaided, but common sense prevailed. She was tired and the drop to the ground was steep. She had no wish to end up prone at his feet. Without more ado she gave him her hand and allowed him to lift her down.

To her annoyance he showed no disposition to release her, holding her against his breast until she was forced to protest.

'My lord,' she said with dignity, 'if you are determined to convince me that your reputation is justified you have succeeded. Must you continue to insult me?'

He grinned down at her and tightened his grip until she thought her ribs must crack. Then he shook her slightly to and fro.

'You are not some schoolroom miss, but a full-blooded woman,' he said softly. 'Is it an insult to be found desirable?'

'As you are planning to wed my niece the answer must be yes.' If she stamped hard on his instep perhaps he would let her go, though she suspected that her small kid boots would make no impression on his Hessians.

He dropped a kiss upon her head as she began to struggle.

'There,' he said. 'Now I have confirmed your worst fears. I am beyond redemption.'

Aurelia felt strangely breathless. For the first time her resolution wavered. This infuriating creature was too. . .too. . .well, he was too much of everything. She did not doubt the size of the task before her. In some odd way he seemed to have the ability to read her mind. He would be a formidable adversary.

She broke his hold upon her abruptly and hurried round to the door of the couch.

'What a journey! I vow I am more dead than alive.' Cassie climbed down stiffly, followed by the others.

The Duke paid them no attention. He reached inside, lifted Jacob in his arms, and strode across the courtyard to the house.

'Ah, Lessing. I'm glad to see you here.' He nodded briefly to a middle-aged man who stood in the doorway holding a lamp aloft.

'This way.' The surgeon led him up the stairs, and waited as he laid Jacob carefully on the bed. 'Now let me see my patient.'

Salterne took Aurelia's arm and led her from the room.

'Lessing is the best. You must try not to worry.' His voice was oddly gentle.

'I cannot forgive myself. . .' Aurelia was close to tears.

'Now, General, you must not give way. The troops rely on you. You have been a Trojan up to this.' A strong hand rested on her shoulder. 'Will you forgive me if I leave you now? You will all wish to rest. . .'

'Of course, and. . .thank you for everything.'

'For everything?' She heard the laughter in his voice, but she did not draw her hand away when the Duke raised it to his lips.

'Take care to redeploy your forces, ma'am,' he murmured softly. Then he looked up as the surgeon joined them.

'How is he, Lessing?'

'Shocked and badly bruised, Your Grace. His head will be tender for a day or two, but I doubt if there will be lasting damage. He wishes to speak to you, Miss Carrington.'

Aurelia slipped into the sick man's room.

'What is it, Jacob?'

'You have not forgot the Frenchie, ma'am. . .the mantua-maker. She is to come tomorrow. You asked me to arrange. . .'

'I have not forgot,' she soothed. She was tempted to assure him that the visit of the dressmaker was the last thing on her mind. Instead she patted his hand. 'You must try to get some sleep,' she told him quietly.

When the Frenchwoman arrived next day Aurelia detected a certain reserve in her manner. It surprised her. Cassie knew the woman well, and the introduction of a new client might have guaranteed some expressions of pleasure.

Madame Claudine looked sharply at Cassie. 'Shall you wish the total, my lady? It is for several seasons.'

Cassie flushed, but before she could speak Aurelia intervened.

'The total, if you please.' Her face was impassive as she studied the enormous bill. She handed it to her sister. 'Is this correct?'

'I—I fear it is. . . I had no idea.'

'These matters are easily overlooked.' Aurelia counted out a pile of sovereigns. 'You should be more importunate, Madame Claudine. You cannot run a business without payment.'

Madame was profuse in her thanks. She forbore to mention that repeated requests for settlement of even a part of the account had met with no response.

She looked with new respect at the slender figure before her. Miss Carrington's dress was not, perhaps, *dernier cri*, but her gentle manner did not disguise a certain air of authority. She signed to her companion and together they began to unpack their pattern books and samples.

Cassie looked uncomfortable.

'Lia, I am so sorry,' she whispered. 'I did not intend that you should pay. Now I cannot order anything new.'

'Nonsense! Did you not assure me that just one outmoded garment will sink us beneath reproach? You shall choose whatever you wish.'

If Madame heard any part of the murmured exchange she gave no indication. She threw open the pages of *La Belle Assemblée* and *Ackerman's Repository of Fashion* and invited the comments of all three ladies.

Later that day she left with a well-filled order book. It had been a profitable afternoon and her black eyes gleamed at the size of Aurelia's commission. She gathered together her samples of tiffany and chambery gauze, sarcenet silks and light muslins, promising the first of the gowns within three days.

'Lia, you are like to outdo the Regent in extravagance!' Cassie exclaimed. But it was a half-hearted protest. As the days went by and parcels arrived she could not hide her pleasure.

'I vow we shall not find time to wear one half of them.' She sighed happily as she twirled before the mirror in a pale pink muslin with puffed sleeves. The low neckline was trimmed with a frill in the same shade, and a satin ribbon of deeper pink confined it beneath the bust. 'I am so glad I did not choose that vile pomona green. It turns my skin to the colour of cheese.'

Aurelia looked at her reflection in the glass. The blue reflected the colour of her eyes. It was patterned in gold, with a gold flounce at the hem, and a ribbon of the same colour was held with a jewelled buckle at her breast.

'You do not think this gown a trifle ornate?' she said doubtfully.

'It is perfect, Aunt Lia. You look like a queen.' Caro's expression was rapturous.

'That is what I was afraid of. I should not have allowed you to persuade me, Cass.'

'Nonsense! On a dark person it would be too much, but on you. . .well, my dear, it is the height of elegance. Caro, stop pulling at the neckline of your dress. It is quite low enough for a young girl.'

'Madame Claudine suggested a bust improver to wear beneath it, mama.'

'Madame Claudine may suggest what she wishes, but I will not permit it. The very idea! You will fill out in time, just as your aunt and I have done.' Cassie looked with satisfaction at her creamy bosom. 'There is no denying that one does need a little flesh to do justice to these styles.'

'I see I shall have to drape gauze scarves about my person,' Aurelia twinkled.

'Do not say so! You are not bony, Lia, though you do not eat enough. If you would but listen to me——'

'Yes, yes, I know. Now, what do you say to a drive? I have hired a chaise. . .'

Cassie looked doubtful.

'Is Jacob fit to drive?'

'I shall drive myself.'

Cassie's dismay caused Aurelia to hide a smile.

'I shall not overturn you,' she promised.

'But the Duke said. . .'

'I do not require Salterne's permission for anything I choose to do. Will you trust me or not?'

'I suppose so.' Cassie stifled her misgivings. The prospect of a drive at the fashionable hour of five was sufficient to persuade her to change her gown, and to hurry Caro into doing the same.

They found themselves in a slow-moving line of carriages. The town had filled up rapidly in daily expectation of the Regent's arrival, and several people looked with interest at the smart little equipage with its elegant occupants.

'Oh, there is Lady Bell!' Cassie waved to a plump little woman who was speaking to a young officer. 'Do bow to her, Caro. We met her in London, you will recall.'

Caroline inclined her head, blushing at the young man's frank look of admiration.

It seemed as if Cassie knew half the world. Aurelia

was forced to stop time and again as greetings and invitations were showered upon them.

'I am so glad we came here.' Cassie was flushed with triumph as they turned for home.

Aurelia smiled at her. She was satisfied with the result of their outing. Now they would be drawn into society. It was clear that during her daughter's season Cassie had made many friends and acquaintances among the *ton*. If there was speculation as to why the lovely Caro was not yet spoken for it was no matter. Salterne's offer was not yet public knowledge.

Cassie, she knew, would be the envy of all matchmaking mamas when it was known that her daughter had captured the biggest prize of the season, but Aurelia was determined to delay that moment for as long as possible. Once Caro was formally betrothed all chance of further offers being made to her would be at an end, and Aurelia's hopes for her niece would be dashed.

'Do not mention Salterne's offer yet,' she warned next day.

'Why not?' Cassie bridled. 'Not everyone was kind to us in London. Caro had a host of suitors until that odious Mrs Ingleby told everyone that she had no fortune. How I long to give her a set-down. Her own girls are the plainest creatures. . .'

'Not yet,' Aurelia insisted. A spark of mischief lit her eyes. 'Shall you not enjoy the furore when the announcement appears without warning?'

'It will cause a stir,' Cassie said with satisfaction. For the moment she appeared to have forgotten her objections to the match.

'Matthew will drive you if you wish to pay some

calls tomorrow.' Aurelia thought it time to change the subject. 'He is quite capable of handling the chaise.'

'You will not accompany us?'

'No. . .if you'll forgive me. The scarf I bought at Hanningtons is quite the wrong shade. I shall walk to North Street and exchange it.'

It was a small deception. After the bustle of the last few days Aurelia longed for some time to herself, and during her walks she had seen several bookshops. A quiet hour or two spent browsing would restore her spirits.

Next morning she set off across the Steyne to Mr Donaldson's. She would take out a subscription to his library.

Her slender figure in the new bronze pelisse and bonnet attracted some attention, but she saw none of her acquaintance. She slipped through the crowd outside the shop and made her way to the counter, glancing at her watch.

'I have but one hour.' She smiled at the assistant. 'Will you remind me if I forget the time?' She knew herself of old. How often had she lost half a day in Rye or Tunbridge Wells, absorbed in the treasures on the shelves?

The young man announced himself at her disposal. He produced several volumes for her inspection, including one by a new author.

'*Pride and Prejudice*?' Aurelia glanced at the first page and was struck by the humour of the opening lines. How delightful! She was chuckling aloud when a shadow fell across the book.

'Good morning, Miss Carrington.'

Aurelia stiffened. There was no mistaking that

deep voice. She looked up into Salterne's smiling eyes.

'Your Grace.' She gave him the slightest of bows, annoyed to find that the colour had rushed to her cheeks. A multitude of emotions swept through her mind as she gazed at him, but she was appalled to realise that her first reaction was one of joy.

She averted her face, striving to remember that this was her enemy. Had he not insulted her, with his cavalier disregard of the conventions?

She made an effort to regain her composure. She had, she told herself, no wish for his company, but it would be ill-mannered to move away without exchanging a civil word or two.

Salterne took the volume from her hand and looked at the title.

'You have read this?'

'Not yet, but I intend to do so. If you will forgive me, Your Grace, I am pressed for time.' She signalled to the assistant.

'Not even an hour to spare?'

Aurelia blushed. He must have overheard her.

'I will take this for the moment,' she announced.

'Then you must allow me to escort you,' he said coolly. 'I hope to pay my respects to Lady Ransome and to Caro.'

'They are not at home. My sister is paying calls this morning.'

'I shall not object to wait for them.' The Duke led her through the crowds on the pavement. Mr Donaldson had done his best to attract custom by setting out tables where one might take tea, play cards, or read the newspapers. Salterne nodded to his acquaintance. Then he turned towards the seafront. Aurelia stopped.

'My lord, my house is across the Steyne, as you know. We must go straight ahead.'

The grip on her arm did not relax, and through the thin fabric of her sleeve Aurelia could feel the warmth of his hand. For some reason she felt unaccountably breathless.

'You can have no objection to a little exercise, Miss Carrington. Forgive me, but you are looking rather pale.'

'It is not surprising. . .' She bit back the rest of the sentence. She could not admit that his sudden appearance had unnerved her.

'I had not thought to find you still in Brighton,' she said coldly. 'We have not seen you since. . .'

'Since the unfortunate incident with your carriage? May I hope that you have missed my company.'

'You may hope, but it would not be the truth.' Aurelia was tempted to assure him that his ego matched his size, but she bit back the words. It would be too childish to indulge in petty sarcasm.

His lips twitched with amusement as he looked down at her, but he did not take up the challenge.

'I hear from Lessing that your man goes on well.'

'Jacob is recovering, I thank you. Do you not go to London, sir?'

The Duke laughed.

'Anxious to be rid of me, my dear?'

'I was merely making the enquiry. . .but if you care to take my words amiss. . .'

'Why should I do that, Miss Carrington? You are a marvel of tact. I hang upon your every word, it is true. Each pronouncement is—er—pregnant with meaning.'

Aurelia stalked along beside him, too furious to reply, but she found that she was shaking. The less she was in the company of this insufferable creature the better. He had the most unfortunate effect on her, ruffling her feathers, disturbing her composure, and destroying her peace of mind.

'In answer to your kind enquiry, I am come to Brighton for the season,' the Duke continued imperturbably.

'But the Prince is not yet arrived.'

'Perhaps I am come to restore my health.' The grey eyes gleamed with laughter.

'What nonsense! I never saw anyone look better in my life.' Aurelia stopped, and blushed to the roots of her hair, wishing that she could recall the indiscreet remark.

'A compliment! I am overwhelmed. Can it be that you are beginning to discover my true worth, or is this merely another attempt to throw me off my guard?' He was enjoying her discomfiture to the full. 'Appearances can be deceptive, ma'am. You see before you a broken man. . .crushed by your disapproval.'

'You are impossible!' she ground out bitterly.

'So I am told. I should point out, by the way, that you are destroying the volume in your hand. A pity! It is a charming book.'

Aurelia glanced down. In her agitation she had almost crushed the book in two.

'Please to release my arm, Your Grace. I must go home at once, and I prefer to go alone.'

'Do I sully your reputation, my fair adversary?'

'I am aware that your own cannot be tarnished further,' she burst out hotly. 'But I must have some care for my own.'

For answer he settled her arm more comfortably within his own. Then, bending down, he peeped beneath the brim of her bonnet. He was much too close, but in that fashionable crowd she could not struggle without making a scene. He knew it as well as she and the corners of his mouth crinkled with laughter.

'I thought you scorned the opinion of the world, Miss Carrington.'

'I hope I am not so foolish. Only a dowager may flout the dictates of society. . .' She stopped again, aware that she had given him the opportunity to make some cutting remark.

'And you are not quite that,' he said solemnly. 'Must I remind you, dear relative-to-be, that our acquaintance is beyond reproach? We are almost family, so to speak.'

'Your betrothal is not yet public knowledge.'

'That is easily remedied. . .an announcement in the *Morning Post* perhaps?'

Aurelia looked at him in alarm. An announcement at this stage would ruin all her plans. She lifted her face to his and gave him her most charming smile.

'Now, in truth, I am worried. Am I to believe that you see me suddenly in a different light?'

'You misjudge me, Your Grace. Perhaps on further acquaintance. . .?' She hoped that her reply sounded convincing, but she was speedily disillusioned.

'You feel that your antipathy might lessen?' Salterne threw back his head and gave a shout of laughter. 'You raise my hopes, Miss Carrington. I wonder why I imagined that you had taken me in deep dislike at our first meeting?'

'On that occasion you were not yourself, my lord. The long ride. . .the worry. . . I appreciate how you must have felt.'

'You are too kind!' He made her an ironic bow. 'We are almost at your door. I will leave you here, and promise myself the pleasure of a visit tomorrow.'

'No!' The sharp refusal was out before she had time to consider.

His Grace raised an eyebrow.

'Then how are we to further our acquaintance, my dear? You do not care to be seen with me in a public place. If we are to learn to appreciate each other's sterling qualities we cannot do so at a distance.'

Aurelia flushed at his mocking tone, but she made an effort to retain her dignity. She knew quite well that he relished throwing her off balance. It should have been easy to treat him with the freezing disparagement she had used to others during her London season, but it was not.

Her own reactions to him puzzled and dismayed her. Antagonism she could handle. It was his teasing, almost tender way of slipping under her defences that was difficult to understand. She was not a child, to be perplexed and thrown into confusion by a word or a smile. The contempt which she had tried to show him appeared to offer him nothing but amusement.

She looked up to find him watching her intently.

'I am persuaded that Lady Ransome and your charming niece will be overjoyed to see me,' he continued. 'I must not be wanting in my attentions. . .'

'My sister is fatigued at present, and after Caro's— er——'

'Escape?' he supplied helpfully.

Aurelia gave him a look of acute distaste.

'I was about to say that after our journey Caroline would welcome the opportunity to recover her spirits.'

'Strange!' he mused. 'When the ladies passed me

not an hour ago they appeared to be in the best of health.'

There was nothing left to say, and as the hard grey eyes gazed into her own Aurelia felt a sense of panic. What a devil he was! He could read her mind without difficulty. She wanted to run and hide. . .anything to get away from his disturbing presence.

'At a loss for words, Miss Carrington? Surely not?' He was in no hurry to help her out of her predicament. She had told him herself that Cassie and Caro were paying calls, and then she had tried to indicate that they were too fatigued to receive him.

'You intrigue me, ma'am,' he said at last. 'What can you hope to gain by your opposition to my suit? Ransome, I fear, is not like to take it kindly.'

'That wastrel!' Aurelia's hand flew to her mouth. Again she had been betrayed into saying more than was right or proper. However she might feel about her brother-in-law, it was unbecoming in her to speak ill of him to others. She could have wept with vexation. If only the Duke were not so provoking. She could not think of another human being, apart from Cassie, to whom she would have made such an unguarded remark, and Salterne was almost a stranger to her.

The knowledge brought her up with a start. Less than a week ago she had never met him. It seemed incredible. That dark, expressive face was almost as familiar to her as her own. She knew exactly how the laughter began deep in his eyes, suffusing their greyness with warmth, and grew until it lifted the corners of that mobile mouth. And she was aware of every nuance in his voice.

Now it was silky smooth.

'I am glad to see that family feeling has not blinded

you to Ransome's faults,' the Duke said softly. 'What a pair we make, he and I. Me with my arrogance, my evil reputation. . .and this. . .' He lifted a hand to his scarred face.

'Do not say that!' Impulsively Aurelia reached out a hand towards him. She had almost forgotten the scar, but now she noticed again the thin line, half hidden on his brow by the thick black hair, and curving down his cheek. How nearly the sabre-cut had missed his eyes. He might have been blinded.

'I should be proud to bear that wound,' she said earnestly.

His mocking expression changed, and in his eyes she saw wonder.

'I am half inclined to believe you. Yet it would be a pity to mar that perfect face.'

His words succeeded in robbing Aurelia of speech.

'I shall observe your machinations with great interest,' he observed in a lighter tone. 'You are like to be a worthy opponent, but I warn you I shall give no quarter. I wonder who will win this contest. . .you or I? Do you care to place a wager on the result?'

'You are insufferable!' All her resentment returned at his taunts.

For answer he raised her hand to his lips, but instead of the conventional courtesy he turned it over and pressed a kiss into her palm. Even through the silk of her mittens she felt that it burned her skin.

He bowed, and to her utter fury she saw that he was smiling as he walked away.

CHAPTER FIVE

AURELIA hurried indoors, blind and deaf to all about her. How could she have allowed herself to be drawn into yet another duel of wits with Salterne?

Her lips tightened. She'd beat him yet. The encounter had been unexpected and it had come as a shock, so that she'd been unprepared. Next time she would be ready for him. If only she had more time, she mourned. She'd been hoping for a breathing space. . . some turn of events. . .perhaps another offer for Caroline which might cause Salterne to withdraw; but it was too soon for that.

And he had spoken no more than the truth. He held all the cards. One word to Ransome and the announcement of the betrothal would appear in the *Morning Post*. Then Caroline's fate would be sealed.

She sat down at her desk and tried to think clearly about the situation. The Duke's attitude puzzled her. He was not lover-like in the least towards Caroline. He had shown no disposition to seek her niece's company either at Marram or in Brighton. He was buying a wife, she thought indignantly, and the transaction did not require him to play the fond suitor. It was an insult to the girl, to say the least.

It was also a relief. She would say nothing of her encounter with Salterne to Cassie or Caro. Time enough to ruin the girl's peace of mind when it could no longer be avoided. In Brighton other diversions might serve to keep the Duke from their door. She had no doubt that he would not lack feminine company. He was a womaniser. His every word and look proclaimed the fact.

Hot colour flooded her cheeks as she recalled her own response to him. She could not treat him with indifference, she lamented bitterly. His touch excited her, though she prayed that he was not aware of it. Yet the man seemed to read her mind with ruthless clarity. The less she saw of him the better, yet in the circumstances that would be impossible.

I won't give up, Aurelia vowed to herself. If Salterne wishes for a trial of strength I'll be happy to oblige him.

She picked up a pile of invitations from the tray. Card parties. . .balls. . .? She was leafing through them when Cass and Caro returned.

'Only think, sister! We are invited to the Broomes' tomorrow.' Cassie's eyes were sparkling. 'I knew Anne as a girl. 'Pon my soul, I believe that all the world is here, and the Regent arrives within the week.'

Aurelia held up a card.

'What do you say to the ball on Thursday?'

'The Old Ship Inn? That is the usual weekly affair. Do let us go! I should enjoy it beyond anything. . .' Cassie's face was lit from within. Once more she was the beautiful Cassandra Carrington, one of the Incomparables.

'I believe I shall wear the jonquil crêpe with the *dents de loup*,' she announced. 'A first impression is of the greatest importance. Caro will look well in her white muslin with the silver sprigs, and possibly a wreath. What of you, Lia?'

'The lavender, I think, with the overdress of spider gauze.'

Cassie looked doubtful.

'It is elegant, of course, but is it not a little subdued?'

'It will suit me well enough,' Aurelia said firmly. 'You would not have me in spangles, like the Prince?'

'Of course not, but——'

'Set your mind at rest, Cass. We shall be quite *à ravir*. I shall send for Monsieur Pierre. He is thought to be a genius with coiffure.' She laughed. 'I wonder how we managed before the refugees arrived from France.'

Her eyes rested on Caroline's face. If the child was missing Richard she gave no sign of it. She had already attracted a good deal of attention, and Brighton was full of eligible beaux, especially the regiment of the 10th Hussars, the Prince's Own. Caro would not lack for partners, and the wider their circle of acquaintance, the more chance there might be of another offer.

She hesitated, knowing full well that she should mention her meeting with Salterne, but that would cast a cloud over Caroline's pleasure. It was apparent that neither she nor her mother knew of his continued stay in Brighton. Aurelia decided to keep her own counsel. Caro should have another few hours' peace of mind.

Then she remembered. Had he not promised to call on the following day?

'I thought we might drive along the coast tomorrow,' she announced. 'If the weather is kind we shall take a picnic to St Mary's Well.'

Caro clapped her hands, but Cassie looked doubtful.

'Had we not better rest? We are promised to the

Broomes for the evening, and, Lia, you know how I freckle in the sun. I am quite out of chervil water as a remedy.'

'Then let us take a morning drive,' Aurelia said patiently. 'You may rest in the afternoon, and we shall deny all callers.'

To her relief Cassie agreed. It was merely postponing the inevitable meeting, but it would serve for the moment.

Her precautions proved unnecessary. On their return she scanned through the pile of calling cards, but Salterne's was not among them. She was seized by the uneasy feeling that he would always be one step ahead of her. Perhaps he intended to lull her into a false sense of security. It would be like him to think of such a devious manoeuvre.

Next day brought Monsieur Pierre and again Aurelia gave instructions to deny all visitors. Even so, she jumped each time she heard a knock at the door.

'Lia, what is the matter with you? Are you not well? I have asked you twice for your opinion on this style for Caro's hair.'

Aurelia gave a guilty start and looked at her niece. The blonde hair had been cropped to form a halo around the girl's face.

'It is cherubic,' she chuckled. 'It suits you quite delightfully, my love.'

The little Frenchman was rightly proud of his reputation. With infinite care he coaxed Cassie's heavy locks into a chignon, training a few tendrils to fall on either side of her brow. It made her look years younger, and as Aurelia caught her sister's eye she was rewarded with a happy smile.

'Now, Miss Carrington, you will trust to my judgement?' Monsieur Pierre regarded Aurelia in the mirror.

'Of course, *monsieur*, but nothing too extreme, if you please. . .'

The Frenchman picked up his scissors with a flourish, ignoring her faint admonishment.

'*À la Grecque*, I believe,' he said firmly. 'We shall not cut these magnificent tresses, but shape them merely.'

Aurelia's misgivings vanished as he combed the cloud of fine fair hair away from her face, and pinned it high into a knot of curls. A swift turn of his fingers caused one or two of them to cascade from the highest point.

'That is better, yes?' He stood back to approve his work. 'Now one may see the full beauty of the eyes, and the classic features. You approve, *mademoiselle*?'

'Indeed, *monsieur*, I like it very much.'

'One sees such styles on Grecian urns. They are in harmony with the present fashion for the draperies of antiquity. And observe how one may continue the theme. . .' He picked up a silver fillet and bound it around her brow. 'One may use ribbons in this way, or jewelled headbands, and sometimes a fillet of three strands. It is a simple matter to catch it at the back of the head.'

He smiled as Aurelia looked doubtful.

'You have perfect carriage of the head, *mademoiselle*, and the style is simple. You may dress it as you will. Perhaps a flower or two besides the curls on top.' To prove his point he chose a cluster of silk roses in the deepest pink and held them against her fair hair.

Aurelia had to admit that he was right. She might

not choose to follow the more extreme of his suggestions, but a flower to match her gown would please her.

That his efforts had been successful was evident when the three ladies entered the ballroom of the Old Ship Inn that evening. A buzz of interest greeted their appearance and a dozen pairs of eyes focused eagerly upon their jewellery and their gowns.

Aurelia scanned the room for the towering figure of the Duke, but he was nowhere to be seen. Satisfied that he was engaged elsewhere, she allowed herself to relax. Perhaps he had returned to London. The Prince liked his friends about him, and he was known to take their absence amiss.

'Lia, do bow! Lady Jersey is beckoning to us.'

Cassie drew her sister's arm through hers and led the way towards the famous London hostess.

'She was kind to Caro,' Cassie whispered. 'We owe her marked civility. Had she not procured us vouchers for Almack's. . .well. . .I do not need to explain what that would mean. The Duchess of Bedford was blackballed, you know, though I hear she was admitted later.'

Aurelia felt the old stirrings of rebellion. It was all so familiar. Arbitrary decisions by the Lady Patronesses of that exclusive establishment could make or break a reputation, and anything was better than the refusal of a voucher to attend. To be without one was to be banished to the outer perimeter of society.

Aurelia found it ludicrous. Almack's rooms were sparsely furnished, the food was indifferent, and the only liquid refreshments permitted were orgeat, lemonade, or the weakest of claret cups. A strange choice of venue for a marriage mart, Aurelia thought to herself, for such was its undisguised purpose.

She moved towards Lady Jersey with a feeling of restraint, and was at once disarmed.

'How pleasant to see you again, Miss Carrington!' Her Ladyship was all civility. 'Country life agrees with you. You are in famous looks.'

Aurelia smiled and thanked her.

'Your father was highly thought of, my dear. I was saddened to hear of his death. Tell me, do you stay in Brighton for the season?'

'For some weeks at least, Your Ladyship.'

'I am glad to hear it.' Lady Jersey nodded her approval. 'When the Prince arrives you may be sure he will invite you to one of his musical evenings.'

She turned away and Cassie squeezed Aurelia'a arm.

'If she speaks to the Regent we are sure to be invited,' she whispered.

Aurelia nodded, though she had no particular desire for such an invitation. But Lady Jersey had great influence with the Prince, and to move in such exalted circles could do no harm to Caro's prospects.

Lady Jersey raised a finger to summon a young man to her side.

'May I present Ensign, the Lord Weekes?' she said. 'I believe he hopes to lead Caroline in the country dance.' She smiled at Caro, who went off happily on the young man's arm.

'Unexceptionable, Lady Ransome.' Her Ladyship at once understood the troubled look on Cassie's face. 'Prince George's officers are beyond reproach.'

Privately Aurelia doubted the truth of that statement, but Cassie was reassured.

'Do you care to dance, Miss Carrington?' Lady Jersey inspected the crowd of hopefuls standing close beside them. 'Leggatt, I vow, has had eyes for no one else since you entered the room.' She beckoned to a tall young man, clad in immaculate regimentals. 'Will you take pity on Captain Leggatt?'

Aurelia looked at the eager face. The captain looked absurdly young, and it would have been churlish to refuse. She took his arm and joined the throng on the crowded floor.

She felt a little shy at first. It was so long since she had danced, or even entered into conversation with a personable young man. But her companion's easy manner soon set her at ease.

'I have not seen you here before,' he said. 'Do you know Brighton well?'

'It is some years since I was last in the town,' she answered. 'I see so many changes.'

'It is a splendid place. There is much of interest here. . .and yet. . .'

Aurelia looked at the wistful face.

'You would prefer to be elsewhere?'

'Not at this moment, ma'am, I assure you, but I should like to see some action. We are a joke among the other regiments. They see us as toy soldiers.'

'That is a harsh judgement. You do not lack courage, I'm sure.'

'Nor does our colonel, Miss Carrington. The Prince has begged to be allowed to serve in the field, but permission is always refused.'

'It is hard indeed.' Aurelia gave him a sympathetic smile. 'Yet the heir to the throne must put his duty first.'

'I understand that, but we. . .the rest of us? I'm

sorry, I must not bore you. The ladies do not care for military matters. Shall you attend the races?'

'I hope to do so. They are a famous sight.' She stumbled as a heavy foot caught the hem of her gown. The gentleman behind her was profuse in his apologies, but the damage was done. Aurelia glanced down in dismay to find that a length of gauze had been torn from her skirt.

'Clumsy fellow!' Her partner looked his disgust. 'Melton is more at home on the hunting field, I fear.'

'It is no matter, but I must catch it up at once, or I shall be a danger to all about me. Excuse me, sir.'

Her companion led her off the floor.

'I believe there is a retiring-room,' she murmured. 'Please do not trouble to escort me. I shall find my way.'

The rest-room was further away than she remembered, but she found it after passing through a series of small apartments. Torn flounces were no rare occurrence, as the maid assured her. With the aid of a needle and thread the damage was soon repaired.

She had intended to return at once to the ballroom, but the inn had been altered since her last visit, and she was soon lost. In the distance she could hear the sound of music, and she made her way towards it.

It was as she was passing a small embrasure that she noticed an elderly woman lying on a couch. She heard the stertorous breathing, and was alarmed by the pallor of the wrinkled face.

'May I be of assistance, ma'am?' Aurelia paused beside the couch. 'You do not look at all the thing. Perhaps a restorative?'

The papery eyelids opened, and a pair of sharp black eyes inspected her.

'I thank you. . .but my grandson. . .he is gone to fetch something for me. It is just the heat. . .'

'It *is* very warm,' Aurelia agreed. The Regent lived in a hothouse atmosphere, and stuffy rooms were all the rage in Brighton. She pulled up a small gilt chair, and then, disturbed by the old lady's laboured breathing, she leaned towards her.

'Perhaps if I fanned you it might bring relief.' She unfurled her fan, moving it gently to create a current of air.

'That is civil of you, my dear. I am an obstinate creature. Rollo warned me that I should rest, but I paid him no heed.' She lifted her face towards the swaying fan. 'There! I feel better already.'

Even as she spoke she collapsed with a sigh into Aurelia's arms.

'Let me!' The deep voice startled her. Salterne set down the glass of brandy in his hand and took her burden from her.

'I will fetch some water.' Aurelia hurried back to the retiring-room, and returned with a small bowl and a cloth.

'This lady should be taken home at once,' she said quietly. She laid the moistened cloth on the unconscious woman's brow.

'I agree. If I might leave my grandmother in your care for a moment I will order my coach and send a servant for the doctor.'

Aurelia nodded. She poured a little of the water over the old lady's wrists and saw with relief that her patient was recovering consciousness.

'Do not try to speak,' she urged. 'The Duke will be back at once.' She held the brandy to the old woman's lips.

'Stupid of me!' The faint words barely reached Aurelia's ears. 'Rollo is like to be insufferable since he is proved right again.' She gave a low chuckle.

'His Grace will be pleased to find you better, ma'am.'

'You are very kind.' A tiny claw-like hand gripped her own with surprising strength. 'It was fortunate that you chanced by. Will you tell me your name? We have not met before, I think.'

'I am Aurelia Carrington, Your Ladyship. You may know my sister, Lady Ransome?'

'Ah, yes. . . Ransome. . .'

There was a silence which Aurelia did not attempt to break. Was she to be classed with her unscrupulous brother-in-law? She would not blame anyone for repudiating his connections. As she attempted to withdraw her hand the old lady spoke again.

'Your father was very dear to me,' she said. 'What a man he was! You must miss him sadly.'

'I do. No one could have had a happier childhood than my sister and myself.'

'Poor Cassandra. She thought the world well lost for love. And you, miss? Are you of the same opinion? You are perhaps betrothed?'

'No, Your Grace.' From anyone else the question might have been an impertinence, but somehow Aurelia could not take offence.

'You do not answer my first question, Miss Carrington.'

Aurelia smiled and rose to her feet.

'You will tire yourself, ma'am. Then His Grace will regret having left you in my charge.'

'Stuff! Rollo worries too much. 'Tis naught but a dizzy spell and to be expected at my age. It has passed off, as you see.' She struggled to sit up, but the effort was beyond her and she closed her eyes.

'How is she?' Salterne stood beside them.

'A little better, I believe. . .but weak.'

He bent and lifted the frail figure in his arms.

'The door on the left,' he said briefly. 'Will you lead the way?'

Aurelia gathered up the old lady's scarf and reticule. Then she hurried ahead of him.

'Get in,' he commanded. 'I shall need your help.'

Aurelia settled herself in the corner of the coach. This was no time to raise objections. As Salterne laid his burden on the seat she took the Duchess's head in her lap.

Their journey was a short one, but Salterne was out of the coach before it had stopped moving.

'Come!' he said in an abrupt tone. He took his grandmother from Aurelia's arms and ran lightly up the steps of a large house.

Flambeaus burned by the door, illuminating the anxious faces of a group of servants. Brushing aside their offers of help, he called to his steward.

'The doctor?'

'On his way, Your Grace. We are keeping watch for him.'

Salterne started up the stairs.

'Miss Carrington!' It was a peremptory command, and she followed him without question. He threw open the door of a bedroom on the first floor, and laid his grandmother down against the pillows. The frail old lady looked pathetically small in the massive four-poster with its heavily carved upright columns. The roof piece supported a high canopy covered in damask drapery, and curtains in the same material, lavishly fringed and tasselled, were half drawn around the bed.

The Duke thrust them aside impatiently as Aurelia busied herself in removing the satin turban from the Duchess's head. She loosened the ribbons of her upper clothing, and then pulled off her slippers.

'I will attend her, madam.'

Aurelia moved aside as the Duchess's maid bent over her mistress. She was about to leave the room when she heard a whispered request.

'Stay with me, please.'

Aurelia looked towards the Duke, but he was gazing through the window, drumming his fingers on the sill.

'At last!' He strode towards the staircase and hustled the doctor into the room.

Aurelia stood back. There was nothing more that she could do. The Duke took her arm and led her into the corridor.

'She is in good hands,' he murmured, as if to reassure himself as much as Aurelia. His tortured expression went to her heart.

'Pray do not distress yourself,' she said gently. 'The old are surprisingly resilient, and the Duchess appears to have an indomitable will.'

He had been gazing into space, but her words struck a chord. He looked deep into her eyes and then he smiled.

'That is one of her problems,' he admitted. 'Miss Carrington, you have been most kind. May I offer you some refreshment?'

She was about to refuse, but a feeling of pity stayed her. She would wait with him until the doctor had given his verdict.

'I thank you. I must confess I am a little thirsty.'

He led her down to the salon and rang for wine.
Then he began to pace the room.

'The Duchess assured me that her disposition was
due entirely to the heat,' she offered.

'To that. . .and a heart condition which is like to
kill her at any time. . .' His face was grim. 'I begged
her not to attend the ball. She should have taken my
advice.'

Aurelia did not speak. She had suspected something
of the kind from what the Duchess had told her.

'Women!' he went on furiously. 'Of all the stubborn, self-willed creatures on this earth. . .'

Aurelia permitted herself the ghost of a smile.

'Something amuses you?'

'Women do not have a monopoly of such traits,
Your Grace.'

He stared at her. Then he put up a hand to acknowledge the hit. 'You are right, of course. I am not myself
the best of patients.'

He sighed to his servant to set down the tray beside
him. Then he turned to Aurelia.

'You will take wine, Miss Carrington? It is not
ratafia, I fear.'

Aurelia blushed. He had not forgotten their first
meeting.

'That was ill done of me,' she said. 'It is not. . .not
my usual way.'

'You had cause for anger. . .but so had I.'

Aurelia changed the subject. She had no wish to be
drawn into a discussion of Caroline's behaviour. She
gazed about the room.

'You are interested in paintings, Your Grace?'

The salon had surprised her. Plain walls painted in
the palest possible shade of green formed a perfect

background for a fine collection of pictures. She could guess at the value of the furniture, which bore evidence of an expert craftsman's skill. It was clear that the Duke did not share the Regent's taste in matters of interior decoration.

Her host appeared to have read her mind.

'Astonished?' he said lightly. 'The Prince's "farmhouse" is somewhat overdone for me, though he is a noted patron of the arts.'

Aurelia felt that she was on dangerous ground. The Regent's flamboyant tastes were no concern of hers, and incautious comment might well reach his ears. She rose to her feet and walked over to the window. It faced the sea and beyond it the lights of the fishing fleet were strung out like a necklace of jewels on the dark waters. Above the sea a rising moon sent a shaft of silver light towards her.

What an evening it had been! And now to find herself in the house of her enemy after all her efforts to avoid him.

She was lost in thought when the doctor entered the room, and she stayed out of hearing while he made his report to the Duke. Then she glanced at Salterne's face with a look of enquiry.

'She is recovering,' he said heavily. 'In future I shall be firm with her. She must follow the physician's orders. She still believes that she may go about as she was used to.' The harsh lines on his face were even more pronounced, and the scar showed white against his tanned skin. For the first time in their acquaintance Aurelia thought that he looked weary.

'I must go,' she said gently. 'Cassie must be wondering. . .'

'I beg your pardon. I had forgot to mention it, but I sent a message to Lady Ransome to explain. . .'

'That was thoughtful, but even so. . .it is late, Your Grace.' Aurelia gave him her hand. 'Try not to worry, sir. When the Duchess is rested you will see an improvement.'

His eyes searched her face. 'You have some experience, I believe. Your sister told me something of your life at Marram. It must have been hard for you.'

'Not in the least. I loved my father dearly. It is three years since his death, and I miss him yet. We were so close, you see.' Her voice was not quite under control. 'He teased me into forming my own opinions on many subjects. I still feel the need. . .'

'For stimulating conversation?' He had understood her perfectly. 'And for affection too, I imagine. It is hard to lose a loved one. They are not easily replaced. . .'

Aurelia's eyes met his, and she looked away. The depth of misery there appalled her.

'You have a daughter, I understand. She must be a joy to you.'

'Charlotte arrives tomorrow.' Salterne's expression changed. 'She is an imp of mischief, Miss Carrington, and my grandmother indulges her. They are two of a kind, I fear.' His severe look was unconvincing.

'Then you have much to look forward to.' She picked up her scarf and reticule. 'Now, if you will allow me, I must leave.'

'Of course. Forgive me, I am being thoughtless.'

Aurelia murmured a disclaimer, and suddenly felt shy. Tonight she had seen a side of the Duke's character which was totally unexpected. She frowned. Could she have been wrong about him? She was unusually silent for the duration of the journey to the Steyne.

As the carriage stopped Salterne took her hands in his.

'I am in your debt, dear enemy. I shall not forget.'

In the darkness she could not see his face, but the warmth in his voice caused her heart to pound. He was having the most unfortunate effect upon her equilibrium, and to her dismay she found that she had not the slightest wish to draw her hands away from his.

'It. . .it was nothing. I beg you will not speak of it. I was happy to be of service to the Duchess.' Aurelia found that she was trembling, and she could not disguise the fact.

'You are cold. Let me take you to your door.' He handed her down, bowed, and was gone before Cassie could greet him.

'Lia, what happened? You have been gone this age. I was never so surprised as when I received the Duke's message.'

'The Dowager Duchess felt faint. I happened to be there.'

'Is that all? I fancied her at death's door. How uncivil of Salterne to ruin your evening!'

'He did nothing of the kind,' Aurelia said shortly. 'Don't fuss, Cass. I should have done the same for anyone.'

'But you dislike him so! Had he but asked I should have gone myself.'

'There was no time, and you could not leave Caro.'

'You might have stayed with her. . .'

'Cassie, let us forget the matter. Did you enjoy the ball?' Aurelia's patience was wearing thin.

'My dear, what an evening! I enjoyed it above anything. . .and the invitations we received!' A thought struck her and her face fell. 'Now that Salterne is here we must consider his wishes, I suppose. I confess I was surprised to find him here.'

'Why so? The Prince is expected, and the Duke is a friend of his.'

'I know, but Salterne may not be best pleased to find Caro behaving as if she were unattached.'

'She *is* unattached as yet. And she has not agreed to marry him.'

Cassie's lips set in a thin line.

'She will do so. There is no alternative. Ransome is in desperate case. We must not lose Salterne now.'

'Things cannot be as bad as that.'

'They could scarce be worse. The duns are closing in. . .' Cassie shuddered.

'How much is involved? I know I said I would not help, but I cannot see you in such straits. . .'

'No!' Cassie was adamant. 'I had no right to ask you. I would not reduce you to our level.'

'I see.'

'No, you refuse to see. When it is known that Caro is to marry the Duke our creditors will hold off. Salterne scarce knows what he is worth. I could not begin to guess at his income.'

'And Ransome would then feel at liberty to continue his present way of life? Where is it to end, Cassie? I may not like the Duke, but I do not consider him a fool. He will not spend his fortune on a gambler.'

'Neither would he countenance Ransome's bankruptcy,' Cassie persisted stubbornly. 'Salterne bears a great name. He will not see it disgraced.'

'Disgraced even further, do you mean? You seem to have forgot his reputation.'

Cassie shrugged. 'We may discount at least one half of the gossip.'

'The other half would be enough for me.'

'Lia, please! If we can but come about this time, Ransome may have learned his lesson.'

Aurelia stared at her sister in amazement. If, after all these years, Cassie still hoped that her husband would have a change of heart there was no more to be said on the subject.

'I am tired, my love.' She dropped a kiss on Cassie's brow. 'I will speak to you in the morning.'

A disturbed night did nothing to refresh her spirits and the others were up and about before she came downstairs.

Cassie was standing by the window, gazing at the rain-swept street.

'We must forgo our drive,' she said in petulant tones. 'There would be no pleasure in setting off in this miserable weather.'

'Then we shall occupy ourselves indoors, though I confess that I have finished my book.' Aurelia looked up in surprise as a knock sounded at the door. 'Is it not too early for morning callers?'

'It is doubtless Captain Leggatt.' Cassie gave her a mischievous look. 'He asked if he might call.'

'The captain must imagine that he is still on campaign,' Aurelia said drily.

'Perhaps he is. It was clear that he admired you.'

'Now, Cass, you are not to be at your matchmaking already.'

'Of course not.' Cassie bent over her netting, that

Aurelia might not see the twinkle in her eye. 'But did you not say. . .?'

The sentence was left unfinished. Her face changed as the door burst open. She rose to her feet and the netting fell unheeded to the ground.

'Ransome!' she whispered. 'What are you doing here?'

CHAPTER SIX

RANSOME inspected them from the doorway. He was smiling, but his eyes were cold.

'How could I stay away, my love?' He sauntered over to Cassie and caught her by the upper arm. To all appearances he was about to salute her as any man might greet a beloved wife, but she gave a gasp of pain as his cruel fingers nipped her flesh.

'Ransome!' Aurelia's voice cut the air like a lash.

'Yes, dear sister-in-law?' The guileless blue eyes looked into hers. Behind the apparent innocence was a gleam of such malevolence that Aurelia gasped. She had not thought to see such evil in a human face. It was gone in a flash, and Ransome strolled towards her.

'Forgive me!' His smile deepened. 'You are the mistress here, so Frederick tells me.' He bent to kiss her cheek.

'Spare me your embraces!' Aurelia looked pointedly at the red marks on her sister's arm.

'Was I too urgent in my greeting? You cannot blame me. I have been deprived of Cassie for so long.'

'And much against your will, I make no doubt. Your eyesight must be failing, sir. Have you no word for your daughter?'

'I imagined she was trying to make herself invisible.' His tone was smooth, but Caroline began to tremble. 'Doubtless she is attempting to hide her delight at my

94

arrival. Come to me, my dear. Will you not greet your father with a kiss?'

With lagging steps Caroline walked towards him. As she reached his side he seized her hand in an iron grip, forcing her to her knees. Then he dropped a kiss upon her brow.

'Nervous, my dear child? Perhaps the excitement is too much for you, but you must try to contain your transports of joy.' He looked at Aurelia as he spoke, challenging her openly.

'What brings you here?' she asked abruptly.

'My family, of course.' His eyes widened in feigned astonishment. 'It was kind in you to spirit them away so suddenly for—er—a change of scene. . .but now I must insist that they are restored to me.' He shot her a swift look of triumph, knowing that she was power-less to stop him.

Without a word she handed him a card from the pile beside her. He whistled as he looked at the invitation. 'A musical evening with the Prince? You move in high circles, my dear Aurelia. Why this sudden wish to return to society? I thought you con-tent to moulder away at Marram.'

'I have changed my mind.'

'I wonder why? You cannot be hoping for an offer after all these years.'

Aurelia was silent.

Ransome laughed then, and it was not a pleasant sound.

'Have I hit on the truth of it? If so, you must persuade Caro to follow your example. She has some foolish notion that she does not wish to marry.'

'Of course she will marry.' Inwardly Aurelia upbraided herself for antagonising him so quickly, but his cruelty had incensed her. 'Surely another week or two in Brighton cannot signify? If you would but consent. . .'

'Pleading, my dear? That is somewhat out of character, is it not?' Ransome was enjoying himself. 'I know you well, Aurelia. You do not approve of Salterne, is that it?' He gave her a hard look.

'I do not know the Duke well. How am I to judge?'

'Oh, you'll judge! Nothing could be more certain. After all, your standards are so high. No one was good enough for you. Tell me, does your fortune make a warm bedfellow?'

'Ransome, please. . .' Cassie was stung into a reproach, but a look from Aurelia silenced her.

'The Regent will not take kindly to a refusal,' she warned.

'Prinny will understand,' he answered carelessly. 'Cass, make your preparations. We leave today.'

'So soon?' Salterne was standing in the doorway, regarding them with a benevolent gaze. He bowed to the ladies and favoured Ransome with the briefest of nods. Then he walked over to Aurelia.

'I crave your pardon for entering unannounced, Miss Carrington. In view of our forthcoming connection I felt that we might dispense with the formalities.'

He turned to Caro and took her hands, giving her a smile of singular sweetness.

'We go on so well, my dear Ransome,' he murmured. 'Caro has promised to drive with me today. I shall take it amiss if you steal her away.'

Aurelia was tempted to laugh aloud at the look on Ransome's face. Cassie was speechless, and Caroline stood as if turned to stone. Aurelia was the first to recover her composure.

'Do not keep His Grace waiting, Caro,' she said briskly. 'Do you put on your pelisse and make haste. The horses must not stand, you know.'

She turned to Salterne.

'We had not expected you quite yet,' she said in perfect truth. 'The rain was so heavy. . .'

'It is clearing, ma'am.' His expression was imperturbable as he looked at Ransome. 'I hope I may persuade you to delay your departure, my dear sir, but naturally if you insist I must give way.'

'Not at all! I did not know you to be in Brighton, Your Grace. I had imagined, you see. . .' His voice tailed away.

'Yes?' Salterne prompted.

'It is no matter. . .' Ransome looked uncomfortable. 'I was concerned to think that the ladies were alone.'

'A proper sentiment from a loving father and husband.' With exquisite grace His Lordship proffered his snuff-box. 'When Miss Carrington and Lady Ransome approved this delightful expedition I could not believe my good fortune. Such an opportunity to woo my bride-to-be! I trust it has your approval? We should have applied for your permission, but we had no notion as to where you might be found.'

An ugly flush stained Ransome's cheeks.

'I beg that you will allow your anger to fall upon me and not upon the ladies, if you have some objection,' Salterne continued.

Aurelia dared not meet his eye. She had seldom seen her brother-in-law so thoroughly routed, and she kept her countenance with the greatest difficulty. The thought of Ransome chiding this formidable creature brought her sense of humour bubbling to the surface. When His Lordship chose he could be insufferable.

'We dispatched Frederick to beg you to join us,' His Grace said smoothly. 'But perhaps you do not care for Brighton?'

'It is well enough.' Ransome quickly recovered his ease of manner. 'If the ladies had but explained. . . Aurelia, I fear you have been teasing me.'

'Miss Carrington enjoys a joke,' the Duke observed with a straight face. 'May I beg you to accompany us, ma'am? Lady Ransome will not wish to leave her husband as he is but just arrived.'

'I shall not keep you above a moment.' Aurelia hurried from the room, praying that Cassie would have the wit to support the Duke's story.

On her return she was not surprised to find that he was embarked upon a plausible account as to how and why he had escorted Cassie and his betrothed into Sussex to visit Marram.

'We had scarce hoped to persuade Miss Carrington to join us,' he said without a flicker of expression. 'But I added my entreaties to those of your family and here we are.'

That was doing it too brown. Aurelia's shoulders began to shake as she met his bland look, but her amusement vanished when Ransome spoke to her.

'I may stay here, I suppose? The town is crowded. There is nothing to be had in the way of lodgings.'

Aurelia forced a smile.

'Of course you shall stay. Hannah will see to the arrangement of the rooms.' The thought of having Ransome under her roof filled her with dismay, but there was no avoiding it.

'My apologies, Miss Carrington.' Salterne's voice

was low as he handed her into his carriage. 'This can be no pleasant prospect for you.'

'It is no matter.' For her part she was glad that Ransome appeared to be in charity with his wife again. 'I fear you have a vivid imagination, Your Grace. What a tale you told!'

'Merely in the interests of family harmony. Or shall I say rather that needs must when the devil drives? On occasion the normal rules of conduct do not apply. One fights fire with fire. You of all people will know that.'

She refused to rise to the bait.

'You must think me remiss,' she said. 'How is the Dowager Duchess today?'

'She is much recovered, I thank you. It was she who asked me to call upon you. She will be happy to see you.'

'Surely she should rest? Did not the doctor say. . .?'

'He has forbidden all visitors for a day or so, and I have insisted that she obey him.'

Aurelia made an unsuccessful attempt to hide a smile.

'You are quite right,' he told her ruefully. 'It was not easy. I was forced to point out that if she wished to enjoy the Prince's company she must save her strength. They are quite the best of friends. She has known him since he was a child.'

'You know the Prince well, my lord? Caro was asking about him only yesterday. . .' Aurelia attempted to hide her irritation as she looked at her niece. Caro was pale. She had not recovered from the shock of her father's sudden reappearance, but she had been rescued from a difficult situation. If only she would make some effort to be civil.

His Lordship did not seem troubled by her silence.

'I believe I know the Regent as well as anyone may,' he replied. 'His is a complex character, and he has been much abused by his enemies. His countrymen are disinclined to favour a patron of the arts, or a connoisseur of food and wine, especially as his pleasures are so costly. Had he been bluff and hearty like the Duke of Clarence he might have been better understood. Yet the Prince has many sterling qualities. . .'

'I was conscious only of his charm,' Aurelia admitted. 'And one hears everywhere of his generosity. The old woman who sells gingerbread and apples at the corner of the Steyne? Did he not give her a pension from his own pocket?'

Salterne smiled. 'You are speaking of Phoebe Hessell. Her story intrigued him. She joined the army as a man and followed her lover to the Indies when she was fifteen.'

'What happened to her?' Caroline forgot her fear of the Duke and leaned forward, her face alive with interest.

'She went into battle with the troops and received a bayonet wound.'

'And then she was discovered to be a woman?'

'Not even then. She was tall and broad, and she had a deep voice. It was only when her man was severely wounded that she disclosed her sex. She was sent home with him.'

'And did they marry?' Caroline asked.

'The story had a happy ending. She nursed him back to health, they wed, and enjoyed twenty years together before he died.'

'How wonderful!'

'The Prince shared your opinion, Caro. To save her from the poorhouse he supports her from his private funds.'

'I am glad that he is so charitable.' Caroline's voice was warm.

'His very generosity adds to his debts, alas, and they, you must know, have always been immense.'

Aurelia looked mystified.

'Was it not said that when he married his difficulties would be at an end? The King and Parliament promised financial help, did they not? I remember my father speaking of the matter.'

'That was the Prince's understanding, ma'am, but it was not as he hoped. His Royal Highness is much embittered. He considers that he was betrayed into a marriage which——'

His eye fell on Caroline and he stopped. He must not discuss her namesake, Caroline of Brunswick, nor the scandals which surrounded that lady. He changed the subject.

'You have not yet seen the interior of the Prince's "cottage"?' he enquired.

Caroline shook her head.

'It is most interesting.' He was smiling as he spoke. 'The Prince is much influenced by Chinese art.'

'I hear that he plans to change the exterior. Will it be in oriental style?'

'It is to be reminiscent of the Indian continent, so I understand. The plans are based on the design of Sezincote, the home of an Indian nabob.'

He glanced at Aurelia's face and his lips twitched.

'Neither to your taste nor to mine,' he said agreeably. 'But the Prince will have his way.'

'An Indian palace by the English Channel. . .?' she

mused. 'Well, it will most certainly be different. . . We have been invited to a musical evening there.'

'You cannot fail to enjoy it.' He turned to Caroline. 'The musicians are of the best, and Prince George has an excellent voice. One cannot help but share his pleasure.' His eyebrows lifted at her look of surprise. 'You are interested in the arts?'

Addressed directly, Caroline grew shy.

'Why, y—yes,' she stammered. She relapsed into silence and gazed through the window.

'Caroline paints,' Aurelia said with a touch of impatience. Really, the child should make some effort to preserve the basic courtesies of social life. Her incommunicative behaviour was becoming a trial.

'Indeed!' The Duke's eyes glazed. Drawing and painting were considered necessary accomplishments for young ladies and he had been forced to examine some dire examples of their effort.

'She has some talent.' Aurelia's eyes glinted. She did not bestow praise lightly, even on a beloved niece. Caroline's work was far removed from the usual daubs.

Salterne sensed her mood.

'I did not know.' He looked at the silent girl. 'Do you prefer portraiture or still life?'

'I. . . I like to paint landscapes,' Caroline said in a low voice.

'Then I shall show you one of the finest sights in England.'

He rapped out an order and the coachman changed direction. As they travelled east the Duke exerted himself to name the villages through which they passed, pointing out the Norman churches, and the ruins of several castles.

Aurelia found that she was enjoying herself. Her companion's extensive knowledge of the countryside surprised her.

When they stopped and he handed her down she found that they had reached a high point of the downs, and in the distance she could hear the sea.

Salterne looked at her yellow kid half-boots.

'The ground is still damp, I fear, but if we keep to the sheep track we may walk a little way.'

Caro was already hurrying on ahead, but Aurelia slowed her own pace.

'Your Grace, I have not yet thanked you for your help this morning. You arrived at a difficult moment. . .'

'You would thank me for my duplicity? You. . .of all people? I am shocked.'

'Please do not jest. I am in earnest. Ransome would most certainly have insisted. . .' Her voice tailed away.

'On removing his family from your baleful influence?' He laughed. 'I guessed as much, Miss Carrington, when I saw him enter the house. It was unpardonable of me to come upon you unannounced, and I had some difficulty in persuading your servant. . .'

'I am very glad you did so,' Aurelia said with feeling. 'I had no power to stop him. I could think of no way to prevent him taking them away.'

'You, at a loss? I don't believe it.'

She caught his eye and blushed.

'We have so many invitations,' she said lamely. 'And it would have been discourteous to refuse the Prince.'

'Quite!' A suspicious quiver lingered at the corner

of his mouth. 'And it would not have suited me in the least. However, I am persuaded that Ransome will make no further difficulties.'

She looked at him then and saw that his eyes were dancing. She could think of nothing to say as he strolled along beside her, perfectly at his ease.

'I must compliment you on the speed with which you followed my lead,' he murmured.

Aurelia coloured.

'Do you imagine that Ransome believed your story?'

'It is in his interest to believe it. In any case, it does not much signify, though I must confess that my powers of invention led me on to dangerous ground.'

She gave him a puzzled look.

'I felt that I had gone too far, ma'am, in claiming that you had yielded to my own entreaties to visit Brighton.' The swarthy face was alight with amusement. 'Confess that it almost overset you! We have not been the best of friends, you will agree.'

Aurelia stopped and turned to face him.

'I was unfair to you,' she said frankly. 'Perhaps I was mistaken. . .'

'A sudden change of heart, Miss Carrington? Is it altogether wise? Think of my age, my reputation. . .'

'You are pleased to heap reproaches on my head. I admit that I deserve them. I. . . I am inclined to be hasty on occasion.'

'And fierce in defence of the weak? Your concern for Caro does you credit.'

'It is just that. . .well. . .she is so young.'

'And afraid of me? I shall try to remedy that.'

'I do not understand why——' Aurelia stopped herself. 'I beg your pardon. I have no right to question. . .'

'To question my motives in offering for her, ma'am? Your niece is a beauty. Had you not noticed? She is unspoilt, and her mama assures me that she is biddable. She will make an excellent wife.'

'Excuse me, if you please.' Aurelia hurried on to join her niece. She was scarlet with mortification at her own want of conduct in quizzing the Duke.

'Aunt, do look at the coastline.' Caroline pointed into the distance. 'We are so high above the sea. This might be a map laid out before us.'

'There to your left you may see almost as far as Hastings.' The Duke raised his gold-topped cane, but Aurelia could not give him her full attention. She wished that the ground might open and swallow her. How could she have been so ill-bred as to question him in such an unmannerly way? She had repaid his civility with what he must only regard as vulgar curiosity.

She hardly dared meet his eye until a firm hand slipped beneath her arm.

'Take care,' he warned. 'This ground beneath you is treacherous.'

She looked up at him then, and the heart-stopping smile made her bones melt. The tension between them was so strong that Caroline must surely sense it. Dear God! She could not go on like this.

With what dignity she could command she moved away, affecting to study the curious lichens growing on a nearby stone. Someone else must act as Caro's chaperon, she thought wildly. In Salterne's company she herself was another person. With him there was always a sense of excitement, and she had never felt more alive. Now she knew why women were said to prefer a rake to more sober-minded gentlemen.

But it would not do. She could not allow him to steal away her peace of mind. This was but a passing sensation, due, no doubt, to the long years alone at Marram. With an effort she regained her composure, only to lose it once more as he murmured in her ear.

'Take heart!' the deep voice whispered. 'You will come about. Don't sheathe your sword just yet.'

Then he turned to Caroline to discuss the difficulties of capturing the landscape in paint.

'You shall come to see my own collection,' he promised. 'A part of it is here in Brighton. You know the works of Poussin and Claude?'

Caroline's face glowed.

'You have some of their paintings? How I should love to see them.'

'It will be my pleasure, though Turner is thought to be the coming man. You may care to give me your opinion.'

Caroline was all animation. She had forgotten her dread of him. She chattered on as they returned to Brighton, encouraged by his evident knowledge of her favourite subject.

Aurelia spoke little. Her mind was in a turmoil. The Duke had exerted himself to set Caroline at her ease, but his manner towards herself was very different. His easy gallantry, the teasing, and the unmistakable look in his eyes. . . One might almost suppose that she, Aurelia, was the object of his affection, but that was ridiculous. She could not look at him.

On their return to the Steyne the Duke stayed only to suggest a visit to the theatre that evening. With a promise to call for them at nine he took his leave.

'Did you enjoy your drive, my love?' Ransome was delighted.

'Yes, Father. Did you know that His Grace is interested in paintings? He has asked if I may go to see his collection. That is—if you will permit me?'

'Of course.' Ransome patted her hand. 'Now go to your mama. She will be anxious to hear your news.'

As the door closed behind her he gave Aurelia a look of satisfaction.

'I must felicitate you, dear sister. You have accomplished what I could not. Caro is quite in charity with the Duke.'

Aurelia could take no pleasure in his words.

'You tried to rush her,' she said coldly. 'You gave her no time to get to know him.'

'Time, for me, is short, as Cassie will have told you. Now it would appear that our troubles are at an end. You have surprised me, Lia. I had not thought you would approve the match.'

'I believe His Grace to have many good qualities,' Aurelia said carefully. She must not arouse his suspicions.

'Do you, by gad?' Ransome's eyes were fixed intently on her face. 'Yet he ain't your style, I think. He's an ugly brute, and he ain't in his first youth. You will know of his reputation.'

She sensed that he was attempting to provoke her.

'He is devoted to his daughter and his grandmother,' she snapped, wondering as she did so why she felt obliged to defend him.

'And to a number of lightskirts. . .' Ransome's mocking tone infuriated her.

'Then I wonder how you can contemplate suggesting him to Caro.'

'Money, my dear. That would not count with you. . .an heiress in your own right. Still, if you care to champion him. . .'

He gave her a speculative look.

'Ah, I see it now. With Caro wed your poor relations will be off your hands. I cannot say that I blame you.'

'You are off my hands already, Ransome.' Aurelia trembled with anger at his imputation. 'Whatever happens I shall not continue to pay your debts, whether or not the marriage takes place.'

'It will take place. I give you my word on it. I shall speak to Salterne tonight. The announcement will go in the *Morning Post* this week.'

Aurelia was tempted to beg him to give Caroline more time, but she knew it would be useless. She turned to leave him.

'No thought of marriage yourself, I suppose?' His tone was deceptively casual, but Aurelia had developed a sixth sense where Ransome was concerned. She understood the reason for his question. Were she to die a spinster her sister would inherit her fortune.

She could not resist the temptation to annoy him.

'Why else would I be here? An heiress, you will know, must always please. I shall not lack for suitors.'

She was ashamed of her words even as she spoke, but it pleased her to see his angry look.

'Aye. . .if you keep a guard upon that tongue of yours,' he sneered. His eyes roved over her figure. 'You ain't yet run to fat,' he admitted grudgingly. 'But that will of yours is in need of taming.'

Aurelia's nails dug into her palms. She had forgotten how impossible he could be.

'Excuse me. . .' She hurried to her room, resolved

to be in his company as little as possible. His presence under her roof was more than she could bear.

'Lia, you look flushed. Is something wrong?' Cassie eyed her sister nervously.

'What could possibly be wrong?' Aurelia gave an ironic laugh.

'I thought perhaps you and Ransome had been quarrelling. I am so sorry. . . I did not intend to foist him on you.'

'It is no matter. At least you are to be allowed to stay.'

A frown creased Cassie's brow.

'He does seem pleased with Caro, but had it not been for Salterne. . . Lia, did you not find the Duke's behaviour strange this morning?'

'You may thank his ready powers of invention,' came the crisp reply. 'He prevented what promised to be a most unpleasant scene.'

'I do not understand him in the least. . .'

'Is it so strange that he should wish to keep you here?' Aurelia said with some asperity. Her head was beginning to ache.

'That he might be with Caro?' Cassie's face cleared.

'He has invited us to the theatre this evening. Did Caro tell you?'

The question was enough to divert Cassie's attention from further discussion of the Duke's behaviour. She slipped away to consider her toilette.

Aurelia summoned Hannah and asked for a tisane. She longed to beg off from the proposed entertainment, but concern for Caro forced her to make the effort to attend. If she could but close her eyes for an hour. . .

When she awoke she found that the tisane had

driven away the dull ache in her temples, and she felt
able to take an interest in her appearance. She had
intended to wear her pearls with the pale blue sarcenet, but she laid them aside in favour of her diamond
drops. Let Ransome accuse her of flaunting her wealth
if he wished. She intended to look her best, but to
what end she could not quite decide.

Aside from a calculating look at the flashing stones
Ransome made no comment, and when Salterne
arrived he greeted his host with all the easy address of
a man of fashion.

Yet he did not seem to be quite comfortable. Beside
Salterne's massive figure and swarthy countenance
Ransome's classic profile and blond good looks
seemed a trifle insipid to Aurelia's eyes. Both men
were dressed in evening breeches and coats of perfect
cut, but no one could mistake the Duke's position in
life. As always he gave an overwhelming impression
of power and authority.

Caro sensed it too. In her father's presence she
could not be easy with Salterne. As she lingered in the
background, lost for words, Aurelia saw Ransome's
growing annoyance.

'Caro,' she murmured softly, 'do try to be a little
more forthcoming. Today you have enjoyed His
Grace's company, have you not?'

Caro turned her face away.

'I liked him better, but I shall not marry him. If I
cannot have Richard I will marry no one.'

'Be quiet, for heaven's sake! You must not anger
your father. Do you wish him to take you home?' The
words were said in a whisper, and under the cover of
general conversation, but Aurelia looked up to find
the Duke's eyes upon her. Her heart gave a small

unnerving leap. He raised an eyebrow in enquiry, but Aurelia smiled and shook her head. If Ransome noticed the exchange he gave no sign. Instead he exerted all his charm to give the impression of a happy family gathering.

Aurelia was undeceived. When things were going Ransome's way he was at his best. Let anyone oppose him and the charm fell away like a cloak, revealing the vicious nature of the man beneath. He lost no time in attempting to embarrass her.

'You have made yet another conquest, Your Grace,' he said slyly. 'My sister-in-law has been singing your praises.'

'An exaggeration, I'm sure. Yet if it is so I am honoured.' The Duke bowed to her, but there was no trace of mockery in his look. He had seen through Ransome's ploy at once and would have no part in it. His face was impassive, but his jaw tightened. She guessed that he was angered by the clumsy remark.

To her relief he suggested that they leave at once if they were to see the opening of the play.

CHAPTER SEVEN

THE exterior of the small theatre in Duke Street had little to recommend it. The building, of wood painted to resemble stone, could not be described as anything other than ugly. A portico above the entrance offered some pretension to grandeur, but the place had a ramshackle appearance.

Yet the inside was furnished charmingly, inviting comparison with the most stylish of London theatres.

Aurelia looked at the scene below from the comfort of Salterne's box. The performance to come, a revival of *An Agreeable Surpise*, had attracted a large audience, most of them members of the *haut ton*.

She guessed that speculation was already rife. Her own appearance and that of the Ransomes, in the company of the Duke of Salterne, could not fail to lead to comment. Cassie, she noticed, was already waving to her friends.

'Lia, do you not see Charles Leggatt?' Cassie drew her attention to the boyish figure who was bowing to them from the pit.

Aurelia nodded an acknowledgement. Then, as the lights dimmed, she settled back to enjoy the play.

It was a slight piece, and she found it impossible to concentrate upon the action on the stage. Her thoughts strayed to her conversation with Caroline. Her niece's unyielding determination to marry Richard had surprised her. A wry smile touched the corner of her mouth. It was a family failing. She had seen it in Cassie, and who could be more stubborn than she herself. Blood will out, she thought with some dismay. At least the girl was steadfast in her devotion.

She looked at her companions. Cassie, secure in her belief that all was well, was on good terms with Ransome. For his part he seemed determined to attract attention. His loud comments on the performance drew angry looks and one or two admonitions to silence from the neighbouring boxes. Caroline had moved away, and was seated in a corner intent on the play.

'You seem preoccupied this evening, Miss Carrington. The performance is not to your taste?'

Aurelia jumped. She had not realised that the Duke was beside her.

'I. . . Yes, of course, Your Grace. I beg your pardon. I was not attending.'

'Something is troubling you?' His words were inaudible to the others. 'If I may be of help. . .?'

'It is nothing, I assure you.' Aurelia found his attention disturbing. The Duke should not single her out in this way. Ransome would be furious to see him by her side when Caro sat alone.

'You would prefer to leave? I should be happy to escort you. . .!'

'Pray do not consider it. Perhaps I am a little tired. At Marram I lead such a quiet life. . .'

Her blue eyes, fringed with dark lashes, looked up at him, and she caught her breath. Some indefinable spark had passed between them in that moment, and it unnerved her. Then the hooded lids came down to veil his expression. It was unfathomable once more.

Aurelia glanced uneasily at Ransome. Where his

own interests were concerned her brother-in-law possessed a sixth sense. He had missed nothing of the exchange between Salterne and herself, and he gave her a inimical look.

With an effort she turned her attention to the play, but Ransome's chatter had ceased. During the interval he came to her on the pretext of offering refreshment.

'Must you make an exhibition of yourself?' he hissed. 'The Duke is not interested in your vapourings. . .'

She was spared the need to reply as the box filled with Salterne's friends.

'What a pleasure to see you again, Miss Carrington!' Charles Leggatt came over to her at once. 'You owe me the favour of another dance, ma'am.'

'You must forgive me. My sister did explain, I believe.'

'And I must claim responsibility.' Salterne stood beside them, dwarfing the younger man. 'It was I who spirited Miss Carrington away. She was good enough to lend me her assistance.' The grey eyes searched one face and then the other. 'I am sorry to have spoiled your evening, Charles.' He moved away.

'Lady Ransome agreed that I might call on you. Did you see my card?'

'I saw several of your cards,' Aurelia admitted with a twinkle. 'You have been unlucky not to find us at home.'

'Then perhaps tomorrow. . .?'

'We shall be happy to see you.'

He flushed with pleasure and stepped aside to allow the other members of his party to be presented to her. She turned to give her attention to the man who was bowing over her hand. He was older than the others, and unlike them he was not in uniform. His flawless evening clothes had an air of understated perfection, contrasting sharply with the ornate dress of his companions. They gave him an air of sophistication which the younger men could not hope to match. His eyes sparkled as he read her thoughts.

'I am quite outshone, Miss Carrington, but I refuse to admit defeat. I have a claim upon your indulgence. Your sister is an old friend.'

'Beware, Aurelia!' Cassie laughed as she tapped his shoulder with her fan. 'Robert Clare is an accomplished flirt.'

'Not so!' Their companion threw up his hands in protest. 'We Irish have a reputation for exaggeration, but tonight I stand on firm ground. We have all Three Graces in this box. Ransome, you are a fortunate man.'

Thus appealed to, Ransome bowed and was at pains to agree, but his eyes were cold. In their depths Aurelia saw undisguised hostility.

She shrugged and looked at Robert Clare with interest. His attractive voice held traces of a Irish accent, and she guessed him to be a member of the Regent's inner circle. Many of the Prince's intimates were of Irish origin. He was said to enjoy their ready wit, their eccentricities, their penchant for late hours, and their love of life. The man beside her appeared to possess those qualities in abundance.

'My countrymen are sadly maligned,' he continued in mock-dismay. 'Our most sincere professions of regard are found to be—er—excessive.'

'Pearls before swine?' she murmured.

'I suspect, ma'am, that I am destined to become

your slave.' His look recorded his appreciation of her sally. 'When wit is allied to beauty I am lost.'

'You are hoist with your own petard, I fear,' Aurelia told him demurely. 'That, sir, is a gross exaggeration.'

She found his manner disarming, and he showed no inclination to leave her side. It was only when the lights dimmed for the resumption of the performance that he rose to his feet. Unlike Charles Leggatt he did not beg for the privilege of calling upon her, but she had no doubt that she would see him again.

She was not mistaken. From then on Robert Clare was a frequent visitor to the house on the Steyne, much to the disgust of Charles Leggatt. The two men vied with each other in proffering invitations to open-air concerts, balloon ascents, and other entertainments.

Aurelia bore Cassie's teasing with equanimity. Neither man had touched her heart, and she suspected that Clare in particular was simply amusing himself.

Ransome, meantime, was growing more surly, and the reason was not far to seek. Caro's betrothal had not yet been announced. Aurelia wondered at the delay, though she was much relieved. Had Salterne decided to play a waiting game, rather than forcing the girl into open defiance?

Her surmise was confirmed when Caroline sought her out.

'We have spoken together, the Duke and I,' she confided. 'He was very kind. I said that I wished to have more time. He looked a little stern, but he made no objection. I was afraid that he might mention it to Father, but he cannot have done so. . .else we should have known.'

Nothing could be more certain. Had Ransome suspected the reason for the delay he would have made their lives unbearable. As it was he grew increasingly morose, and spent as little time as possible in the house.

Aurelia found it a relief. His temper was uncertain, and she dreaded an explosion which might bring matters to a head.

When Salterne called upon them later in the week he brought a message from the Duchess.

'She begs that you will visit her today, Caro, if it is convenient.'

'She is quite recovered. . .? The doctor. . .?'

'Lessing has given his permission, Miss Carrington, and my grandmother has not yet met my bride-to-be.'

'I am so sorry, but Ransome and my sister are not at home.'

'I know,' His Grace said smoothly. 'The invitation is to you and Caro.'

Caroline looked uneasy and Aurelia frowned at her. The Duke gave the ladies a bland look.

'You find some objection, Miss Carrington?'

'Not at all.' It was not quite true. Ransome would be incensed to find that he had not been included in the invitation, but there was nothing she could do. 'It is a splendid idea,' she said hurriedly.

'Then if I might suggest. . .?' Salterne strolled over to the window and looked into the street. 'There is a chill wind this morning, but doubtless the horses will not suffer overmuch if they are kept standing. My groom is looking anxious. . .though naturally I should not wish you to imagine that I am at all impatient.'

'Of course not.' Aurelia's tone was dry. 'How could I have gained that impression.

'My felicitations, ladies!' he exclaimed some five minutes later. One grows accustomed to a lengthy wait for members of the opposite sex. I trust I was not too importunate?'

'The horses must always be considered, Your Grace.' Aurelia gave him a limpid look.

Salterne chuckled.

'Shall you always pop in a hit when my guard is down, Miss Carrington? I shall come about,' he promised.

He was laughing, and she caught a glimpse of fine white teeth. How could she ever have thought him ugly? she marvelled. When he laughed his face was transformed. The stormy grey of those deep-set eyes could change in a moment into a shining gleam of silver. The lines about them would crinkle and the beautiful mobile mouth would turn up at the corners.

Yet her heart sank as she looked at him. She sensed that she was faced with danger, but not from him. The danger lay in her own heart. He was too much in her mind these days, and she had grown accustomed to his easy camaraderie. She had always been honest with herself, and she could not deny that she looked forward to their gentle *badinage*. What a joy it was to find an intelligent man who relished a battle of wits. He picked up her thoughts almost before she had time to formulate them. She had no need to explain. . .to spell everything out. . . But therein lay the danger.

She folded her hands in her lap. She was becoming fanciful. He had a fine mind, that was true, but of late she could not deny that there was also a powerful sexual attraction. She was not a child, and she could not mistake his look, or her own reaction. She wanted him, she realised now, and the thought appalled her. Of course it was not love. . .just simple animal lust. She had not imagined herself capable of it, but it was true. She wanted this man to hold her in his arms, to whisper words which she had never thought to hear, and to take her without fear of the consequences.

And he was to marry Caroline. A pang of anguish stabbed her. The child did not even wish to be in his company. What hope of happiness could there be in such a match? Both lives might be ruined.

She was still lost in thought when they reached their destination.

In daylight the house on Marine Parade was larger than Aurelia had at first imagined, and Caroline's eyes grew wide with dread. The size of the establishment served to confirm all her fears, and this was but one of the Duke's houses. She had neither the desire or the ability to take charge of any of them.

Salterne led them up the curving staircase and into the Dowager's room. There, propped up against a mass of pillows, lay the tiny figure of the Duchess.

'So you have come!' The voice was faint, but the black eyes were as sharp as ever. 'And this pretty child must be Caroline. Will you give me a kiss, my dear?'

Caroline moved towards the bed. Although she was shy, and obviously in awe of the old lady, her manner was charming. She dropped a curtsy and bent to kiss the withered cheek.

'I am glad to hear that you are better, Your Grace,' she murmured softly.

'I am well enough, I thank you. It is trying to be confined to one room, but Charlotte does her best to entertain me.'

She threw back the coverlet to reveal a small child, who gave them solemn look. Then her face gleamed with mischief.

'I was hiding, Papa, and you did not guess.'

She slid down the coverlet and ran towards the Duke, squealing with pleasure as he lifted her to his shoulder.

'I had thought you lost,' he assured her. 'I should have searched everywhere for you.'

'To take me to see the donkeys? You promised. . .'

'Indeed I did, my puss, but you must be patient. Miggs shall take you later.'

The child's lip quivered. 'I want you to come.' A plump little arm crept about his neck.

'We shall see.' Salterne looked at the Duchess. 'I hope she has not tired you, ma'am. You promised to rest. . .'

The old lady snorted.

'Time enough for that in the churchyard,' she snapped. 'Don't fuss, Rollo! Send for Miggs, if you must. It is time for Charlotte's walk.'

The child's face crumpled and she hid her face in the Duke's coat. 'I don't want Miggs. . . I want you to come.'

For once the Duke was at a loss, and the Duchess's enjoinder not to be a watering-pot resulted only in Charlotte tightening her arm about her father's neck.

As she watched his gentle attempts at comfort Aurelia was filled with wonder. She was seeing yet another aspect of this complex man's character, and one which was unknown to her. He bent his dark head, so like Charlotte's own, towards the little girl, and dropped a kiss upon the child's brow. His face had softened, and she heard the tenderness in his voice. With his daughter Salterne was a different person. Gone was the forbidding hauteur of his manner, and the mocking drawl which she so disliked.

The love apparent in his eyes made him at once look younger and more vulnerable, and Aurelia found herself smiling at the pair of them with undisguised warmth. The sensation was disquieting and she strove to compose herself.

'I heard a story about a donkey,' she announced to no one in particular. 'His friend was a little girl, but she lived in the sea. Sometimes I look through the window to see if she is here.' She strolled over towards the sweeping curve of glass.

A tearful eye inspected her cautiously, but Aurelia paid no attention. She looked down at the beach.

There was silence for a moment, then, 'Is she there?'

'Not at present, but I can see the donkeys. There. . .that is the one; he wears a blue hat. He must be waiting for her.'

'Is she in the sea?'

'I expect so. She is a mermaid, so she can swim.'

'Does the water come over her head?'

'It does, but she doesn't mind. If you come to the window I will show you where she lives.'

In another moment a small hand stole into hers.

'Did you know that a mermaid has a tail like a fish instead of legs like yours?' Aurelia continued conversationally. She settled herself on the window-seat with Charlotte on her knee.

'How does she walk?'

'She doesn't. When the tide comes up to the donkey's feet she reaches up and climbs into his saddle. Then he gives her a ride.'

'Does she talk to him?'

'Oh, yes. Mermaids are clever. They can talk to anyone.'

'Would she talk to me?'

'I believe so. . .if you were lucky enough to meet her.'

'When does she come to see the donkey?'

'She waits until it is quiet. She is rather shy, you see. She doesn't come when the sun is shining because it dries her skin.'

'She could come when it was raining.'

'So she could. That is when the donkey takes her for long, long rides across the sand.'

'To the bathing houses?'

'Far beyond there. Do you see those cliffs? It was there that they found lots of shells.'

The little face brightened. 'I found some shells when Papa came with me. Would you like to see them? I was showing them to Grandmama.' Charlotte reached into her pocket and produced the treasures. 'Papa knows their names,' she said proudly. 'But I have forgotten.'

'They are very pretty. Perhaps you may find some more. Does Miggs like shells?'

'Yes, but she is not as clever as Papa. I could show her, though. . .'

'She would like that. . .' Aurelia looked across at Salterne to find him pulling the bell-rope.

Miggs led the unprotesting child away.

'She is sadly spoiled, I fear. . .' Salterne said heavily.

'Not at all. She is a delight.'

'It is kind of you to say so. In the usual way she is a cheerful child, but her grandmother and I have been away, and. . .'

'And she has missed you? It is but natural. You would not wish it otherwise, I'm sure.'

'Rollo, your daughter has monopolised Miss Carrington! Do you intend to do the same? I shall not permit it. Come here, my dear, and tell me all your news.'

Salterne laughed and strolled towards the bed.

'Caro and I will leave you to your gossip,' he announced. 'She wishes to see the paintings in the salon. . .'

'Then off you go.' The Duchess waved a hand in dismissal. As the door closed she turned to Aurelia.

'You will forgive me for being blunt, but really this will not do. Has Rollo taken leave of his senses?'

'Your Grace, please! I cannot discuss. . . I mean, I have no right to express an opinion. . .'

'Stuff! The child is a beauty, that I'll grant you, and she has a charming manner, but she is not the wife for Salterne. He would be bored within a week. Aside from that, she is afraid of him. You will not tell me that she holds him in regard?'

Aurelia looked away.

'She respects him. That may be enough. . .'

'Fiddlesticks! You believe that no more than I. I do not hold with nonsensical transports of devotion. We are past the days of medieval romance, I hope. But Rollo has suffered enough. He needs a woman of character who will give him more than an heir.'

'Caro is young,' Aurelia offered. 'His Grace may be sure that she will be kind to Charlotte. Then, too, she may develop. . .'

The Dowager sniffed in disbelief.

'Is she like to lose her dread of him? Rollo is no saint. His needs are those of any other man. It would try his patience beyond belief should she shrink when he approaches her. No matter what the world believes, he is not a brute.'

'I am sure of that,' Aurelia told her warmly. 'I place no reliance on hearsay, ma'am. The Duke has been all civility.'

A crow of laughter greeted her words.

'You have had no differences, you and he? Do not ask me to believe it.' With her head on one side the Duchess looked like some small exotic bird, alert and sharply aware of the tension in Aurelia's manner. She had not missed the way in which the colour flooded to her companion's cheeks when Rollo's name was mentioned, or the highly charged atmosphere in the room whenever he was present.

'We have not always been in perfect accord,' Aurelia admitted. 'I find the Duke somewhat difficult to understand at times.'

'So do I, and never more than at present.' Her Ladyship settled back against her pillows. 'Now tell me the truth, Miss Carrington; you like this match no more than I?'

Aurelia was at a loss for words.

'Yet you do not altogether dislike my grandson, I believe?' The question was apparently artless as the Duchess searched among the rumpled pillows for her handkerchief.

'Our—er—disagreements cannot be laid entirely at his door.' Aurelia's face was burning with embarrassment. The question was unexpected and she did not know how to reply. How could she hope to hide her inner turmoil from the shrewd mind of the Dowager?

Dislike? The word was too mild to describe her initial reaction to Salterne. She had detested him. But now? She could not say with honesty that her feelings had not changed. He still had the power to annoy her almost beyond endurance, and of course he had no right to challenge her with his sexuality, as he did each time they met.

No other man had the power to cause those indefinable longings which seized her at his merest touch. With a smile or a look he could throw her into utter confusion. What had happened to the cool Miss Carrington? she wondered. In the past she had always been in command of her thoughts and her emotions.

She looked up to find the Duchess's eyes upon her face.

'I find the Duke an enigmatic person, ma'am. He can be formidable, can he not? Yet when I see him with his daughter and with you I cannot doubt his gentleness.'

'Rollo has a loving heart.' The old lady closed her eyes and lay back among her pillow, but her expression was still troubled. 'Well, they are not yet wed, or even formally betrothed. I had best see Cassandra, I suppose, and Ransome too, though the thought gives me no pleasure.'

Ransome was surprised by the invitation.

'Salterne must have persuaded the old harridan,' he announced. 'We had best put a civil face on it. He won't marry to disoblige her. She has a handsome fortune of her own.'

Peace did not reign for long. When Ransome returned from his visit to the Duchess his face was dark with rage.

'Well, madam, what is your game?' A small vein pulsed in his temple as he walked towards Aurelia. 'You have set the old hag against me.'

'You need no help from me in that respect,' Aurelia told him coldly. 'This is my house, I must remind you. Either you are civil or you leave.'

'I intend to do so, and I'll take my family with me. We are doing no good here.' He began to curse and stormed out of the room.

'What has gone wrong?' Aurelia turned to Cassie who was sobbing quietly. An ashen-faced Caroline stood beside her. Cassie was incapable of speech. She shook her head and buried her face in her hands.

'Caro, what is the matter?'

'The Duchess was kind, but it was as you thought. She. . .she said that I would make an excellent wife, but not quite yet. She counselled waiting for some months. . .' The tears began to trickle down her cheeks. 'Papa is very angry.'

'And Salterne agreed with her. That was the worst of it.' Cassie gasped out the words between her sobs. 'Ransome could scarce contain his rage.'

'I hope he did not disgrace us, Cassie.'

'He would not openly antagonise the Duke. Salterne is very large, you know, and he is said to have a punishing left, whatever that may mean. Ransome did not dare to argue. . .and that made him worse. I cannot tell you what he said as we left the house.'

'Some tea will restore your spirits. Caro, my love, will you speak to Hannah?'

Aurelia closed the door and returned to Cassie's side.

'Well, sister, what did he say?'

'I had not thought he could be so coarse, especially with Caro. It was dreadful. He told her that if she encouraged Salterne in. . .in a different way he would not be content to wait. The child was bewildered, Lia.

She had no idea what he meant. He said that if she did not know how to go about the matter he would tell her.' Her sobs redoubled. 'He used the foulest language about the Dowager Duchess. I cannot repeat his words. He said also that Salterne could not be much of a man if he allowed Her Grace to lead him by the nose.'

'I notice that he did not care to face the "punishing left",' Aurelia said drily. 'Cheer up, Cass. Nothing appeals to Ransome more than the opportunity to torment his victims. You must not let him think you fear him.'

Cassie raised her head and Aurelia was shocked by the bitterness in her eyes.

'Don't look like that,' she begged softly. 'Ransome shall not have money to gamble away, but I am prepared to pay his more pressing debts.

'You will ruin yourself if you try to help us further.'

'Let me be the judge of that. I cannot allow him to take you away. He must agree to leave you here, at least for the next few weeks.'

Cassie was too distraught to argue further. With an anguished cry she left the room.

It was late that afternoon when Ransome returned.

'Are they ready?' he snarled. 'The carriage is at the door.'

'Then you had best dismiss it. I have something to say to you.'

'You may save your breath.' He thrust his face close to hers and she could smell the fumes of wine. 'I have you to thank for this change in Salterne. Don't trouble to deny it. You want him for yourself.'

Crimson with fury, Aurelia rose to her feet.

'How dare you speak to me like that?' she cried.

'Touched a nerve, did it? It's obvious, my dear. You're behaving like a bitch on heat.'

The crude vulgarity of his words turned Aurelia to ice. She was trembling with anger and the knuckles of her clenched fists whitened, but she made a supreme effort to control herself.

'That remark is all that I would expect from you,' she said quietly. 'Sit down and listen to me. It is to your advantage.'

'Be quick about it, then.' He flung himself into a chair. 'We leave tonight.'

'Is that wise? The Duchess, I understand, has suggested merely a delay.'

It was then that he began to curse—loudly and with great violence. Aurelia scarcely heard him. Her mind was still reeling from his accusations. It wasn't true. It could not possibly be true.

A sick feeling of dismay threatened to overwhelm her, combined with a feeling of self-disgust. She had allowed herself to drift almost imperceptibly into friendship with the Duke. How obvious it must have been to everyone that he sought her company rather than that of Caroline.

She stifled a groan of dismay. Coarse as Ransome's words had been they could not have wounded her so deeply if there were not some truth behind them. In an agony of mind she recalled her own reactions to Salterne's touch. It was all true—she did want him, and honesty demanded that she face the fact.

Wearily she lifted a hand to stem Ransome's flow of words.

'If you will but listen,' she said, 'I am offering you a way out of your difficulties.'

She had his attention then.

'I will give you a letter to my bankers. They will pay your more pressing debts. It will give you time. . .'

'Aye! If Salterne comes up to snuff. . .and if that little bitch can be brought to see reason. . .'

'Curb your tongue! You have not heard my conditions yet.'

'You wish me to kill myself?'

The sneering suggestion did not merit a reply.

'You will leave Cassie and Caro here while you deal with your affairs. If you do not agree I shall not lift a finger to help you.'

He gave her a calculating look.

'I might. . .if you throw in some blunt as well.'

'You may have one hundred pounds in gold. Give me a list of your debts. As the matter is urgent you should leave at once.'

He shrugged and walked over to her desk. He wrote for several minutes and then handed her the paper. Aurelia was shaken as she looked at the total, but her face remained impassive.

'Is this everything?' she enquired.

'Do you wish to see the accounts?' His laugh was ugly.

'You may show them to my bankers. Give me half an hour and I will write the letter. You had best see Cassie before you go.'

He hesitated, seemed about to speak, and then thought better of it. With a shrug he left the room.

Aurelia dropped her head in her hands. At that moment she felt that she would never have peace of mind again. She blamed herself entirely. How could she have been so blind? If she had stopped to think. . . had considered truthfully where her disturbing emotions were leading her, then she might have avoided her present anguish. Her throat ached with unshed tears, but at last she picked up her pen and began to write.

The letter completed, she reached into her bureau for a leather bag and counted out the gold. She had bought a little time, but to what end? All she had achieved to date was the destruction of her own happiness.

When he returned Ransome looked at her averted face.

'Expecting thanks, my dear? I won't embarrass you with that. Were it not for Cass you would see me rot in hell. My thanks must go to your father, for leaving you so warm.'

She rose to face him then and he recoiled from her look. He turned on his heel and left her.

'Lia, I want to thank you. . .'

At the sound of Cassie's voice Aurelia looked up.

'Not another word! I could not bear it.' Her nerves were close to breaking-point. 'I wish to forget what has happened here today. Did we not promise ourselves to Lady Bellingham this evening? If we dine at seven we shall be in time for Lady Hamilton's performance.'

'Shall you wish to see it?'

'Any performance will suit me well enough, as long as I am not involved.' Aurelia hurried from the room.

CHAPTER EIGHT

LADY BELLINGHAM'S rooms were hot and crowded. As their hostess led them through the crush Aurelia looked about her, praying that for tonight, at least, the Duke would be otherwise engaged.

Now that she had faced up to the truth she could not meet him with any degree of equanimity. Her treacherous heart had led her into the worst of situations. That she could find herself drawn to the man who was to marry her niece did not bear thinking of. At the very least it showed an appalling breach of taste.

Yet she could not repress a most irrational sense of disappointment to find that he was not present. The lights did not seem so bright, and the chatter of the fashionable crowd seemed more meaningless than ever.

She took her seat on a small gilt chair set before an improvised dais which was hidden by a velvet curtain.

'We are almost ready,' Lady Bellingham announced. 'You will forgive me if I leave you for a moment, but I must see Lady Hamilton.'

She bustled away, leaving the audience to await the appearance of the woman whose reputation had set the country by the ears in Nelson's day. Some of the surrounding faces were disapproving, but most were avid with curiosity.

Aurelia sighed as she thought of the tragic ending to the famous love-affair. After Trafalgar and the death of the Admiral a grateful government had showered wealth and honours upon Lady Nelson. Her husband's dearest Emma, the woman he loved with all his heart, had been left in poverty to bring up his daughter as best she might, in spite of his dying wishes. Now Lady Hamilton was eking out a living by relying on the charity of her friends.

'She's drawn the crowd, I'll say that for her.' The speaker behind Aurelia did not trouble to lower her voice.

'Wait until you see her.' There was malicious amusement in the reply. 'She is grown so fat, my dear. One finds it hard to imagine what the Admiral found to admire.'

'She was the loveliest creature in the world.' Salterne took the seat beside Aurelia. Ostensibly his words were for her ear, but the deep voice carried easily to the row behind. 'I saw her once in Naples. So exquisite! She was the jewel among Sir William Hamilton's treasures.'

His words had silenced the gossips for the moment and soothed Aurelia's indignation at their cruelty. She had resolved that when they met again she would keep him at a distance, but now, forgetting her vow, she gave him a warm smile of thanks. It was returned with interest, and she coloured slightly. She would persuade Caro to change places with her. . . Before she could suggest it, however, the draperies parted. They revealed a figure alone on the stage. It was covered completely by a large shawl. The silence was intense as the audience waited. Then a corner of the shawl was lifted.

Aurelia gasped. The gossips had not exaggerated. It was difficult to believe that this blowsy woman, heavy to the point of grossness, could ever have captured a man's heart. All traces of her former beauty had vanished, obliterated in the folds of flesh.

A lump came into Aurelia's throat. It was tragic to see Nelson's beloved mistress reduced to peddling her notoriety in this way. She had no wish to watch, but escape was impossible. They were close to the stage, every seat was taken, and a number of people were standing by the doors. A sudden departure could only give offence.

'Wait!' A large hand closed over her own. 'You will be surprised.' Once again Salterne had read her mind, but Aurelia would not be comforted. She looked at her sister in despair, but Cassie's attention was fixed on Lady Hamilton.

Aurelia forced herself to look again. Then she leaned forward in amazement. By some curious alchemy the figure was suddenly transformed. Now its very solidity gave truth and dignity to a classical pose. The shawl was drawn further aside, and the white tunic, held only by a ribbon beneath the breasts, fell into graceful lines. The uplifted arms and the curve of neck and head spoke of loss and endless yearning.

In the hush that followed Aurelia knew that she was witnessing true artistry. The enveloping shawl was raised once more as the audience burst into a storm of applause. When it fell to the ground a moment later the figure was supported by another—a young girl kneeling in prayer. A murmur rippled through the room, and stilled in horror as the woman grasped the child's hair. In her other hand she held a dagger. There was not a sound as one emotion after another flickered across the woman's face. Pity was followed by despair, then forlorn desperation gave way to the first faint gleam of hope. The dagger was cast away as the child was gathered to her mother's breast.

There were shouts of 'Bravo! Bravo!' and the sound of tumultuous clapping.

This should be trumpery, Aurelia thought to herself, and yet it was not. For the next half-hour she watched enthralled as Lady Hamilton, with the aid of a shawl or two, a lyre, and a tambourine, took her audience with her into flights of poetic fantasy with only the slightest of improvised gestures.

The curtain fell at last, to a furore of clapping and requests for an encore.

Lady Bellingham held up a hand for silence.

'We cannot ask for more,' she pleaded. 'Lady Hamilton is too exhausted to appear again. You will find refreshments in the dining-room.' She stepped down from the stage and paused by Cassie's chair.

'Did you enjoy the performance, Lady Ransome?'

'Her Ladyship is a true artiste,' Cassie assured her warmly. 'Lia, I'm sure, will agree.'

'I do indeed. It was a triumph. Your guests will not soon forget this evening.'

'Poor soul! It is little enough that I can do for her. She is very low at present.'

'And well she may be!' Aurelia heard the whispered voice again. 'She is on the verge of bankruptcy, so I hear. These performances are her only source of income. Even so, one must question her taste in dragging the child about with her. . .'

Aurelia turned and glared at the speaker. She was happy to see that the woman had the grace to blush.

'Lady Hamilton's is a remarkable gift,' Aurelia said in a high, clear voice. 'We must be grateful to her for allowing us to share it.'

'I agree, Miss Carrington.' Salterne too had raised his voice. 'It is strange, is it not. . .this magic? I have observed it before. Physical appearance is naught if the gift is there.'

His eyes were half veiled by the thick dark lashes, but she sensed that he was about to give the gossips a set-down.

'The best will, of course, always be a target for the worst,' he observed in the same placid tone. 'I do not refer to Lady Hamilton in particular, though she must always be at risk from vulgar minds.'

Aurelia heard a snort of indignation and the scrape of chairs as the gossips made a hasty exit.

'Thank you,' she said shortly. 'That was somewhat trying. The remarks were unkind, and spoken so loud that I feared that Lady Hamilton must hear.'

'It would not be the first time. She is no stranger to insult, ma'am, and she is accustomed to the censure of the world. When the Admiral was alive it had no power to harm her. . .but now. . .'

'I think you have no taste for hypocrites, Miss Carrington.' Robert Clare had joined them. 'And you are right. Mrs Fitzherbert is still treated like a queen, though the Prince has tired of her.'

Aurelia was still furious. 'That is what I mean,' she said.

Cassie gasped. 'Lia! I beg of you. . .remember where you are! Come, let us find Caro and Leggatt. They are gone into the dining-room.' She rose to her feet, dropping her reticule and her fan in her haste to hurry her sister away. She was relieved to see that the Duke had been drawn into conversation by Lady Bellingham and did not appear to have heard Aurelia's remark.

Robert Clare bent down to retrieve the fallen objects, and then he gave Aurelia a quizzical look.

'Nelson is still idolised,' he said. 'But the gratitude of the country does not extend to his mistress. As to the other matter. . .you have heard the rumours?'

Aurelia looked at him in silence.

'It is said that Mrs Fitzherbert is the Prince's true wife,' he went on. 'Though Fox has denied it in Parliament.'

'That cannot be,' Aurelia protested. 'He married Caroline of Brunswick. It would mean. . .'

'Bigamy?' The room had emptied, but his voice fell to a whisper. 'Remember that Mrs Fitzherbert has never consented to receive Fox since he denied her marriage. . .and there were witnesses.'

'Please!' Cassie was beside herself with anxiety. 'Must we discuss these matters? The world abounds with gossip, and it is naught but hearsay.'

Robert Clare gave her an ironic smile, but he did not pursue the subject. As he moved towards the door, Cassie caught her sister's arm.

'Do take care!' she pleaded. 'Clare is close to the Prince. If your remarks should reach the Regent's ears I cannot answer for the consequences. Neither he nor Mrs Fitzherbert ever forgets an insult.'

'I shall not say another word,' Aurelia promised. 'But it does seem unfair, you will admit.'

'I admit nothing of the kind. It is none of our concern. I wish you will not always be taking up some lost cause or other, Lia. It can lead to nothing but trouble.'

How true that was, Aurelia thought ruefully. Not for the first time she doubted the wisdom of her decision to come to Brighton. It had been a disaster from the first, and what had she achieved? She might as well have stayed at Marram and paid Ransome's debts. Instead she was trapped in a situation which she found intolerable. She could not avoid the Duke's company, sweet torture though it was. She could think of no way to persaude him to alter his manner towards her, and to behave with cool formality. It was the only way they could deal together.

Perhaps if she had a frank talk with him and explained that he should direct his gallantry at Caroline. . . No. . .that would never do. He could only regard it as an impertinence, and in any case the girl would not welcome it.

The answer, she knew, was to return to Marram as quickly as she could, away from his disturbing presence, but for the moment it was out of the question. Caro and Cassie were both dependent on her, and she could not let them down.

The solution to her problem lay in her own hands. Perhaps if she showed an interest in Captain Leggatt, Robert Clare or one of her other suitors Salterne might direct his attentions elsewhere. The town was filled with charmers, many of them beauties, and he had shown that he was susceptible to the female sex.

The thought caused her a pang. There must be other women who could cause that lazy smile to appear behind his eyes. Would he laugh and tease with them as he had done with her? A small green imp of jealousy rose in her heart, but she crushed it at once. A fictitious interest in another man would be her answer.

She was still preoccupied as she walked into the dining-room. Absently she accepted a plate of oyster patties from Charles Leggatt, but she found she could not eat. As she raised a glass of wine to her lips a feeling of nausea assailed her.

'It is so very warm in here,' she murmured to Cassie. I must have some air.'

Without waiting for a reply she walked towards the open windows and stepped into the garden. There was a slight breeze, and the air felt pleasantly cool against her skin. She wandered down the path towards a small gazebo. It had been sited to take advantage of the view. In the night sky the moon was full, paving the sea with a path of molten silver. Above her she could see a scattering of stars.

'You have forgot your wrap, Miss Carrington.' Charles Leggatt had followed her. 'Forgive me if I intrude. . .but I feared you were not well.'

'I found it excessively warm.' Aurelia smiled up at him. 'Pray do not trouble yourself. I wished only for some air. I must not keep you from your friends.'

It was a clear dismissal, but to her extreme discomfiture he attempted to take her hands.

'May I claim you as one of them?' he said urgently. 'I could wish it were something more. Miss Carrington. . .Aurelia. . . I have longed for an opportunity to speak to you alone. You. . .you do not hold me in dislike, I think?'

'Of course not !' Aurelia attempted to draw her hands away, but he held them in a firm clasp. 'We are all sensible of your kindness. It has been delightful to attend the entertainments in your company. . .'

'I do not mean that.' The captain was clearly struggling with some strong emotion. 'I dared to hope that in these past few weeks. . .well. . .you must have suspected—although perhaps you have not.' He sat down on the bench beside her and put his head in his hands.

'Captain Leggatt, please. . . I beg of you. . .' Aurelia had no wish to hurt his feelings, but he was clearly determined to propose.

'Please allow me to tell you of my regard for you. From the moment I saw you I knew that I could love no other woman——'

Aurelia stopped him before he could go on.

'I do not mean to be unkind, but let us not continue this conversation. We are good friends. I should be sorry to find some awkwardness between us.'

He released her with reluctance, and gave her a solemn look.

'My dearest wish is that you become my wife.'

'But I have no thought of marriage.'

'Then your affections are not engaged elsewhere?'

'Captain Leggatt, that is not a proper question, but no, they are not.' To her own ears the lie was unconvincing. Her heart, her mind and her soul were engaged elsewhere, but she must not admit it, even to herself. Had she not resolved to guard her thoughts, directing them away from a tall, athletic figure with a tanned face and laughing eyes? Such infatuations passed in time.

As she saw the expression on the captain's face she knew that her disclaimer had been a mistake.

'That, at least, is one comfort. Perhaps I may hope. . .when we are better acquainted? Lady Ransome gave me to understand. . .'

'My sister wishes for my happiness,' Aurelia told him gently. 'She believes that I should marry, but. . .'

'You do not agree? Will you not tell me why?'

She hesitated. 'It is hard to explain,' she said at last.

'My parents were so happy together, but marriage can be destructive when those concerned are unsuited to each other.' Her look was a plea for forgiveness. 'Each partner must give their heart.'

'You have mine,' he said simply. 'I shall not lose the hope of winning yours.'

Aurelia laid her hand upon his arm. 'Believe me when I say that it can never be. Let us continue to be friends. That is worth something, surely?'

'It is worth a great deal. . .but. . .'

'Let us say no more. Reflect a little. Your own good sense must convince you that without the same feeling on both sides a marriage is not to be considered.'

He gazed at her with stricken eyes. 'I cannot blame you if you do not. . .do not reciprocate my regard; but I thought. . .'

'If I have given you cause to misunderstand me I am sorry, but, believe me, I had no thought of doing so.'

'You did not. . .but I hoped that you would learn to love me.' He was about to launch into another impassioned declaration, when a shadow blotted out the moonlight.

'Miss Carrington, your servant.' Robert Clare stood before them, his eyeglass swinging idly from his hand. 'Lady Bellingham bids me convey her compliments, Captain Leggatt. She is making up her tables and needs a fourth at whist.'

'You were unable to accommodate her?' There was open antagonism in the question.

'Whist is not my game,' Clare said smoothly.

'Just what is your game, may I ask?'

Robert Clare looked amused.

'I am thought to be lucky at Macao. . .and other games where fortune favours the bold.'

It was not the most tactful of replies, and Aurelia sensed the tension in the air. Before the captain could reply she turned to Robert Clare.

'I had forgot my wrap,' she said swiftly. 'Captain Leggatt kindly brought it out to me. Now I am about to beg another favour of him. Should you see my sister on your way to the tables, sir, will you tell her that I shall be with her directly?'

He had no alternative but to acquiesce, but his rigid back was eloquent as he walked away.

'Your wrap? Well, I cannot deny that the atmosphere was chill.' Robert Clare stifled a laugh. 'Young puppy! I trust that he did not annoy you?'

'You shall not make sport of him,' Aurelia said quietly. 'He is a dear friend.'

'I crave your pardon, Miss Carrington. I was not aware that young Leggatt was a particular favourite of yours. . .'

For once the soft Irish accent failed to charm her, and Aurelia rounded on him sharply.

'Must you be quite so foolish, Mr Clare? Captain Leggatt did not annoy me, but you will most certainly do so if you persist in reading unintended meanings into my words.'

'Am I to suffer your displeasure? You may ascribe my ill behaviour to a violent case of jealousy.'

'Please! You are jesting, I know, but that is unworthy of you.'

'I do not jest, Miss Carrington.' He turned to face her and she saw that he was serious. 'The young have no monopoly of strong affections. I would suggest that only an older man could value you at your true worth.'

'Great heavens!' Aurelia looked about her wildly for some means of escape, but the sinewy fingers were entwined in the long fringe of her shawl. 'Mr Clare, I beg of you——'

'This garment would appear to be entangled.' A long arm reached from behind her and shook the fringe free. 'Miss Carrington, I am charged with a message from your sister. She insists that you rest here quietly until you are feeling quite restored. The lady will excuse you, Clare.'

Aurelia's importunate suitor laughed, and gave way gracefully to Salterne. In no way did he betray is annoyance at being thus rudely interrupted. With a low bow to Aurelia and a wave of his hand for the Duke, he sauntered away.

Aurelia wished that the ground might open and swallow her. She was torn between the warring emotions of relief at her rescue and utter mortifiction at being found at such a disadvantage. Salterne had appeared from the shrubbery, and she had no idea of how much he had overheard or how long he had been there.

He did not leave her long in doubt.

'Do you care for a stroll, Miss Carrington?' He offered her his arm. 'I give you my word that I shall not propose marriage. Three offers in one evening would be the outside of enough. . .'

'You were listening? How could you? You should have discovered yourself, Your Grace. That was not——'

'The act of a gentleman? I believe you mentioned as much to me on another occasion. You are right, of course, but this time I have some excuse. The offers came so thick and fast, there was no time. . .'

Her annoyance deepened as she felt his shoulders shaking. How could he dare to laugh at her predicament? She stalked along beside him, her head held high.

'And then, you know, on these occasions thwarted suitors have been known to get above themselves. Either of them might have called me out.'

'What nonsense!' Aurelia's anger vanished as she tried to stifle a giggle.

'That's better!' He tucked her hand through his arm. 'You lead an exciting life, Miss Carrington. Never a dull moment, one might say.'

'I was surprised myself,' she admitted frankly. 'I came out merely for a breath of air.'

'You did not reckon with the lure of the enchantress?'

'Now you are making sport of me. Forgive me, sir, but I must go back to Cassie. I have been gone this age.'

'You will wish to compose yourself, will you not? These situations can be unnerving.' The gentle teasing did much to restore her spirits, and she was tempted to ask him how he knew. She thought it unlikely that impressionable females were in the habit of declaring themselves to him, only to be rejected, but she did not comment on his words.

'But did you not say that Cassie——?'

'A subterfuge, my dear. I have not spoken to Lady Ransome, but I felt that I should rescue you before other hearts were laid at your feet.'

'It is no laughing matter,' Aurelia said with feeling. 'I have not given either of them the least encouragement.'

'But that is the trouble. A citadel, you must know, is always a challenge.'

'You make me sound cold and unfeeling. . .'

'You? Never!' The warmth of his reply made her heart leap in her breast. 'I should not accuse you of either of those traits of character. Rather the opposite. Moreover, you are a rarity in my experience. . .a beautiful woman who is neither vain nor a coquette.'

'Really, Your Grace, you must not. . .'

Though she demurred, she was grateful for his words. At least he did not think her a heartless flirt.

'I must not speak the truth? Come, that is unlike you. You set great store on honesty, do you not?'

Now was the time to speak, if ever. After what had happened she had no hope of convincing him that she had any interest in Clare or Leggatt. Taking her courage in both hands, she faced him squarely.

'I do, my lord, so you will forgive me if I speak of a matter which troubles me. It is not easy for me to do so, but it must be said. Ransome has suggested. . .at least he said. . .well, the fact is that—er—Caroline is not sufficiently in your company. . . I mean, by your side.'

She was crimson with embarrassment by the time she had finished the stumbling explanation.

'Please do not think that I mean to criticise,' she continued lamely. 'It is not for me to advise you, but he feels that. . . Well, I am sure that the fault is mine. . .but he imagines that I have been somewhat indiscreet in my attitude.'

The garbled words did not lessen her feeling of discomfort. She was rambling like a fool, and still she had not asked him to avoid her company. Would he understand? It was a humiliating situation and he might well reverse his opinion as to her lack of vanity. She wished that she had not spoken of the matter.

'Does he indeed?' Salterne's eyes were slits of silver in the moonlight. 'That is most interesting.'

'I must go back to Cassie,' Aurelia went on nervously. 'I have been out here for an age. My reputation will be in shreds.'

She heard a cynical laugh.

'Few of Lady Bellingham's guests can boast of unsullied character. Half of them have foisted other men's children on their husbands, and as for the rest. . .well, as you know, they thrive on gossip. You do not hope to escape unscathed?'

'I intend to provide them with as little opportunity as possible for the exercise of their tongues, so you see I must return.'

'You disappoint me, Miss Carrington. Who knows what further surprises the night may have in store for you?' Salterne looked up at the sky and shook his head. 'The full moon is said to have a curious effect on the minds of men. I am half inclined to believe it. Will you take the risk? Your next discarded suitor is like to fall upon his sword.'

Aurelia stifled a laugh. 'Really, Your Grace. . .!'

'I am serious,' Salterne said wickedly. 'Think of the scandal, ma'am, and Lady Bellingham's dismay at the possible damage to her carpet!'

She could contain herself no longer and her peals of laughter rang across the garden. The vision of moonstruck swains was all too much for her composure.

'No vapourings, Miss Carrington? What a relief! I have not a single burnt feather about me at this moment.'

'An oversight, Your Grace?'

An appreciative chuckle greeted her words. Salterne turned his back on the lighted windows and led her further into the garden.

'Then it is true? Your affections are not engaged? I was not sure. . . There is a fashionable convention which insists that a lady does not give her consent at once to an offer of marriage.'

'You felt that I was following convention?' Her tone was dry. . .so dry that he chuckled again.

'I confess it would have surprised me. . .but you have not answered my question.'

Suddenly Aurelia was seized by panic. Since their first meeting the Duke had shown an uncanny ability to read her mind. She could lie to him, but would he believe her? Here, in the romantic setting of this moonlit garden, with the delicate scent of summer jasmine perfuming the air, she was in danger, and she knew it.

She dared not look at Salterne, but there was no need. His image was forever printed on her mind. The dark, unruly curls, the lean, sardonic countenance, his eyes, his mouth and the graceful poise of his head were as familiar to her as her own face. Pray heaven he would not guess.

Through the thin silk of her wrap he could feel her trembling.

'You are cold?'

'A little,' she lied.

'I have been thoughtless.' He drew her into the lee of the garden wall. 'Will you continue to evade my question?'

'You heard my reply to Captain Leggatt, I believe?' To her relief her voice was under control. 'That is not a proper question, sir.'

'And no business of mine? I must disagree. As I'm soon to become a member of your family it is very much my concern.'

The recollection of his imminent betrothal to Caroline stabbed Aurelia to the heart. She felt sick with jealousy.

'I have not forgot that you hope to marry my niece,' she said coldly. 'But I must remind you, sir, that I brook no interference in my affairs. I am mistress of Marram, and I may do as I please.'

'Then we must hope that you do not please to throw your life away on some man who is unworthy of you.'

'You believe me to be a poor judge of character?'

'I cannot say, though I suspect that your heart will always rule your head.'

He could not know how close he had come to stumbling upon the truth. How he would despise her if he ever guessed that he was the object of her thoughts and dreams.

Aurelia refused to rise to the bait.

'Captain Leggatt is young,' she said evenly. 'At present he chafes at the restrictions on the Prince's regiment. He found me a willing listener, though I find it hard to understand why any man should seek the miseries of the battlefield.'

'Inexperience, ma'am! One need only take part in an engagement such as Talavera to understand that death and glory do not always go hand in hand.' In the moonlight his face was grim. 'Sickness accounts for much of the army before the enemy is seen. Casualties are to be expected in battle, but it is hard to lose one's friends when the wounded are left untended.'

Aurelia glanced at the harsh countenance. 'Did

you. . .did you meet a Captain Elliott at Talavera?' The quiver in her voice caused the Duke to give her a sharp look.

'Tom Elliott? Was he a friend of yours?'

She nodded, unable to speak.

'Wellington thought highly of him. Were you aware that the great man cried when he saw the list of dead? Elliott was a favourite with all the general staff, and his men would follow him anywhere. They would have died for him. Instead he died for them. You knew that he was killed when trying to save his sergeant?'

Aurelia swallowed the lump in her throat which threatened to choke her. 'No one would tell me anything,' she whispered. 'The details were thought unsuitable for my ears, and. . .and we were not formally betrothed.'

'Then you were the lady?' Salterne stopped and looked at her. 'Elliott had always an air of inner joy. I knew it from my own experience. It comes from the knowledge that one is truly loved, and loves in return. It happened to me, and I understood his secret.'

He did not say more, and Aurelia did not dare to break the silence which fell between them. Long years of private anguish told her that no words of sympathy could ease his pain. It would be insensitive to offer them.

'Will you not tell me something of the Peninsular campaign?' she ventured at last. In the brilliant moonlight the strong planes of his features were etched into light and shade, illuminating the fearsome scar and giving him a sinister appearance, but Aurelia sensed only a fellow human being in need of comfort. Anything she could do or say to draw his thoughts from his dead wife must be of help to him.

For a moment she thought he had not heard her words. Then, with an effort, he gave her his attention.

'It is not a pretty tale,' he said slowly. 'I fear that it may distress you.'

'I want to know,' she insisted. 'In his letters Tom made light of the conditions in Portugal and Spain, but I am not foolish enough to suppose that it was pleasant. I wished to feel close to him, to share the life he lived out there, yet I could understand his wish to spare me.'

Salterne's smile was grim. 'Whatever he told you it would be impossible for you to imagine the heat, the dust, the poisonous snakes, the lack of food and water, and the mosquitoes. . . My God! The mosquitoes! They feasted well on tender English flesh. Some of the men were a living mass of agony, and the local population laughed at their sufferings. It was too much for one young officer—I will not give you his name. . . No inch of his skin was free from bites. After days and weeks of such torture he shot himself.'

Aurelia gasped, but she pressed him to go on.

'Our allies failed us, supplies did not come through, and the men were barefoot and ragged. Yet still, in that campaign, they fought with matchless courage to turn the tide against Napoleon. It was the beginning of the end for the French genius.'

'You see him as a genius, and not the monster of popular belief?'

'He is a brilliant man, Miss Carrington. Think of the Napoleonic code. . .to say nothing of his generalship. The flaw is his quest for world domination. We cannot let him have England.'

Aurelia murmured her heartfelt agreement.

'Thank you for answering my questions,' she said.

'Our brother too was killed at Talavera, and we have wished so much to know of his life in Spain. You knew him?'

'Not as well as I knew Elliott, but I have spoken of him to your sister. She had a look of him, but you. . . you are an original.'

Aurelia sensed that his eyes were upon her face. She began to tremble again.

'Here!' The Duke shrugged out of his coat and placed it about her shoulders. It still held the warmth of his body and the sensation was so intimate that he might have been holding her in his arms. She could detect a faint scent of soap and tobacco rising from the expensive cloth.

She gave a nervous little laugh.

'My brother was used to have two men to help him in and out of his coat,' she said inconsequentially.

'I fear I am too large for such refinements. Besides, I cannot bear to feel constrained.' He looked enormous as he stood before her, the white sleeves of his shirt billowing slightly in the breeze.

'I had best take you back,' he said abruptly. 'You will not care to be exposed to Ransome's insults.'

'He. . .he is gone to London.'

'A sudden departure? I had thought he would not dare.' He looked at her intently. 'Ah, I understand! You have paid his debts once more. I am sorry for that.'

'The decision was mine,' Aurelia said with dignity. 'My sister and Caroline are my first concern. . .' She stopped. She had intended neither to admit to paying Ransome's debts nor to let the Duke know that he was in such desperate straits.

Again he seemed to read her mind.

'The facts are known to me,' he said mildly. 'You need not fear that you have been indiscreet.'

Aurelia was silent as he hesitated, before he continued. 'A word of warning, Miss Carrington. Beware of Robert Clare. He is a dangerous acquaintance.'

'Your Grace, you presume too much,' she said in an icy tone. 'You may not choose my friends. . .'

In her haste to get away from him she turned sharply and caught her foot in the hidden root of a tree. With a low cry she put out a hand to save herself from falling, and found herself in Salterne's arms. She struggled wildly, but then his mouth came down on hers and she was lost.

His kiss was gentle and caressing, but insistent. The warm lips promised untold delights, robbing her of all caution. Of her own volition she surrendered to his passionate embrace, her hands reaching up to hold him close as she melted into his arms.

'My darling!' His murmured words were soft as he held her to his breast. Beneath the fine cambric of his shirt she sensed the sheer power of the man. His heart was pounding, as was her own, but the sound of his voice brought Aurelia to her senses. With an inarticulate cry of self-disgust she tore herself away from him and fled back along the path towards the house. Her head was reeling. It had taken but a single kiss to destroy her calm resolution to keep the Duke at a distance. And once in his arms she had offered no resistance. At that moment she loathed her own treacherous femininity. Her body had betrayed her at his touch.

Bitterly she remembered Ransome's cruel accusations. His contemptuous words were justified, she knew that now. She had realised the danger in that moonlight stroll, but she had not sought to avoid it. Hers were the actions of a woman lacking in all proper pride. And what must Salterne think of her? Her cheeks burned. Perhaps he had taken advantage of the moment because he'd imagined that she expected it.

She could not forgive herself for her folly. That she, Caroline's aunt, could behave so ill with the girl's betrothed! She would never have peace of mind again.

As she stumbled across the terrace Cassie caught her arm.

'Lia, where have you been? You have been gone this age. I thought you taken faint.'

As the light fell on her sister's face Cassie gasped.

'You are ill! I knew it! Your eyes are wild, and you are so flushed! We must go home at once!'

'Let me sit quietly in this corner behind the curtain. Do you summon the carriage, Cass.' Aurelia sank into the nearest chair as Cassie bustled away. She had only the vaguest awareness of being led through the crowd minutes later. Then they were in the darkness of the carriage, driving towards the house on the Steyne.

It was not until she was safely in bed that Aurelia allowed herself to dwell on what had happened in the garden. She could hardly bear to think about it. Deeply ashamed, she was also furious with both herself and the Duke.

She moaned and buried her face in the pillow. Everything had conspired against her. Salterne had found her first with Captain Leggatt and then with Robert Clare, when any well-bred woman would have been accompanied by a chaperon. In spite of her protestations, no doubt he believed that she had given encouragement to her suitors, permitting liberties as she had done with him.

She had behaved so badly, and she could hardly blame the Duke. To walk through a jasmine-scented garden, with the moonlight turning the trees to silver, and a shimmering curtain of stars above. . . She must have been out of her mind. She might have guessed what would happen. Salterne was a well-known libertine. The normal rules of conduct did not apply to him. He had given her evidence enough of that.

A tear trickled slowly down her cheek. It was no excuse, but for those few forbidden moments she had felt like a woman again instead of an old maid. Her face flamed as she recalled the sensual smoothness of his flesh against her skin.

Once more she had felt beloved, but it was an illusion. The Duke intended to marry Caroline. He had said as much this very evening.

She cried herself to sleep.

CHAPTER NINE

AURELIA awakened heavy-eyed next day. Her head ached, and she felt tired and listless. She was in no mood to cope with Cassie's scoldings.

'To leave those warm rooms and wander about without your wrap in the chill night air—'tis enough to set up an inflammation of the lungs. . .'

'Cassie, please. . . Doubtless you are right, but I do feel wretched. . .'

Faced with this admission, Cassie was all sympathy, and Aurelia felt a pang of guilt. It was true that she felt out of sorts, but the reason was not a chill. How could she ever face the Duke again? She closed her eye and Cassie tiptoed out of the room.

Until yesterday Aurelia had imagined that nothing could be worse than the difficulties in which she found herself. Now they were compounded. She should have fought against the Duke's embrace, or flayed him with cutting words. Instead she had returned his kiss with a passion that had shaken her to the core.

Her own behaviour had astonished her. Her gentle encounters with Tom Elliott had left her unprepared for the unfamiliar sensations which now troubled her so deeply. If this was infatuation she wanted no more of it.

She blamed herself rather than Salterne. Men, she knew, were said to be carried away by primitive instincts which took no account of civilised observance, but that she should have allowed herself to do the same did not bear thinking about.

The Duke's reputation should have warned her, she thought mournfully, but he had disarmed her over the past few weeks with his quick intelligence and his sense of humour. She had enjoyed his wit and their verbal battles. She could not deny that she was drawn to him, but she had been an easy conquest. A stifled cry of agony escaped her lips.

Writhing as if she were on the rack, she thought of their conversation in the garden. What a hypocrite he was! Had he not told her that she should find a man who was worthy of her? Apparently she had done so. Salterne's lack of integrity was matched only by her own. What man of honour would make an offer for a girl and devote his attentions to her aunt?

She had no doubt that a man of his temperament did not lead a life of celibacy, but surely he might have restricted the fulfilment of his needs to the many lightskirts who already filled the town. The thought gave her no comfort. She could not think of him in another woman's arms even now, when his behaviour had disgusted her. She knew her despair for what it was—a simple case of jealousy.

She rose and dressed and then began to pace the room. Somehow she must recover her peace of mind. In her present mood she was a prey to every kind of nonsensical idea.

After all, the Duke had not tried to rape her. She was refining too much upon a single kiss. As far as he was concerned it was probably but the impulse of a moment, in the worst of taste, considering the circumstances of his attachment to Caroline, but understandable. Easy dalliance was a way of life for him, but she could not be flattered to think that she had been the most recent recipient of his favours. Gently bred women did not expect or welcome such familiarity and, rake though he was known to be, his behaviour had surprised her.

Ransome's words returned to haunt her. He had accused her of wanting Salterne for herself. Surely the Duke could not suspect her motives to that extent? Had it crossed his mind that her stated reasons for wishing to prevent his marriage to Caroline were a sham, and that her own interests were her paramount concern?

The thought was acutely painful. She had done nothing to convince him otherwise. . .rather the reverse. Self-loathing occupied her mind to the exclusion of all else.

If only her father were still alive she might have taken his kindly counsel. In the three years since his death she had not missed him as she did now.

A wave of homesickness swept over her and she longed to return to Marram. Yet even as she considered the prospect she was seized with doubt. She had been content, but it was a cloistered view of the world. She began to wonder if she knew herself at all. Questions posed themselves and she had no answers. The cocoon in which she had wrapped herself had split. It was she who had changed, and now she wanted all that life might offer her.

Perhaps she had grieved for overlong, for her father, her brother, and Tom Elliott. It was a form of self-indulgence, she realised. Those who turned away from the world would be asked to pay the reckoning, as she was doing now.

She straightened her shoulders. Last night must

serve as a warning to her. She would take good care that such a thing did not happen again. Her next meeting with the Duke might be awkward, but she would not allow him to think that his unseemly behaviour had affected her. If he should mention it, which seemed unlikely, she would put it down to over-indulgence in Lady Bellingham's excellent wine. She must be discreet and, above all, she must put him out of her mind.

She picked up her book. *Sense and Sensibility* promised to be entertaining, and the author's calm good sense and ironic humour would distract her unruly thoughts.

For the rest of the day she revelled in the unaccustomed peace, and fell that night into a deep and dreamless sleep.

'I am glad you are recovered,' Cassie said next day. 'I was persuaded that we should miss the Prince's evening.'

'We shall be there,' Aurelia promised. In spite of her resolutions she was disturbed by the thought of meeting the Duke again, but she had a few days' grace. Would he embarrass her by giving some indication. . .a look or sly smile. . .to show that he recalled the memory of their kiss? She would attach herself to some dowager for the evening to prevent an attempt at conversation should the Duke approach her.

On the other hand it was possible that Salterne himself regretted the incident in the garden and had no wish to be reminded of his folly. His visits to the house on the Steyne had ceased abruptly, though Cassie saw nothing to remark upon in this. The

Regent, she surmised, had first call upon the Duke's attention.

Aurelia could only be thankful for the respite. Her peace of mind was only partially restored, but as the days went by she managed to convince herself that the matter was best forgotten. She could now, she felt, meet His Grace with perfect equanimity.

Her fragile confidence was quickly shattered. It was at the fashionable hour of five when she and Cass drove out with Caroline along the promenade.

'Shall you think of bathing, Aunt?' Caro's eyes were upon the blue and red bathing huts at the water's edge.

'I doubt if I have fortitude enough for the waters of the Channel,' Aurelia said with a smile. 'My preference is for Mr Williams' New Baths, which are heated. Cassie, do you not agree?'

A silence greeted her words and Aurelia looked at her sister in surprise.

'Cassie?'

'Over there!' Cassie gestured towards an expensive equipage which had drawn to a halt by the roadside. The occupants were surrounded by a crowd of young bucks.

'It is a trifle *outré*,' Aurelia agreed. 'A lining of pale blue satin would not by my own choice.'

Cassie reddened. 'Look the other way,' she whispered fiercely. 'We cannot recognise those. . .those creatures.'

'Why, Cass, what on earth. . .?'

'It is Harriet Wilson. . .*the* Harriet Wilson. . .and her sister. The brazen hussies! I wonder that they dare show themselves in daylight and in a public place.'

'How beautiful they are!' Caroline stared avidly as

the crowds parted and the occupants of the carriage were fully revealed. 'Mama, they are dressed like Hussars.'

'Such impudence! To copy the uniforms of the regiment is outside of enough, though it is not surprising. They have formed connections with so many of the officers. . .' Conscious of Caroline's interest, her mother stopped in mid-sentence.

The crush had forced their own carriage to a halt, and curiosity caused Aurelia to glance at the more striking of the two demireps. The woman was a beauty, there could be no doubt. A mass of auburn curls framed one of the loveliest faces she had ever seen, and a pair of glorious blue eyes were trained coquettishly upon a tall figure who had been hidden from their view by a passing horseman.

'Why, Mama, it is the Duke!' Caroline was more intrigued than startled.

At that precise moment Salterne looked up. With a word of apology to the voluptuous young woman who strove to hold his attention, he detached himself from the crowd and sauntered towards Aurelia's carriage.

'Your servant, Lady Ransome. . .and yours, Miss Carrington. Caroline, you are in famous looks today.'

His Grace chose to ignore Cassie's scarlet cheeks. With unruffled composure he lifted Caroline's fingers to his lips. Aurelia attempted to avoid his eye, but he was quick to ascribe her silence to another cause.

'I understand that you have not been well, Miss Carrington. 'I trust that I see you fully recovered from your—er—unfortunate indisposition?'

Aurelia bowed stiffly. She heard the amusement in his tone, but she was determined to ignore it.

'It was nothing. . .nothing to trouble me in the

least.' She gave him a steady look. 'You refine too much upon it, my lord.'

'I am glad to hear it.' His dark eyes were dancing. 'Then we shall meet at the Prince's evening?'

Aurelia bowed again, and left Cassie to exchange a word or two of civil conversation. His Grace then stood back to allow them to drive on.

'Well, really! That man has gall enough for anything! To find him in such company! He had no right to acknowledge us.' Aurelia was pink with indignation, and another emotion, which she had no desire to admit, even to herself.

'There is no need to distress yourself. It was unfortunate to find him in such company, but Salterne, as you know, pays no attention to polite observance.'

'He should have pretended not to see us. . .' Aurelia could no longer pretend that her feelings were other than those of jealousy, but Cassie must not guess.

'I cannot understand you,' Cassie sighed. 'Have you not always been the first to make excuses for such women?'

'That does not mean that I wish——' She stopped, afraid that she might betray herself.

'How little you know of men! What has the Duke's acquaintance with Harriet Wilson to say to anything? Married or betrothed, they will seek amusement in the arms of lightskirts. Anyhow, why should you care how he behaves?'

'*I* do not,' Aurelia announced with dignity. 'But you, I imagined, must have felt outraged.' She glanced at Caroline, who was absorbed in this interesting conversation. 'Had you not best explain to your daughter?'

Caroline flushed to the roots of her hair.

'I. . . I think I understand,' she said hastily. 'But it does not signify in the least.'

'Sensible girl!' Cassie beamed her approval. 'I must say, Lia, you astonish me! You were not used to be so strait-laced.'

Aurelia held her tongue with difficulty. She was deeply shaken by her own reaction to the sight of the Duke enjoying the company of the lovely Harriet.

The courtesan, so she had heard, had become the mistress of Lord Craven when she was but fifteen. Other lovers, including the Duke of Beaufort and the Duke of Argyll, had followed her original protector, and who could blame them? Those great violet eyes and that spectacular figure were enough to turn the head of any man.

For all she knew Salterne might, at this moment, be planning to give the woman *carte blanche*. Aurelia's nails dug into her palms. What was the matter with her? She was no schoolroom miss. She was well aware that an expensive mistress was an allowable indulgence for a man of fashion, but that knowledge was no comfort to her.

'I had thought better of him,' she muttered fiercely. 'Other men's leavings——' She stopped suddenly, conscious of Cassie's curious look.

'Salterne? My dear. . .with his reputation? That creature is doubtless but one of many. . .'

Aurelia lapsed into silence, and Caroline seemed momentarily bereft of speech.

But it doesn't matter to her, Aurelia thought sadly. She does not love him. The full import of her thoughts struck her a moment later and she paled. The reasons for her days of depression, her anger and her jealousy

were suddenly all too clear. She could no longer
deceive herself. This was not simply a foolish infatuation. She had allowed herself to fall in love with
Salterne almost unwittingly. The shock of the discovery overset her composure and she began to tremble.

'We had best turn for home,' Cassie said firmly.
'You do not look at all the thing. The drive has been
too much for you.'

'Very well.' Aurelia forced out the words through
stiff lips. She could not wait to be alone. In her
preoccupation with Cassie's troubles she had not
paused to consider the true nature of her own
emotions. She knew now why she had returned
Salterne's kiss with such unbridled passion. It was the
reaction of a woman in love.

On the following day Aurelia rose early, determined
to occupy herself so fully that she would have no time
to think, either of the Duke, her own feelings, or
anything at all but the prospect of the Prince's Musical
Evening.

In the long reaches of the night she had had time to
reflect. Her only hope of contentment or peace of
mind was to crush this love which had come unbidden
before it succeeded in destroying her. She must banish
any hope of a happy outcome, or she might fritter
away her life in dreaming.

She gave orders that all visitors were to be denied
while the ladies gave their attention to the elaborate
toilettes required for the evening entertainment.
Monsieur Pierre had been bespoken well in advance,
and by early evening the deceptively simple hairstyles
were arranged to the satisfaction of Aurelia and
Caroline, but Cassie inspected them with a criti-
cal eye.

'You do not think, *Monsieur*, that perhaps a turban or an aigrette for my sister. . .? Her jewels are so fine, and this diamond clasp. . .?'

'If Miss Carrington would consent to the silver hair ornaments which I suggested? Simple bands in the Greek style would be most effective against her fair hair.'

'Cassie, I like it as it is,' Aurelia said gently. 'Your turban is designed to match your gown. I shall wear my diamond earrings and a bracelet. It will be enough.'

'*Mademoiselle* is right. Her beauty needs no ornament; but let us see.' With deft fingers he trained one or two ringlets to fall from the topknot on her head. 'There. . .that is softer. You are pleased, Miss Carrington?'

'Very pleased, I thank you.'

When he had gone she stepped into her underdress of ivory satin. Over it she wore an open robe of crêpe in the same shade, trimmed with blonde lace.

'Aunt, you look like a beautiful lily,' Caroline announced enthusistically.

'What of your mama? She is like to outshine us all.'

'Fiddlesticks!' Cassie disclaimed the compliment, but she was looking at her best. Her plain round robe of finest white silk was decorated with a formal border of bronze embroidered leaves and edged with bronze ribbon. The Madonna-blue overskirt bore the same decoration around the border of the long train. Her short puffed sleeves were cuffed with the material of the underdress, and the neckline was trimmed with a small ruff of the finest lace.

'You do not think it over-elaborate for tonight?'

'Not at all,' Aurelia said stoutly. 'The Prince is a

stickler for tradition. I cannot think how long it is since I wore a train. In any case you know he will put us in the shade.'

Cassie smiled. 'I fear you are right, but I could wish that you had chosen the pink with the black net overdress rather than that ivory crêpe. The trimming on the skirt is well enough, yet I feel that a contrast would have been more striking.'

'The ivory will not clash with the regimentals,' Aurelia said demurely. 'Who can compete with yellow boots, scarlet trousers edged with gold fringe, and a laced jacket dashingly worn across the shoulder?'

Cassie was suitably impressed.

'How clever of you,' she said thoughtfully. Aurelia had described the uniform of the 10th Hussars to perfection. 'Now I am pleased that I did not yield to Caroline's entreaties to allow her to wear pink. She must see how it would clash, and she looks so sweetly pretty in white. The rosebuds are a charming touch. Your bosom-bottle is quite secure, my love?'

'Indeed, mama, it is stitched into the gown.'

'Then you must remember not to bend forward, or you will spill the water for the flowers.'

Aurelia caught her niece's eye and bit her lip, but she managed to preserve her countenance. It would not serve to upset Cassie on this important occasion.

'Let us dine now,' she said quickly. 'You must both be hungry. The Prince does not rise from the table until after ten, and no food is served before the performance. It will be midnight before we are offered refreshment.'

Her prophecy proved to be correct. As they joined a slow-moving line of carriages on the serpentine drive leading to the Regent's villa Aurelia feared that they would arrive later than the appointed time of ten in the evening.

When they reached the portico she hurried her party through into an octagonal ante-hall already thronged with guests.

The smell of the fashionable crowd was nauseating. Mr Brummell might have counselled frequent bathing and changes of linen—he, she had heard, bathed four times a day—but his words had obviously fallen on deaf ears. Not all the perfumes and pomades could disguise the stink of unwashed bodies.

She moved on swiftly into the entrance hall, a larger room which was decorated in soft shades of green and grey.

'But this is beautiful, Aunt Lia. It looks so cool. Did you not tell me that the Prince's taste was for dragons, serpents and other monsters?'

'This is designed as a contrast with the inner rooms. Come through this entrance and you will see.'

Aurelia led the way into a long, low corridor, and Caroline gasped. A myriad flickering candles illuminated the brilliant scene, aided by vast chandeliers. On the walls huge mirrors doubled the apparent width of the gallery and reflected painted murals of peacock-blue bamboos on a background of pink linen.

Everywhere the eye was held by Chinese porcelain figures. Mandarins and pagodas vied with fantastic carvings picked out in scarlet, blue and amber and richly gilded furniture. Oil-lamps of intricate design provided additional illumination.

'Let us stay by the staircase. Just to the side the crush is not so great.' Aurelia managed to find a space by the stairwell, where Caroline might examine the details to her heart's content.

'What a curious choice,' she said in wonder. 'I had not thought that bamboo would be strong enough to support the handrails.'

'A clever imitation, my love. The staircase is cast iron, painted to resemble bamboo. You will find many surprises here. The furniture is of English beech, which also simulates bamboo. And do but look at the windows above the stair. More mandarins, I fear.'

'You do not care for it, Aunt?'

'The workmanship is very fine, but I find the whole somewhat overwhelming, and I do not care to find a serpent by my ankle, though it is only imitation.'

'Thank heavens we are not late,' Cassie murmured. 'The Prince is not yet risen from the table, though I hear that he sat down at six.'

Aurelia glanced at the small watch in her reticule. It was almost eleven. She was about to speak when there was an expectant hush, and the door to the banqueting-room was thrown open.

As the Prince appeared the crowd drew back to allow him passage. He made his way slowly down the line of curtsying women and bowing men, stopping at intervals to exchange a word or two with his guests. There was no mistaking the resplendent figure, though he was much heavier than when Aurelia had seen him last. His coat was of exquisite cut, embroidered down the front with silver flowers, picked out with foil-stones. Beneath it a waistcoat of white and silver tissue echoed the embroidery on the coat. A blaze of decorations completed his ensemble.

Tall though he was, he was dwarfed by the man behind him. Salterne's evening clothes lacked all orna-ment, but they fitted him to perfection. Those broad shoulders had no need of padding, nor wide revers to emphasise his massive chest. To Aurelia's mind he was the most distinguished-looking man in the room.

As he drew level with their little group the Prince stopped.

'Lady Ransome, I am glad to see you here, and Miss Carrington too. Now, who is this delightful creature? It cannot be your daughter, Lady Ransome. You are much too young.'

'You are too kind, Your Royal Highness, yet it is so. This is my daughter Caroline.'

The Prince was profuse in his compliments, but he was swaying slightly, and Aurelia guessed that he was not quite sober. To her surprise he was carrying an airgun.

'We must have some sport,' he announced. 'Come, ladies, let us go to the drawing-room.'

Seizing Caroline by the hand, he darted off, followed by his guests. As they reached the drawing-room he rapped out an order, and Aurelia realised, much to her consternation, that a target was to be erected at the far end of the room. Her own misgivings were reflected in the faces of the Prince's orchestra, who were seated uncomfortably close to the line of fire.

'Now, my dear.' Prince George pressed the gun into Caroline's unwilling hands. 'Shall you care to try your skill?'

Caroline cast a pleading glance about her, but there was no hope of salvation.

'Will you not show me, sire?' she begged.

'Nothing to it, m'dear.' The Prince took aim and hit the target in the centre. 'Hold the gun so. . .' He stood behind her, enfolding the shrinking figure in his arms. 'Now squeeze the trigger gently.'

Caroline closed her eyes and fired, making a neat hole in the ceiling.

'Well, well. . .better luck next time. Lady Ransome?'

With great dignity Cassie took the gun from her daughter's hands, held it in the prescribed manner, and fired. A yelp of agony followed.

'I fear you have hit a fiddler, ma'am. Now do not distress yourself. The fellow is but grazed. . .' The Prince walked to the far end of the room and handed over a small purse.

He came back beaming. 'No harm done,' he said gaily. 'Now, Miss Carrington. . .'

'Miss Carrington may not be so lucky, sire.' The deep voice behind her startled Aurelia. 'She is so short-sighted as to be almost blind to what goes on about her.'

Aurelia spun round to find Salterne at her elbow. For a second she was tempted to protest, but the thought of being excused from this eccentric target practice was too tempting. She contented herself with smiling at the Prince.

'So!' He bent towards her. 'A pity in one so young, but we all have our afflictions, ma'am. I myself am a martyr to gout.'

He paused for a moment, lost in thought. 'I have it, my dear—you will be able to enjoy the music, at least.'

With the courtesy for which he was renowned, he led her to the far end of the room and seated himself beside her.

'Do you care for glees and catches, m'dear?' He signalled to the leader of the orchestra. 'You shall join in. We do not stand on ceremony here.'

He began to sing in a pleasant bass, with so much enjoyment that Aurelia found herself infected by his own enthusiasm.

'These are your favourites, sire?' she asked.

A piercing blue eye regarded her. 'Shall you like to hear the best of all?'

Aurelia smiled her assent and the Prince began his solo—'By the gaily circling Glass'.

A burst of loud applause and cries of 'Encore!' marked the conclusion of his song, but their host rose to his feet, shaking his head. He bowed to Aurelia and to Cassie and moved away to join his other guests.

'Is he not perfection?' Cassie was glowing at the signal mark of favour shown to her family by the Regent.

'He was certainly very kind,' Aurelia agreed in an absent tone. It was difficult to give Cassie her full attention when her glance would persist in straying towards the tall figure standing by the Prince's side.

It would not do. If they could but steal away unnoticed now that the music had ended. . .

Cassie would have none of it.

'How can you think of such a thing?' she demanded. 'We should never be forgiven. Besides, I long to see that odious Mrs Ingleby. Tonight she has been given the set-down she deserved. I doubt if she will put on her airs with me again.'

Aurelia resigned herself to the inevitable, but she had no intention of putting herself in the Duke's way. She allowed Robert Clare to find her a seat in a corner half hidden by a Chinese screen, and accepted his offer to bring her a glass of wine. The hothouse atmosphere of the room had made her drowsy, and she guessed that it was late. A glance at her watch showed her that it was after midnight. If only Cassie would return. . .

She was roused by the sound of voices.

'I hear that Harriet Wilson has her hooks in yet another noble lord. . .' The speaker was very close.

'And this time there is talk of marriage. . .' A sneering laugh accompanied the reply. 'It may be the only way to stop her publishing her memoirs.'

'She has threatened to do so?'

'Indeed! And Harriet means it. She has caused a certain *frisson* among the *bon ton*, but this latest *affaire* may put an end to it. The thought of becoming a duchess will doubtless weigh with her.'

Aurelia froze. Could this be the reason for the delay in announcing Caroline's betrothal? And why the ravishing Harriet had been seen in public with Salterne? Yet the Duke could not possibly be contemplating marriage with a Fashionable Impure. She could not believe it. Yet she had seen him conversing on easy terms with Harriet, and the woman's previous ducal suitors were known to have tired of her.

If Harriet had the means in her possession to injure him. . .? No, he would never submit to blackmail, she was sure of it. Sir John Lade might take to wife a woman with a past, but Salterne would not stain his ancient name by marriage to such a creature. The speaker must have been referring to some other duke, but try as she might she could not think of a suitable candidate.

'Lost in thought, Miss Carrington?' The subject of her preoccupation seated himself beside her.

Aurelia gave a start at the sound of that familiar voice. She knew only too well why her heart was pounding, and to her dismay she found that her hands were shaking. Why must he seek her out? His nearness made it so difficult to hide her true feelings. She gave him a faint smile and looked away.

'Are you absorbed in the study of this curious piece of furniture?'

'I. . . I had not noticed it.' Pehaps if she gave him no encouragement he would seek more congenial company.

'Really! You surprise me! Personally I feel that the place for an Egyptian river boat is on an Egyptian river. The crocodile feet are charming, of course, but this gilded prow is inclined to catch one at a painful angle.'

The laughing eyes sought her own, expecting her to share his amusement, but Aurelia averted her head. She was about to make some excuse to leave him when Robert Clare appeared.

'Your wine, Miss Carrington. My apologies for the delay, but the rush was appalling.' He gave Salterne a pointed look, but the Duke showed no disposition to relinquish his seat.

'I see I have been supplanted,' Clare remarked cheerfully. 'Perhaps later, Miss Carrington?'

Aurelia nodded. She would not insult her companion in front of Clare, but courtesy dictated that he should have given way to her supper partner. She was about to speak when he forestalled her.

'I believe I mentioned Clare to you before.' There was a hint of steel in his voice.

'And I believe that I informed you that you may not choose my friends. You will perceive that I make no comment upon your own.'

He looked at her for a long moment, and she saw the glint in his eyes.

'Ah. . .the lovely Harriet. . . I see. . .'

'How dare you, my lord? No gentleman would mention such—er——'

'Barques of frailty?' he supplied helpfully.

'I was about to remark that such subjects are unsuitable in mixed company.'

'But you brought this one up yourself, my dear.'

'If you will excuse me, Your Grace. . .' Aurelia gave him an icy look, and rose to her feet.

'No! I think not. Sit down, Miss Carrington.' A firm had closed about her wrist and, short of indulging in an undignified struggle, she had no choice but to obey. 'We were speaking of Robert Clare. . .'

'*You* were speaking of Robert Clare, and I may say that I find your attitude offensive.'

'But you do not know the reason for it, do you?'

'Jealousy, my lord? Clare is close to the Prince, I believe. Do you think that he will supplant you?'

'It is unlikely, and you are mistaken. My reason for warning you against Clare is other than that. He is a dangerous man.'

'I do not believe you. He has been kind and courteous and. . .and all attention.'

'That is a part of his stock-in-trade. A surly manner would not serve him well.'

'I wonder if you realise just how insulting you are?'

'My intention was not to insult you, Miss Carrington, but to open your eyes, if possible.'

'How would that help me, Your Grace, if I am thought to be so short-sighted as to be blind to all about me?'

'Come now.' The corner of his mouth lifted. 'Confess that you were happy to be rescued from a trying situation.'

'I should have begged to be excused from attempting to hit the Prince's target.'

'You might not have succeeded. Prince George can be most persuasive, and I feared that with a gun in your hand you might have aimed elsewhere. . .quite by accident, of course. I was resolved to stand behind you, should you attempt the feat. One quarry was brought down, you will recall.'

Aurelia's composure was sorely tried. The memory of Cassie in full court dress, with plumes in her turban, was all too much for her. Her shoulders began to shake.

'I shall treasure that moment always,' the Duke observed mildly. 'It will be a comfort in my declining years.'

Choking with laughter, Aurelia attempted to hide behind her fan.

'Cruel!' she gasped reproachfully. 'The man might have been badly hurt.'

'But he was not. I believe he was more astonished than injured, as were we all.' His grave look set Aurelia off again.

'Careful, Miss Carrington! I shall begin to suspect you of unbecoming levity. Had you not heard that a polite simper is all that is allowable in society? Laughter mars the features, and is the cause of wrinkles, so I understand.'

'You are impossible,' she told him frankly. 'I cannot imagine why I let you tease me into a better humour when I am determined to be cross.'

'But we deal together extremely, do we not?' A large brown hand reached out and covered her own. 'Will you not trust me in this matter of Clare? It is not personal pique, I assure you. There are reasons, but they are not mine to give at present.'

Aurelia snatched her hand away as if she had been stung. His touch was too disturbing. The warmth of his flesh against her own brought back vivid memories of that night in the garden which she now regretted so bitterly. What to him was casual friendship, or even a mild flirtation, now meant everything to her. And she would never drive him from her mind if she was forced to see him, to hear his voice, and, worst of all, to be so close to him.

Silently she prayed that he would leave her.

'Look at me!' he commanded. 'Do you believe that I have your interests at heart?'

His tender expression set her heart beating wildly, and she rose to her feet, afraid of betraying herself.

'I believe that you mean well, Your Grace, though I cannot understand your aversion to Clare. My sister has known him for years. He is an old friend. . . Now, if you will excuse me?' She was relieved to find that her voice was well under control.

'My grandmother asked me to come in search of you. Will you spare her a few moments?'

'Why did you not say so, my lord? I should not wish to keep her waiting.'

Salterne picked up her scarf and draped it about her shoulders. Did the strong hands linger longer than was strictly necessary? Aurelia stiffened, but she did not speak.

He led her to an ante-room, tapped on the door and entered. The Dowager Duchess was propped up on a sofa, laughing immoderately at one of the Regent's stories. The Prince broke off as Aurelia walked towards them.

'Now, ma'am, that piece of gossip is not fit for
tender ears,' he warned. 'Miss Carrington will think
me no fit company for a gently bred young lady if you
give me away.'

Aurelia murmured a polite disclaimer, but Prince
George shook his head.

'Come, Salterne! Let us leave these ladies to their
coze. Then, ma'am, you shall obey your doctor's
orders. Your carriage will be at the door in precisely
fifteen minutes.'

The Duchess smiled indulgently as the two men left
the room.

'The Prince has a generous heart,' she said. 'In
many ways he is the best of men. . .'

'You have enjoyed this evening, ma'am?'

'I have. The Prince is a matchless mimic. He was
reminding me of his uncle. One might almost think to
hear the old man speaking, with his grunts and his
broken English, but done without malice, my dear. . .'

'His manner is so very affable,' Aurelia said shyly.
'Is he not called The First Gentleman of Europe?'

'He is, and the tile is well-merited, but it was not of
him I wished to speak. I heard that you had not been
well.' The sharp black eyes scanned Aurelia's face.
'You look vastly elegant tonight, but you are not
yourself, I think.'

'I am well enough, ma'am.' Aurelia's heart sank.
Did she give herself away so easily? It was becoming
more and more difficult to hide her secret. She longed
to explain her difficulties to the Dowager. That wise
old head held years of accumulated wisdom. Yet
Salterne was her beloved grandson, and she would
never doubt his integrity. To speak of his behaviour,

and particularly of her own reaction to it, was impossible.

'I am glad to hear it, as I can now pass on to you a message from a faithful admirer. . . Charlotte longs to see you again. Will you not come to visit us? Salterne is with the Prince for much of the time, and I am ordered to rest each day. The child worries me. She is growing subdued, with so little company aside from that of the servants. . . Perhaps I should not ask. . . It is an odd request. . .to bear company with a six-year-old. . .'

'Ma'am, I should be happy to see her,' Aurelia answered warmly. 'Charlotte is so interested in the world about her.'

Her sympathy had gone out at once to both Charlotte and the Dowager, but on reflection she knew that it was unwise to be drawn even further into Salterne's affairs. She sighed inwardly. Events never ceased to conspire against her avowed resolution to put him from her mind.

CHAPTER TEN

'LIA, have you seen Caro?' Cassie looked about her with a frown.

'You will scarce discover her in this crush. Do you stay here and I will find her. Then we must go. It is very late.'

'I suppose so.' Reassured by Aurelia's words, Cassie turned back to Lady Bellingham.

Aurelia walked swiftly through the thinning crowds, but Caro was not to be found. Perhaps the grounds? Aurelia's cheeks burned as she recalled her own experience a few days earlier. Had Caro been tempted into the gardens by some young buck intent on a stolen kiss or two?

Her niece was not within the building. That much was certain. There was nothing for it. She must venture out herself. At least Caro was wearing white. Her gown would be visible in the darkness.

Aurelia looked about her before she stepped on to the terrace. She had no wish to provide food for gossip. Wagging tongues would be quick to credit her with an assignation if she was seen to leave the villa alone.

No one glanced in her direction, so she caught up her train, opened the long window and hurried out of sight around the corner of the building.

'Another promenade in the evening air, Miss Carrington?' The deep chuckle brought her to an

177

abrupt halt. Salterne, of all people! She could have cried with frustration.

'My lord, as you appear to spend your time on these occasions lurking in the shrubbery, perhaps you will tell me if you have seen my niece?'

'Unjust, my dear! But in answer to your question I saw Caroline not half an hour ago. She was walking towards the Prince's stables.'

'Alone?' She could have bitten off her tongue even as she spoke.

'Alone,' he agreed smoothly.

'Then what in the world. . .?'

'The architecture is thought to be very fine. Prince George considers that his horses are better housed than he. It is difficult to appreciate the finer points in darkness, of course.'

'Oh, you. . .you. . .'

'Give yourself time, Miss Carrington. You will find a suitable word to describe my character. Meantime, if you care to go in search of your niece I shall be happy to accompany you.'

'Yes. . .no. . . oh, that foolish girl! She can have no idea. . .'

'None whatever,' he agreed politely. 'Will you take my arm? The ground is somewhat uneven. There is every chance that you may stumble.'

Aurelia's face flamed. So he had not forgotten the false step which had thrown her into his arms. She was tempted to withdraw her arm and order him to leave her, but the grounds were large and lonely, and ahead of her the stable block loomed dark against the night sky.

'How pleasant this is,' the Duke observed in an

affable tone. 'I am glad that you share my enjoyment
of a stroll before retiring.'

He might have been making civil conversation in a
drawing-room, but Aurelia was seized with a strong
desire to give him the worst set-down of his life. No
suitable epithets came to mind, so she vouchsafed no
reply. Instead she scanned the rising ground in the
hope of catching a glimpse of Caroline.

'In here, I believe.' Salterne indicated a narrow
doorway in the great stone wall.

Aurelia stopped and faced him, dreading what she
might find.

'You will not. . .?' she breathed.

'No, I shall not accompany you. I fear I should be
de trop.' With a bow he turned and left her.

Aurelia felt both humiliated and furious. That
Caroline should put any member of her family in this
position! She marched inside the building, and made
her way along a narrow corridor. A dim light burned
at the end of the passageway, and as she reached it
she heard whispering.

'Caroline!'

She heard a gasp. Then Caroline appeared with a
young man by her side.

'We are ready to leave.' Aurelia's tone was icy. This
was neither the time nor the place, but she would have
much to say to her niece when they reached home.
Meantime she would give the young man a piece of
her mind. She paused in surprise as he stepped into
the light.

'I *had* to see Richard.' Caroline was nervous but
defiant. 'I have made no secret of my feelings for him,
Aunt, and they have not changed.'

'And you, Mr Collinge? What have you to say to

me? I had thought better of you. This sneaking way of
going on is not to my taste. Have you no thought for
Caroline's reputation?'

'No one saw me leave the villa,' Caroline told her
sullenly.

'Then how is it that the Duke of Salterne was able
to tell me where to find you?'

'I might have known,' came the bitter reply. 'Am I
to be spied on for the rest of my life?'

'Hush, Caro.' Richard Collinge moved towards
Aurelia. 'I hear. . .' He cleared his throat. 'I hear that
Caro is not yet betrothed. We had hoped to find some
way. . .'

'My niece knows of my desire to help her, but
clandestine meetings will not serve, Mr Collinge. This
is the height of folly. You may be thankful that His
Grace did not accompany me.'

'Is. . .is he waiting outside?' Caroline's courage was
fast deserting her. 'He shall not harm Richard. I could
not bear it.' She threw herself into her lover's arms
and burst into tears.

'The Duke knows only that you entered this building.' Aurelia crossed her fingers behind her back. The
Duke, as she knew from his remarks, was in no doubt
that his bride-to-be had an assignation with another
man. If he chose to ignore her foolishness that was his
privilege, odd though it might appear.

'What do you suppose might have happened had my
sister found you together?' she continued.

The two young people looked at her in silence.

'You know quite well, I believe. Caroline would be
taken home at once to face her father's wrath. Did
you think of that, Mr Collinge?'

'She has been badly treated,' the boy said in a low

voice. His face was pale, but determined. 'I cannot let her suffer.'

'Her suffering is like to be far worse if you do not heed me. Caro, I am surprised at you. Did you not give me your word?'

'I promised only that we should not elope. I did not say that I should not write to Richard, or try to see him.'

Aurelia felt a surge of pity as she looked at the two wan faces. It was mixed with a certain admiration. She had underestimated Caroline. None of the lures thrown out to her, the compliments, or the obvious admiration of the men who clustered about her daily, had changed her devotion to this stocky young man.

'You have two minutes to make your farewells,' she said. 'Caro, I will wait for you by the outer door.'

She knew when she was beaten. Caro had received no formal offers, but whether this was due to her want of fortune or a lack of encouragement she had no way of knowing. She suspected a combination of both.

She was half tempted to release Caroline from her promise. An elopement might be the answer after all. Caro would be safe from both her father and the Duke. Yet Cassie must be thought of too. Aurelia shuddered. She could imagine her sister's treatment at Ransome's hands should such a thing occur.

'Has the Duke gone?' Caroline's voice was a mere whisper.

'I do not see him. You may give thanks for his discretion, Caro. It is more than you deserve.'

She hurried her niece across the deserted lawns, uneasily aware that their light-coloured gowns made them conspicuous as they left the shelter of the trees. They gained the villa undetected, though a scattering of guests still clustered in the entrance hall. Aurelia had feared a tirade from Cassie, but her sister was still deep in conversation with Lady Bellingham. As the ladies whispered together she guessed that some particularly juicy snippet of scandal must be under discussion.

'Cassie, here is the Prince.' Aurelia curtsied deeply as the portly figure of their royal host came towards them.

'Lady Ransome. . .Miss Carrington. . .you have enjoyed this evening?' He appeared to be gratified by their expressions of pleasure. 'You do me honour, ladies. Now tomorrow we have the fireworks. Shall we see you at the display? I can promise you something out of the common way.'

They thanked him prettily as he handed them into their carriage.

'Did you see Mrs Ingleby's face?' Cassie was enjoying her triumph. 'If looks could kill we should be lying dead at her feet.'

The lack of response from her companions did not appear to trouble her.

'Only think, my dear!' She leaned towards Aurelia. 'That creature Harriet Wilson has hopes of becoming a Duchess.'

Aware that she had Aurelia's full attention in response to this startling piece of news, she glanced at her daughter, but Caro was staring into the darkness, lost in her own thoughts.

'Marriage, Lia! What do you say to that? I could not credit my ears. What is the world coming to. . .?'

'I do not believe it.'

'But it is true. I had it from Lady Bellingham. His Lordship made the offer last week. . .'

'And. . .and you do not mind?' Aurelia forced out the words with difficulty. So this was why Salterne was so unconcerned about the evening's events. He had lost all interest in Caroline. She felt as if a giant hand had clasped her throat, choking her in its grip.

'Mind? Why should I mind? It has naught to do with me. If the young man is lost to all sense of propriety then his father is not. The old Duke offered to buy her off. . .'

'The. . .the young man? And. . .the old Duke?'

'That is what I said. What is the matter with you, Lia? One might suppose that you are deaf. You know the parties concerned, though I must name no names.' She gave a significant nod in Caroline's direction.

'Then Salterne is not involved?' Aurelia clenched her hands as she waited for the answer.

'Only to the extent that he has succeeded where the old Duke could not. The slut professed herself insulted by the offer of an annuity, or even a lump sum. As though it were possible to insult a whore! She had her eye on the family wealth. All seemed lost until Salterne spoke to her. He is believed to have issued a certain warning. . .'

'Is. . .is the matter ended?' Aurelia felt weak with relief.

'I believe so. You look oddly, sister. I pray that you have not taken another chill.'

'Cassie, you worry about me over-much,' Aurelia chaffed. She bent a mock-frown upon her sister. 'Had you but heard the questions about my health tonight. Do not, I beg you, continue to fancy me at the gates of death.'

'You must make light of it, I know, but sometimes I think. . .Oh, well, if you do not wish to tell me. . .'

'I am perfectly well, I assure you. Was it not kind of Prince George to invite us to the fireworks? If he claims that the display is to be out of the common way it is sure to be extraordinary.'

The remark served to divert Cassie's attention, and she continued to speculate upon the forthcoming entertainment until they sought their beds.

'I shall not rise early,' Cassie announced. 'It is already past three in the morning. I vow I shall not open my eyes before noon. We shall all sleep well tonight.'

Aurelia agreed, but sleep did not come easily. A niggling feeling of guilt assailed her. She groaned as she thought of the twinkle in Salterne's eyes when she had been indiscreet enough to mention Harriet Wilson. She had not actually spoken the woman's name, but he had taken her meaning at once.

She had been all too ready to impute the worst of motives to him. Yet this evening he had shown himself to be a marvel of tact when faced with Caroline's folly.

She tossed uneasily in her bed until she came to a decision. She must apologise, if he would allow it, and thank him for his discretion. She would be on dangerous ground. A prospective bridegroom might reasonably be expected to take violent exception to unfaithfulness on the part of his betrothed. Again she wondered why he seemed unperturbed. That he knew of the assignation she could have no doubt. What was the matter with the man? He did not lack courage. Perhaps he had waited for Richard and challenged him. Her blood ran cold at the thought. But would he call out a mere boy? No, she would not think that of him.

The thought served to calm her, and she found herself growing drowsy. There was something. . . something at the back of her mind which she could not quite recall. She went over every word of their conversation, and then it came to her. He had asked for her trust.

That in itself was strange. Was she not his acknowledged enemy? Her cheeks grew warm as she remembered that lazy voice and the gently smiling eyes, yet she had seen something behind them. A flicker of steel?

She tried to crush her growing unease. Was he playing some deep game? It would account for so much which she found inexplicable. . . She drifted off to sleep at last.

She was roused by a bustle in the street below and the sound of knocking at her door. Aurelia looked at her watch. It was almost noon. She rang for Hannah and was dismayed to learn that Ransome had returned from London. It was to be hoped that he had settled his affairs. She dressed and went down to the salon.

Her brother-in-law greeted her cheerfully. He appeared to be in the best of spirits.

'I may stable the curricle here?' he asked. 'It will not crowd the phaeton.'

Aurelia forebore to ask if the vehicle was a recent purchase. Ransome's pride in it was evidence enough.

'You saw my bankers?'

'Yes, my dear, and all is well. I thank you.'

His unusual civility disturbed Aurelia. What mischief had he been up to? She might be sure that some nefarious scheme was afoot. Either that or his luck had changed, and he had won heavily at the tables.

'You seem in good spirits, Ransome,' she observed.

'Why not, my dear Aurelia? Your generosity brought me good fortune. Your gold has multiplied.' He pushed a leather bag towards her. 'Naturally I shall wish to repay your loan.'

Aurelia's heart sank. Now she was more convinced than ever that trouble must follow as surely as night must follow day. She straightened her shoulders. Why should she doubt his words? Fortunes were won and lost each day at White's and Watier's. It was not impossible that he was speaking the truth.

'I thank you.' She picked up the bag of gold and locked it in her desk. 'You have seen Cassie?'

'Not yet. . .not yet. . .but I hope to surprise her.' He patted his pocket significantly. 'Just a trifle which I hope will give her pleasure, and something for Caro too.'

He left her then, and Aurelia sank into a chair. In spite of his assurances she could not trust Ransome. He had not mentioned Salterne. Did this mean that the proposed marriage was not now of the first importance? His win must have been large indeed. A feeling of dread swept over her. She should be happy to find him so much changed, and yet she was not. With an effort she put Ransome from her mind, and proceeded to give her orders for the day.

It was a radiant Cassie who came tripping down the stairs.

'Is it not wonderful?' she cried. 'Ransome has had such luck at the tables. See, Lia, he thought of me.'

She held out a trinket in the form of a golden melon. As she pressed a spring at the side the fruit opened out into quarters, each section containing a different perfume.

'Is it not charming?' Cassie allowed a drop or two

to fall on the inside of her wrists. 'Only the French can create such things.'

'Then how did Ransome come by it? All trade has ceased since Napoleon conquered the European mainland.'

'Doubtless it came from one of the refugees. Poor creatures! When they fled the Terror they brought their prized possessions. Now, I suppose, they are forced to sell to keep themselves alive.'

'I see. It is gold, is it not?'

'Of course. Oh, Lia, you will not complain of his extravagance? I am so happy to have it.'

Aurelia forced a smile.

'And for Caro. . .well, you cannot imagine. It is the sweetest brooch. . .a double circle of pearls and dia-monds. It will look delightful with her chamerry gauze. That is, if you think it warm enough for gauze this evening? We shall be out of doors. . . Well, perhaps we may carry our Kashmir shawls.'

Aurelia tried to hide her dismay. At that moment she longed to run away. If she could but saddle up her horse and ride back to Marram she vowed silently that she would lock the door against all callers, and to perdition with the Prince's fireworks.

Instead she expressed her admiration for Caroline's brooch, and allowed herself to be drawn into a discus-sion of a suitable toilette. In defiance of Cassie's pursed lips she elected to wear an underdress of silver-grey tiffany covered with an open robe of her favourite spider gauze. It was understated, but Aurelia felt that it matched her mood. She was unaware that the slender silver column was a perfect foil for her flawless skin, and that it did not detract from the beauty of her hair and eyes.

The Prince was in no doubt.

'Venus rising from the foam,' he announced that evening. 'Clare is right when he speaks of the Three Graces. Salterne, you must agree with him for once?'

'I do, sire.' Salterne bowed, but his eyes were for Aurelia alone, and the warmth of his expression discomfited her. That look should be for Caro. After all, it was she to whom he had offered marriage. His open admiration for herself, and the way in which he almost ignored her niece. . .well, not only was it embarrassing, but it was not the behaviour of a man of honour. Her face was cold as she turned away. How could she have grown to care for someone who lacked integrity?

'Ladies, we must make sure that you are settled in a point of vantage.' The Regent fussed about them. 'You will see to it, my lord?'

He moved away, leaving Salterne to guide Aurelia's party across the park.

Ransome, she noted in surprise, was less than cordial to the Duke. Could it be that his sudden access of fortune had changed his mind about the desired connection? She hung back as her brother-in-law strode ahead with Caro and Cassie on his arm.

'Your Grace, I have something to say to you.' Aurelia kept her voice low, partly from shyness and partly from a wish not to be overheard.

'My time is always at your disposal, Miss Carrington. The matter is urgent, I presume? Shall we—er—lurk in the shrubbery? As you know, it is a favourite haunt of mine. . .'.

Aurelia's face flamed. Perhaps he was merely referring to her acid comment on the previous evening, but she could not be sure. She suspected that he was recalling to her mind that dreadful loss of conduct on her part when she had allowed him to kiss her, and. . . she could not deny it. . .she had returned that kiss with such fervour.

'I wish you will not joke,' she said as calmly as she could. 'I wished merely to say. . .at least, I feel that I should. . .'

'More sackcloth and ashes, Miss Carrington?' She heard the laughter in his voice. 'Oh, dear, I hope not.'

'Not at all.' Would he never be serious? 'It is merely that I wished to thank you for your. . .your forbearance with Caroline last evening. I had feared that. . . that. . .'

'That I might call the gentleman out?'

'Oh!' she cried in exasperation. 'You are the strangest lover I can imagine. Don't you care? You seem to take these matters so lightly.'

'There you are mistaken.' The light tone had vanished. 'But your fears are unfounded, my dear. Your niece's youthful peccadilloes do not interest me in the least.'

'They most certainly should.' Aurelia was indignant.

A pair of large hands rested lightly on her shoulders and the Duke swung her round to face him.

'Must I ask you once again to trust me? The facts, my dear. Remember that you must have *all* the facts.'

'But if you intend to marry her?'

His smile was enigmatic as he drew her arm through his and led her towards the others.

Aurelia drew her Kashmir shawl closer about her shoulders. The slight breeze from the sea promised to increase in strength, and the delicate gauze of her overdress offered little protection. The Duke felt her shiver.

'You ladies have my admiration,' he remarked. 'I cannot understand why fashions which originated in ancient Greece should be thought suitable for the English climate.'

'I have thought the same myself,' Aurelia admitted, and was rewarded by a chuckle. She stole a glance at him. What a mystery he was. She would never learn to understand him. What other man would have turned aside her apologies for Caroline's behaviour to speak of the present fashions? He must be possessed of an iron self-control.

He raised an eyebrow in enquiry.

'Another question, Miss Carrington?'

'I was admiring your panache, Your Grace. Your self-discipline amazes me.'

'It also amazes me, my dear. In the last few weeks my resolution has been sorely tried.'

The words were spoken lightly, but there was something unnerving in his tone.

'You do not care for the present fashions?' she said quickly. It was best to follow his earlier lead and attempt to conduct their conversation on more acceptable lines.

Was he suggesting that he was losing patience with Caroline's delaying tactics? Aurelia's heart sank. If Salterne wished to marry without further delay he might override his grandmother's advice.

'The fashions are charming when they are worn by an enchantress with fair hair and eyes as blue as the summer sky,' he said softly, but his words enraged her.

'I find extravagant compliments foolish and distasteful. Oh, dear, I sound so priggish, but it is true.'

'So is the compliment, my dear, but if you wish I

will change it. Shall I tell you that you are obstinate and headstrong, and also impatient of restraint?'

Aurelia laughed.

'I fear it is a fairer assessment of my character, your Grace. Appearances mean so little. . .'

He did not pursue the subject, and led her back to Cassie.

'Ransome, may I suggest that you move your party closer to the shelter of the trees?' he said agreeably. 'There the ladies will be more comfortable, and you will have an excellent vantage-point.'

Ransome gave him a careless nod and moved away. When Aurelia next looked round the Duke had disappeared.

'Is it not delightful to be *en fête*?' Cassie's eyes sparkled with pleasure. 'Look, Lia!' She pointed as a Horizontal Wheel blazed into the night, decorated with Roman candles and Pots de Brins. Gillocks of Brilliant Fire followed it in quick succession. Then came the transparencies in Rayonant Fire, and Maroons, but by that time Aurelia was trembling with cold.

'I do not propose to stay out here for the finale,' she told Cassie. 'I will wait for you at the Prince's villa. Pray do not hurry yourselves.'

'But you will miss the discharge of the Pots de Grades and the Illuminated Bomb Shells,' Cassie protested. 'Ransome shall fetch you another wrap.' She looked round for her husband but he was nowhere to be seen.

'Don't worry, I shall be perfectly comfortable. It is but a step to the villa.' Aurelia moved away before her sister could argue further.

She found the villa deserted except for the servants.

They were clustered by the tall windows, enjoying as much of the entertainment as they could see.

Thankful to be out of the wind, Aurelia made her way to a retiring-room on the ground floor. The breeze had disarranged her hair. She must tidy it before the later crush prevented her from finding a mirror.

It was the work of a moment to secure her topknot in place. Thank heavens she had yielded at last to Cassie's plea to wear the silver fillets. The sides at least were smooth. She combed back the straying tendrils of curls which marred the perfection of the front, and glanced at her reflection. A flush rose to her cheeks as she remembered Salterne's extravagant compliment. It was a flush of annoyance rather than pleasure, she told herself severely. Had he not only moments before expressed his impatience for the delay in his wedding plans? Not only did he lack integrity, he was also insincere. Had she thought his words came from the heart. . .well. . .that was quite a different matter. One might not then be quite so irritated to be termed an enchantress. Her colour deepened, and then faded.

She was forgetting. A rake must, of necessity, know how to please, and the Duke's success with women was not in doubt. And she had succumbed to his charm as easily as many others. The thought disgusted her. She frowned and turned away.

In the distance she could hear the boom of the shells which signalled the end of the display. If she made her way to the entrance hall she would be certain to find Cassie.

It was as she passed an ornate archway that she heard the sound of voices raised in anger. Surely that was Robert Clare? His Irish accent was unmistakable.

Anxious not to embarrass him, she hesitated. He was too close to the door to allow her to slip by unseen.

Then she froze. The second voice was even better known to her, and Ransome was in a towering rage.

'You'll remember my position, damn you!' he shouted. 'Who are you to tell me what I may or may not do?'

'Be quiet, you fool, and keep your voice down. Do you wish to be charged with treason?'

'I shan't be taken alone.'

'No, my friend? Remember that I am an Irishman. I cannot be held guilty here. England is naught to me.'

'The Regent would be glad to hear it. And the law may not make such a fine distinction.'

'Then use your head. Your circumstances are well-known, yet you come here in the latest curricle, with the kind of horseflesh only the wealthiest can afford. Not satisfied with that, you must present your daughter with a costly gift of French design, which she wears tonight for all to see. I cannot credit such stupidity.'

'A gaming win accounts for all,' Ransome announced in a surly tone.

Aurelia heard a sneering laugh.

'A gaming win? Who will support your story? Where did you play, and who were the unfortunate losers?'

'Must the place be well-known? St James's street is not the only——'

'It is the only place where play is high enough to warrant such a win. And would not the tale be all over London?'

'Who is like to challenge my word?'

'Everyone who knows you, at a guess. And not least those whose eyes are already on the loss of gold to

France. Did I not warn you to avoid any alteration in your way of life?'

'My sister-in-law has paid my debts. I do not care who knows it.'

'Miss Carrington is not a fool. The world thinks highly of her common sense. Not even for her sister's sake would she give away her fortune.'

'That's true!' Ransome sounded bitter. 'She keeps a close eye on the guineas.'

Aurelia was too horrified by what she had heard to take exception to the lie. She was trembling violently, and the world seemed to spin about her. If they should suspect that she had overheard. . .

Panic seized her as a hand closed over her mouth.

'Don't struggle,' Salterne said softly. 'You are perfectly safe.'

Drawing her arm through his, he strolled calmly into the room ahead of them.

'Ah, Ransome, there you are. We have been charged to find you. The entertainment is ended and Lady Ransome was wondering. . .'

'I. . .I felt the need for refreshment.' Ransome's face was grey with shock, but he made an effort to recover himself.

'A splendid idea. I had just suggested to Miss Carrington. . .Do you care to join us, gentlemen?'

'I think not, Your Grace. Affairs call me away, if you will forgive me.' Clare was at his most urbane, though Aurelia sensed the tension in the air. Did he wonder how much of the conversation might have been overheard? If so, he gave no sign.

He left them and Salterne turned to Ransome.

'My lord?'

'No, I cannot. I must find Cassie and Caro. Aurelia, will you come with me?'

A warning pressure on her arm enjoined Aurelia to silence.

'Miss Carrington felt the chill of the evening air,' the Duke murmured. 'I fear she has not yet fully recovered her strength. May I take it upon myself to find her a glass of ratafia? It will restore the colour to her cheeks.'

A glance at Aurelia convinced Ransome that his sister-in-law was far from well. Her face was ashen. With a muttered word he left them.

Aurelia sank into a chair and buried her face in her hands.

'Miss Carrington. . .Aurelia. . .look at me!'

Aurelia shook her head. She could not speak.

'You heard everything?'

She nodded.

'My dear, you must be more careful. You might have placed yourself in the greatest danger. So much is at stake. . .'

She looked at him then with swimming eyes.

'You. . .you know?'

'Let us say that I have suspected for some time. Gold is most certainly being smuggled to France to pay Napoleon's troops. The profits are enormous. In Paris an English guinea sells for half as much again. For that kind of money men will stop at nothing.'

'Blood money!' Aurelia said faintly. 'And Ransome is involved. I might have known, yet, blackguard though he is, I had not guessed him to be a traitor.'

'Hush, my dearest.' A comforting arm slipped about her shoulders. 'There is nothing you can do. Events must take their course.'

'But my sister. . .and Caro?' Aurelia's eyes were wild. 'How are they to bear the disgrace? Yet that is not the worst of it. Our own troops die at Ransome's hands as surely as if he had fired the guns.'

'I asked you once to trust me. I could not explain, but now you know some part of it. The rest I will tell you when it is safe to do so. Do you understand?'

Aurelia was too shocked to do more than stare at him.

'What am I to do?' she whispered. 'Please tell me. I cannot stand by and pretend that I know nothing.'

'If you do not you will be as guilty of costing lives as Ransome himself.' There was a note in Salterne's voice which she had not heard before, and it frightened her.

'We owe it to those who have already died to stamp out this villainy. Would you have others follow them?'

She shook her head.

'Ransome and his kind must be stopped or this French war will go on for years. You of all people know what it has cost in human suffering.'

The reference to her dead brother and her lost love forced a sob from Aurelia's lips, and the arm about her tightened.

'I know what I ask of you,' the Duke said softly. 'And it will be hard. For the next few days you must carry a heavy burden. The net is closing, but we must have them all. Will you. . .can you bear it?'

Aurelia sat with folded hands. She longed to beg for time to think. . .to decide. . .but in her heart she knew the answer.

'I will do as you ask,' she said.

'You are a truly remarkable woman. I knew you would not fail me.' Salterne cupped a hand beneath her chin and gazed into her eyes. He gave her a smile of singular sweetness and Aurelia's heart turned over. How could she ever have doubted him, or thought him ugly? Her hand went out to him and he pressed it to his heart. Then he turned it over and kissed her palm.

'Be very careful,' he warned. 'The danger is extreme. . .You must give no hint of your suspicions.'

He took her arm and led her back to the entrance hall.

Aurelia could not look at Ransome, but she was aware that Robert Clare's keen eyes were fixed upon her face. She turned to Lady Bellingham.

'Do you attend the races, Miss Carrington? I vow I shall apply to you before I venture on a wager. You know I cannot tell one beast from another. . .'

'I shall do my best to help you.' Aurelia felt that she was moving in some dreadful nightmare. 'Appearance is not everything. The jockeys are not always honest; there has been talk of pulling. . .' She rattled on, only half aware of what she was saying, but Clare seemed satisfied, and he moved away. She longed for their carriage to be announced. If he should engage her in conversation she doubted her ability to convince him that nothing was amiss.

'Miss Carrington, would it be uncivil of me to say that you look somewhat out of countenance this evening?' The soft Irish voice held only sympathy, and she realised with a start that he was close behind her.

'Aurelia felt so chilled at the display.' Unwittingly Cassie came to her rescue, putting her arm about her sister's waist. 'See, here is the carriage. Tomorrow you shall rest. You will excuse us, Robert?'

Clare stepped back at once and made them a deep bow, but Aurelia felt uneasy. She was under no illusions as to his quick intelligence. Ransome might claim all the advantage of rank, but it was Clare she feared.

She took her seat in the carriage, leaned back, and closed her eyes, expecting Ransome to make some comment about her sudden appearance with the Duke. He was so quiet that she stole a glance at him. The handsome face wore a surly expression, and even Cassie's constant chatter did not bring the usual snarling rebuke.

A wave of nausea swept over her as she considered the full enormity of his guilt. Then her eye fell on Cassie and she clenched her hands. What a price her sister had paid for a youthful infatuation! If only she could be spared the worst of the disgrace. . . Ransome might deserve a hideous fate, but why should Cassie suffer too?

Her only hope was Salterne. In these shifting quicksands of intrigue and deception he alone offered some hope of salvation for Cassie and her daughter. He had asked for her trust and she had given it unconditionally. She would keep her promise to him.

'Tired, Lia?' Cassie laid a soft hand on her arm. 'I blame myself, my love. I have persuaded you to do too much. Tomorrow you shall have peace and quiet.'

She was as good as her word, but Aurelia could not rest. At the back of her mind was the awful spectre of what would follow when the conspirators were taken. She forced the images away. They were too horrible to contemplate. She would live from day to day, even from hour to hour. For the moment her task was to avoid arousing suspicion.

It was easier than she hoped. Ransome had left the house before she rose next morning.

CHAPTER ELEVEN

'SHALL you care to drive out, Lia? The air might do you good.' Cassie cast a troubled look at Aurelia's face.

'I am promised to the Dowager Duchess this morning, but do you take the chaise. I shall not need it.'

Her forbidding expression stifled any argument. If she had had misgivings about the wisdom of her promised visit to Charlotte they vanished with the certainty that in Salterne's house she would run no risk of meeting Robert Clare.

As she walked along the promenade her thoughts revolved around a number of mysterious questions. What part had Salterne played in the discovery of the plot, and how could he contemplate marriage with the daughter of a traitor? Was this the reason why his attachment to Caroline appeared to be, at best, lukewarm? How long had he suspected Ransome? And worse, had he offered for her niece in order to watch Ransome without arousing suspicion? She could think of no satisfactory answers.

Her mind was still preoccupied as she mounted the steps to the Duke's front door. Then her attention was distracted by a tapping at the window. Looking up, she caught sight of an eager little face which disappeared as she rang the bell.

Aurelia stepped diffidently into the lofty entrance hall. She should have insisted that Caroline accompany her. It was her niece's place to get to know

Charlotte better, but the Dowager had not included Caro in her invitation. Aurelia sighed. It was all so very difficult. Then Charlotte ran towards her.

'Miggs said that I should wait for you in the salon, but I could not. Was that very bad?'

'Poor Miggs! Has she lost you again? She must think you are a little eel which wriggles away and hides.'

The anxious expression on the child's face gave way to a mischievous smile.

'She would not do that. Papa says that eels have no legs. . .Oh, dear, I have forgot my curtsy.' Frowning with concentration, Charlotte sank to the ground, and promptly tumbled over.

'Are you hurt?' Aurelia reached down to help her to her feet.

'No. . .I do it all the time. I wobble too much, you see.'

'It isn't easy,' Aurelia agreed gravely. 'But it will come with practice.'

'Grandmama would like to see you.' A small hand slipped into hers. 'She is tired today, so she is still in bed. We must be very quiet.'

Aurelia allowed herself to be led upstairs to the great bedroom which overlooked the sea. A glance at the Dowager's face convinced her that Charlotte had not exaggerated. Lying amid the mass of silken pillows, the Duchess looked more fragile than ever. Her face was ashen, and Aurelia noticed with misgiving the bluish tone of the skin about her lips.

'It was good of you to come, my dear.' The old lady managed a faint smile. 'I am not at my best today, so I shall be poor company.'

Aurelia bent to kiss her.

'Ma'am, you must rest,' she said in a low voice.

'With your permission I shall take Charlotte for a walk.'

'Would you? Miggs has a heavy cold. Charlotte should not be too much in her company lest she catch the infection.'

'Do not worry, I beg you. We shall enjoy ourselves on the beach.' She looked at Charlotte who was nodding in delight.

'We should not trespass so upon your time,' the Duchess murmured. 'Salterne has been seeking a governess, but the child is over-young, and her old nurse is too infirm to travel.'

'Your Grace, it will be my pleasure. Charlotte has much to tell me and to show me.'

Her words were spoken in all sincerity. Aurelia could think of nothing at that moment which would please her better than to spend an hour or two with this artless little creature who found so much interest in the world about her.

'Will you curtsy to your Grandmama?' she suggested. 'Perhaps if I held your hand. . .?'

Thus supported, Charlotte's curtsy was a triumph.

'It makes it easier not to wobble,' she announced. 'My coat is here. I can nearly fasten all the buttons and the ties, but if you help me it will be quicker.'

Five minutes later they were walking hand in hand along the promenade.

'I haven't seen the mermaid yet,' Charlotte said earnestly. 'But the donkey with the blue hat is over there.' She cast a glance of longing at the patient animals.

'Would you like to ride him if I walk beside you?'

Charlotte's look of rapture was all the reply she needed. Once astride the donkey she was speechless with delight, and Aurelia felt a surge of affection for the indomitable little girl.

'Now who is this fearless rider who is galloping like the wind across the beach?' The Duke had suddenly appeared beside them, and Aurelia jumped at the sound of his voice.

'Papa, you must not tease. Blue Boy is not galloping; he is walking quietly so that I do not fall off.'

'I beg your pardon, Charlotte. You must excuse me. He is such a matchless steed that the mistake is understandable.'

'He is beautiful,' Charlotte said with reverence.

Aurelia glanced down at the ancient animal. The donkey was the picture of dejection. Head down, he plodded along as if even Charlotte's weight was too much for him. Her lips twitched.

'I think we must agree that beauty is in the eye of the beholder, Miss Carrington?' Salterne's dark face was alight with amusement. The breeze had disarranged his thick black hair, and as he threw back his head and laughed Aurelia caught a glimpse of strong white teeth. His delight in Charlotte made him look like a boy again.

'Will you ride him back again, my puss?'

Charlotte nodded, and the Duke signalled to the attendant to take the rein.

'You are too kind, Miss Carrington.' The teasing note had vanished from his voice. 'May I hope that my grandmother's request was not inconvenient for you? Perhaps we are overly concerned for Charlotte's welfare.'

'Not at all. I admire you for it. Children, I feel, are sometimes left too much in the care of servants. Their parents seldom see them. Perhaps it is the way of the world, but I cannot think it right or sensible.'

'I agree. Such parents miss so much pleasure, and the children lack guidance. . .' His fond glance rested on his daughter. 'She was too young to remember her mother well, but one wonders. . .'

Aurelia's feelings threatened to overwhelm her. She longed to offer words of comfort, to gather him to her breast, and to wipe away all memory of the past with her caresses. Reason told her that she must not love him, but she could not listen to reason. How could she convince herself that the man beside her was a roué or that he lacked integrity, when beneath the sophisticated mask she had found a caring heart? His love was not for her, it was true, but his affection for his child proved that he was not the monster she had thought him.

'Again, Papa! Again!' Charlotte's excited voice broke into her thoughts.

'Certainly not!' Salterne reached out to lift her down from the saddle. 'Too much riding on one day means that tomorrow you will be eating nuncheon standing up.'

'Why?'

'You will be saddle-sore. You are not yet accustomed to ride for any length of time.' He looked at Aurelia. 'I thought she might have a pony of her own when we get back to Salterne. Do you advise it? She may be too young. . .'

Charlotte trembled with excitement, but her eyes were fixed on Aurelia's face.

'I think it a splendid idea.' Aurelia was not allowed to continue. She was almost overset as the small body hurtled towards her and wrapped a pair of chubby arms about her knees.

'I knew you'd say yes. Oh, thank you, thank you. . .'

'Charlotte, where are your manners, my dear? You must not tear about like this. Miss Carrington does not care to be tumbled in the sand.'

'I'm sorry. Did I hurt you?' Charlotte's lip quivered.

'No, you did not. Now give me your hand. Were we not going to look for shells?'

'An inspiration! Shells, I confess, are a passion with me. I shall accompany you.' Salterne smiled down at them and Aurelia's heart turned over. She moved ahead so that he might not see the expression on her face. Loving him as she did, she could not fail to betray herself.

'I had thought you occupied with the Prince today,' she said in a voice that was not quite under her control.

'Today the Prince meets with members of the opposition,' Salterne replied. 'These political factions are not to my taste. They lead to much dissension.' He did not elaborate and changed the subject at once.

'I am glad to see you looking more yourself. To learn what you did must have been a severe shock.'

'It was,' she agreed. 'To be frank, I have always considered Ransome capable of any villainy, though I had not thought of treachery. Now I cannot bear to look at him.'

'Yet you will dissemble, as I asked?'

Aurelia nodded.

'It is Clare I fear,' she said quietly. 'He is too quick by half.'

'You are right, but you must not give yourself away. I cannot over-emphasise the danger.'

'What is this, Papa, and this?' Charlotte ran back to join them, bearing a pile of shells. To her delight Salterne was able to name them all.

'Your claims are justified.' Aurelia attempted to lighten his mood and her own. 'You have indeed a passion for shells, Your Grace.'

'Among other things.' His face was inscrutable. 'Did you doubt my words, Miss Carrington? Shall I beg you again to give me your trust?'

'I do trust you,' she admitted in a low voice. Her face was rosy as she bent to pick up the shells. 'Now if you will excuse me. . . Cassie must be wondering. . .'

'Always Cassie?' His tone was dry. 'Will you never consider yourself?'

Aurelia was about to reply when she caught sight of Charlotte's stricken look.

'Is something wrong?' She stooped down to the little girl.

'Are you going home? I thought you would stay with Papa and me. Don't you like us?'

'I do indeed! You are my friend, are you not?'

Charlotte hid her face in Aurelia's skirt.

'You could stay for nuncheon. I am supposed to have mine in the nursery, but sometimes Papa allows me. . .' She peeped hopefully at her father.

'You are a witch!' Salterne tugged gently at a shining curl. 'But you remind me of my manners. Miss Carrington, may we not persuade you. . .?'

He stood very tall and straight beside the tiny figure of his daughter. Two pairs of grey eyes, so much alike, were fixed eagerly on her face, and Aurelia had not the heart to refuse; but still she hesitated. The child must not grow too fond of her.

'A message shall be sent to Lady Ransome, if that is what is troubling you. . .'

'Then I thank you. You are very kind.' Aurelia made a quick decision. Perhaps it was sheer folly, but she could not disappoint the child. Nor, a small voice deep inside insisted, did she wish to disappoint herself. Every moment spent in the company of the Duke and his daughter was precious to her.

At nuncheon a joyful Charlotte kept them entertained with her plans to learn to ride the promised pony.

'John will help me,' she said earnestly. 'Then, when I am very good, I shall be able to ride with you and Papa.'

Aurelia had not the heart to explain that she would never visit the great house at Salterne until after the Duke and Caroline were married. And not even then, if she could avoid it, she told herself.

Dear as Caroline was to her, she could not face the prospect of seeing the man she loved wed to another woman. Her own plans for Caroline's future had come to naught. It was clear that the girl was still in love with Richard Collinge, and Caro had received no other offers. If the Duke could bring himself to wed the daughter of a traitor the marriage might yet take place, but even if it did not. . . Depression overwhelmed her. Salterne did not love her, and what hope did she have that he might ever return her affection? She too was tainted with Ransome's betrayal of his countrymen. Unseeing, she allowed her thoughts to wander.

'Miss Carryton, you look sad!' Charlotte tugged

insistently at Aurelia's hand. 'Shall we play a game to make you smile?'

'Miss Carrington, if you please, my puss.'

Charlotte tried again, frowning in concentration.

'It is very difficult,' she announced. 'May I not call you Aunt Lia, as Caro does?'

'That is not respectful,' the Duke said sternly. 'I doubt if Miss Carrington will permit it.'

'Of course I will. It is much easier to say.' Aurelia smiled, though she felt a pang of regret, knowing that she should not encourage the child in any form of intimacy. But what did it matter? When she returned to Marram she would not see the Duke or his daughter again.

'Papa and I play a splendid game,' Charlotte confided. 'It is called "Guess what I am?"'

Aurelia looked up at the Duke. Did he think her too forward in allowing Charlotte to call her by her given name? His face reassured her. He was gazing at his daughter with an expression which she could only describe as smug.

'We play in the Grand Salon,' Charlotte explained. 'Papa needs plenty of space when he is pretending.'

Aurelia gave in to temptation.

'Now that I should like to see,' she admitted.

'I go first,' Charlotte told her, once they had entered the salon. Without more ado she got down on all fours. 'I'll do an easy one first because you haven't played before. I'll be an animal, and you have to guess which one.'

She pretended to lick her imaginary fur, miaowing like a cat.

'Gyp the dog?' The Duke lay back in his chair, his eyes closed in concentration.

'Papa, it isn't your turn, and I'm not a dog.'

Aurelia pretended to think hard.

'You must be a cat,' she said.

'Yes, I am. You win, so you may go next.'

'Your papa is disappointed because he did not guess correctly. Will you allow him to go next?'

Charlotte nodded, quite missing the expression on the Duke's face.

'Thank you very much, Miss Carrington,' he said with heavy irony. 'I see that you cannot wait for my performance.'

'I am all impatience, Your Grace.' Aurelia smiled.

Salterne gave her a withering look and walked to the far end of the room.

'Will you do the frightening one, Papa?'

'Only if you promise not to tell Miss Carrington what I am supposed to be.'

Charlotte took Aurelia's hand.

'Don't be afraid,' she said. 'Papa is only pretending.'

The Duke shambled towards them, rolling his head from side to side and growling.

'Can you guess?' Charlotte whispered in a conspiratorial tone.

Aurelia shook her head.

'You must try. If he reaches us before you guess he will eat us.'

'I have it now,' Aurelia whispered back. 'Your papa is pretending to be a mouse.'

A peal of laughter rang through the room.

'No, no. . .not a mouse. Papa is a fierce bear.'

Charlotte rolled about the floor in glee, only to be scooped up in the Duke's arms and nuzzled.

'Right, my puss. Now it is Miss Carrington's turn.'

Salterne grinned at Aurelia. 'I shall promise you some inspired guesses, ma'am.'

Aurelia thought for a moment. Then she sat down before them, blinking solemnly and hooting like an owl.

'My turn to guess,' the Duke announced. 'Now, Charlotte, you must not help me, even though I am puzzled. This cannot be an animal. . .Miss Carrington is much too pretty. . .'

'She is, isn't she?' It was a stage whisper, 'She looks like the princess in my book, Papa.'

'So she does!' The Duke grinned again as Aurelia blushed. 'Do you think she is pretending to be a rose?'

Aurelia threw him a reproachful look.

'No? Then perhaps the morning star?'

'Only one more guess, Papa. . .then it is my turn.'

'Perhaps she is the princess after all, though I cannot guess which one. Was there not a lady who was awakened. . .?'

'With a kiss? I remember. . .but Papa, do you not see? Aunt Lia is pretending to be an owl.'

'So she is! I should have known. The owl. . .who is the wisest of all creatures. . .'

The Duke was unrepentant at having been the cause of Aurelia's blushes.

'Wisdom dictates that I return home, Your Grace.'

'You are offended? I beg your pardon. The temptation to repay you in kind was too much.'

'I am not offended, but I must go. . . I thank you for a most delightful day.' Aurelia bent to drop a kiss on Charlotte's brow.

'You will come again, Aunt Lia? You promise?'

'I will.' She could promise that at least before she returned to Marram.

Charlotte clung tightly to Aurelia's hand.

'I don't want you to go,' she whispered tearfully.

'You are importunate, my puss.' The Duke swept her up in a pair of massive arms. 'We cannot keep Miss Carrington with us, much as we should like to do so.'

He stretched out a hand to Aurelia.

'What can I say? We are much in your debt, my family and I.'

'And I in yours,' Aurelia admitted shyly. 'Today I have forgot my worries, thanks to Charlotte.'

'And to me, I hope. It is not given to everyone to see my impression of the bear.' The fine grey eyes were full of humour as they looked down at her.

At that moment Aurelia loved him more deeply than ever. Once again he had surprised her. She had not thought to see this tough, intimidating man so far forget his consequence as to romp like a boy. That he loved his daughter she could not doubt, but he also had a deep understanding of the child's needs. He realised that it was not enough to provide Charlotte with material possessions. She also had a claim upon his time and his attention, and those he gave gladly.

She could not wish for a better father for her own children, should she be lucky enough to have them. A shadow crossed her face. She was dreaming again and it was naught but folly. Salterne was not for her.

Then she looked up and his expression startled her. Blue eyes were held by grey, and something passed between them. She could not be mistaken. His look was both tender and passionate and her own feelings must be plain for him to see.

She stood as if mesmerised until Charlotte reached out to her.

'Another kiss?' she begged.

'Take care! You may awaken the sleeping princess,' the Duke said softly.

'Papa! You have forgot the story. It is the prince who kisses her.'

'Not the Duke?' Salterne moved towards Aurelia with his daughter still in his arms.

Aurelia felt unable to stir. Her heart was pounding so violently that he must surely hear it. It was only too clear that he had not forgotten that night in Lady Bellingham's garden. She flushed to the roots of her hair. He could not intend to kiss her again?

With an effort she moved back a pace, though her legs were trembling so that she doubted if they would support her. He was much too close, and once again she was aware of the faint scent of fresh linen, soap, fine wool and tobacco.

As he lowered the child towards her she found herself wishing that he would gather both of them within the circle of his arms. There she would feel both safe and. . .beloved? No, that could not possibly be. She disengaged herself from Charlotte's embrace as gently as she could.

'I will order the carriage for you,' the Duke said quietly.

'If you please. . .I should prefer to walk back to the Steyne.'

'As you wish.' The grey eyes rested intently upon her face. 'Do you attend the races tomorrow?'

'I believe so.' Aurelia tied the strings of her fashionable bonnet, thankful that the brim protected her in some sort from that searching gaze. She would not ask if he too would be there. His eager look assured her that he welcomed the prospect of another meeting.

She must do something. . .anything. . .to stop the exquisite torture of being in his company. Was she not beginning to suspect that he returned her love? She must be out of her mind. If it was so then he was playing a dangerous game, and it did him no credit. Off with the old and on with the new while he was still unofficially betrothed. . .?

A prey to a thousand conflicting emotions, she walked back slowly along the promenade.

By next day the wind had dropped and the clouds had blown away. The sun shone from a sky of flawless blue as Aurelia and her party set out towards the east of the town, attended by Captain Leggatt and two of his friends.

Ransome had not returned to the house on the Steyne, but no one remarked on his absence, as much for Cassie's sake as for any other reason. Her spirits were much depressed.

'He will appear at the races, never fear,' Aurelia whispered. 'Cheer up, Cassie. You must not play the part of the injured wife.'

Cassie's depression lifted at the sight of the fine horseshoe course, built on the downs within sight of the sea. The gaiety of the three young men, and the brilliant spectacle of the crowd, served to chase away her sombre mood. Within minutes she was engaged in greeting her acquaintances as the ladies, in their light cambrics and muslins, strolled by escorted by the splendidly uniformed officers of the militia.

Captain Leggatt pointed down the course.

'The Prince, you must know, prefers to keep to his barouche. Over there. . .with the six black horses, and Sir John Lade on the box.'

'The crowds do not trouble him?' Cassie eyed the Regent in wonder.

'He is all good nature, ma'am. . .and they think the better of him for his easy manner.

Aurelia gave a rueful smile. As a patron of the arts the Prince might expect only scorn from his fellow countrymen, but when it came to the sporting life that was a different story. On a day such as this he could bask in unaccustomed popularity.

She glanced at the men in the barouche, but Salterne was not among them, nor was he to be seen in the stand. She felt a pang of disappointment, for which she at once took herself to task, deploring her own inconsistency.

Common sense dictated that she must avoid his company, but in view of the dreadful knowledge of Ransome's treachery she would feel safer with the Duke at hand. It was easier to be brave with him beside her.

She could only be thankful that Ransome and Robert Clare were also absent from the gathering. The Duke had counselled courage and expressed the belief that she would not fail him, but she would prefer not to have that courage put to the test.

'Do you care to go down to the paddock before the races start?' Captain Leggatt looked into the distance. 'If you wish to place a wager I will arrange it for you.'

'May I go, Mama?' Caroline looked as if she expected a refusal.

'You may, my love, and I will go with you. Lia, do you care to come?'

'I think not. I shall stay here. Oh, wait! Here is the Dowager Duchess come to join us.'

Caroline looked uncertainly from one face to the

other as the old Duchess, leaning heavily on Salterne's arm, made her way towards them.

'No, no. . .off you go!' An imperious wave of her silver-topped cane dismissed the party of young people. 'Rollo was against this expedition, but the day is so fine, and all the world is here.' She looked about her in some satisfaction, daring her grandson to contradict her. A slight twitch of the lips was his only reply to this admission of disobedience. 'I am told that Basset is the horse to beat in the first race,' she continued. 'Is that so?'

'I should not care to wager on him myself,' Salterne said with a smile. 'Warren and Sherry will know his form.' He beckoned to the men behind him.

The Dowager Duchess was soon involved in a discussion of the merits of the various horses and their jockeys. At last she made her choice and turned to the others.

'Aurelia, do you care to wager? Rollo will see to it.'

'I think not, I thank you. Not for the moment, at least.'

'Cassie?'

'I cannot resist.' Cassie picked up her reticule. 'Since Ransome won so heavily in London I must believe that luck is with us.'

A silence greeted her words. The Honourable George Warren raised an eyebrow and looked at Sir Francis Sherry. Both of them glanced at Salterne, but his countenance was inscrutable.

'Is. . .is something wrong?' Cassie had sensed the tension in the air.

'Not at all, my lady. It is some time since we left London. We had not heard of Ransome's good fortune. I felicitate you.' Sherry's smooth words had a hollow ring, and his lie was unconvincing. They had travelled down from the capital on the previous day, as Aurelia knew.

'We are wasting time,' Salterne said quickly. 'The race will be over before we have settled on the horses.' He strode away, taking his two companions with him.

At the sight of Aurelia's stricken expression the Dowager turned to Cassie.

'I trust that Caro makes use of her parasol? In my young day we were used to dread the sight of freckles. Do you believe in crushed strawberries or chervil water as a remedy?'

Her words reached Aurelia through a mist of terror. Should a doubt arise in Cassie's mind about the fictitious gaming win, her sister might question Ransome, and Cassie could be persistent when she chose.

The possible consequences were too terrible to contemplate. With an effort she forced her attention back to the conversation.

'I am persuaded that distilled water of pineapple is the best, Your Grace, though Caro will take care. She is so fair, and her skin is like to suffer in the sun.'

The Dowager Duchess directed Cassie's attention to the Regent's barouche.

'Prince George is in spirits today,' she observed. 'He has waylaid Sir Francis, as one racing man to another. Sherry is one of his favourites.'

'I do not doubt it.' Cassie blushed a little. Sir Francis had not attempted to hide his admiration when they were introduced.

'I vow I never laughed so much as when he told me the story of Lady Haggerstone.'

'Is she not Mrs Fitzherbert's sister? I beg you will share the joke.'

'It is a piece of nonsense, but I confess I was much diverted. The lady, you must know, was taken with the fashion for rusticity. If Marie Antoinette could play the milkmaid then so would she. She transformed her garden into a farmyard, hired three Alderneys, and invited the Prince and his friends.'

The Duchess paused for effect, her black eyes gleaming.

'And then?' Cassie prompted.

'Why, then, my dear, out she came from her dairy, attired in the most fetching milking-hat and with the sweetest little apron over her silks. She carried a stool and a silver pail. Her intention was, I believe, to offer Prince George a fresh syllabub.' The Dowager's composure threatened to desert her. She raised a handkerchief to her lips.

'Do go on, dear ma'am.'

'Her Ladyship essayed to milk the nearest of the cattle, but the animal was of the wrong sex.'

'A bull?' Cassie's peal of laughter caused heads to turn in their direction, and Aurelia too was smiling.

'I hope the creature did not take offence,' she said.

'He did not take it kindly, Aurelia. Milady was forced to flee to her dairy. She did not appear again.'

'And the Prince?'

'A marvel of tact, my dears. His manner did not falter. He remarked upon the neatness of the farm-yard, and the fineness of the day, before he returned to his carriage. One may imagine his amusement later.'

'Poor Lady Haggerstone!' Cassie wiped her eyes.

'Pray do not waste your sympathy on her. Such nonsense! I have no patience with these sentimental fancies. Neither she nor the French Queen had the least idea of how the rustics live. Some small experience would soon shatter that idyll.'

'More scandalous stories, my dear ma'am?' Salterne had reappeared beside them, his tone of reproof belied by the fond glance which he bestowed upon the old lady. His keen eye searched the faces of the other two ladies and, attuned as she was to his every mood, Aurelia sensed that he was not displeased to find them laughing together. 'You distract Lady Ransome and Miss Carrington,' he continued. 'They are like to miss the start of the race.'

'We have been waiting for you.' The Dowager tapped him with her fan. 'How it can take so long to set a man upon a horse I do not know.'

She continued to mutter at intervals, claiming to have lost her reticule, and searching for her shawl, until Cassie was only too pleased to accept an offer from Salterne to escort her to the paddock.

The Duchess turned to Aurelia.

'What is amiss, my dear? I thought you about to faint when Sherry and Warren disclaimed all knowledge of the gaming win. Is Ransome up to his tricks again?'

'I have not the full story, Your Grace. . .'

'I shall not upset Cassie, if that is what you fear, though I do not doubt that he had lied to her.'

Aurelia was silent.

'It will not be the first time that a man has deceived his wife. . .nor the last, I fear. . .But why should it frighten you so?'

'Are my feelings so obvious, ma'am?'

'Perhaps not to others, but you are grown so dear to me. Is Salterne involved?'

The sudden question took Aurelia by surprise. She cast about wildly for a reply, and jumped as Salterne answered for her. She had not known he was so close.

'I must always be involved when Miss Carrington's interests are at stake. . .and Caroline's too, of course.'

'Of course!' The Dowager's ironic tone was not lost on him and he gave her a disarming smile.

'Sherry begged the privilege of escorting Lady Ransome,' he explained. 'I could not refuse.'

'So you hurried back to me?' The irony was even more in evidence. 'I am flattered, but you shall not change the subject, Rollo. I hope you know what you are about.'

Salterne sank into the seat beside her and stretched out his long legs.

'Why, ma'am, I believe I do.' His voice was calm and untroubled as he took her tiny claw-like hand and raised it to his lips. 'You have all my thanks. I know I might trust to your diplomacy.'

'I cannot come at your meaning, Rollo.'

'I think you can, my dear ma'am.'

'Such a farrago of nonsense! Diplomacy? Trust? Half-hints and the like. It sounds like a hum to me.'

'On the contrary, it is extremely serious.' He was still smiling, but the Duchess straightened suddenly as her eyes met his.

'This girl is frightened,' she said grimly.

'She will not be harmed if she follows my advice.' Half unconsciously he moved closer to Aurelia.

'Very well. I shall say no more.' The Duchess closed her eyes and took no further interest in her companions.

Salterne drew Aurelia a little apart.

'We cannot speak here,' he said in a low tone. 'Shall you attend the concert in the park tonight?'

'I cannot say, but I will speak to Cassie. Ransome is still away. . .'

'He will not return tonight, and nor will Clare. Shall we say at nine?'

His face was impassive, but Aurelia's feeling of dread returned. Some of the brightness had vanished from the day. She longed to ask him what was afoot, but his look enjoined her silence.

It was in no contented frame of mind that she set out for the park that evening. Salterne's suggestion of a meeting had disturbed her. She guessed that he would not be the bearer of good news.

To add to her worries Sir Francis Sherry approached them with a message which she could not welcome.

'I am charged to tell you that your son is in Brighton, Lady Ransome. I chanced to meet him at the races. He will wait upon you presently.'

'Frederick is here?' Cassie shot a nervous look at her sister.

'Your elder son, I believe. He expressed an urgent wish to see you. I mentioned that he might find you here this evening.'

Aurelia stifled a feeling of dismay. A true son of his father, Frederick's visits invariably heralded trouble of one kind or another. Pray heaven he was not involved in Ransome's dealings with the French.

On reflection she decided that it was unlikely. Frederick was a loose fish. When foxed with drink he would not guard his tongue. None of the conspirators would trust him. He would give their game away within a week.

'I cannot understand it, Lia.' Cassie took advantage of a particularly stirring military march to whisper to her sister. 'How is he able to afford to travel here? Ransome may have offered to fund him, of course. . . though he did not mention it to me. And where is he to stay? The town is full.'

'You may ask him yourself. Here he is. . .'

Frederick strolled towards them in a group of his cronies. He greeted Aurelia's party civilly enough, kissing his mama, and bending low over his aunt's hand. As handsome as his father, Aurelia thought cynically, and just as untrustworthy. Frederick seemed to sense her thoughts.

'Don't worry, Aunty, dear, I shall not trouble to ask for your hospitality.' His lips were close to her ear, and the words were inaudible to the others. 'It would scarce be offered willingly, but I have no further need of your crumbs of charity.'

'I am glad to hear it, Frederick. And to what do you owe this sudden access of fortune?'

'A run of luck.' He waved his hand in an expansive gesture. 'No need to mention it to Mama.'

Aurelia was strongly tempted to box his ears. She quickened her pace to catch up with the others. Caro, as always, was surrounded by a bevy of admirers, and Cassie was deep in conversation with Sir Francis. There was no sign of Salterne.

Aurelia glanced at her watch. It was long past nine. Perhaps he had been called away. If events had overtaken him he might be in danger at this moment. She prayed that her fears were unfounded. Without his support she felt lost and vulnerable.

Then she saw him. He was walking towards her in company with the Prince. Her heart sank. Now there would be no opportunity for him to speak to her in private.

The Regent was at his most affable.

'More music, Miss Carrington? I see you are of the same mind as myself. There is nothing like it to lift the spirits, but we are too far away. You cannot see the uniforms of the band. I designed them myself, you know. Let us go closer and you shall give me your opinion.'

'Your fan, Miss Carrington. I believe you dropped it.' Salterne held out the pretty trifle, and pressed it firmly into her had.

Aurelia was about to disclaim ownership when his expression stayed her.

'How careless of me!' She was conscious of Cassie's eyes upon the fan.

'Are you not mistaken, sister? Look at it close. I do not recognise the design.'

Salterne intervened before Aurelia could reply.

'Sadly it is broke. The fall has damaged the sticks.' With a barely perceptible movement of his fingers he gave a slight tug at the central ribboning and the fan opened to reveal a solid core between the struts. She caught a glimpse of writing, but she had no time to read it before he snapped it shut.

'A charming object! May I see?' The Prince took the fan from Aurelia and examined it with the eye of a connoisseur. 'I commend your taste, Miss Carrington. These Chinese brisé fans look delicate, but see how the copper end sticks protect the inner ones of ivory. Were you aware that some of them hold secrets?'

To Aurelia's dismay he pulled at the ribbon. The fan separated, but after one brief glance the Regent closed it and returned it with a bow.

'I was mistaken,' he said easily. 'It is of a different
type. The struts are damaged, but it is not beyond
repair. The less it is handled the better. May I suggest
that you put it in your reticule?' Still chatting about
the programme of music, he led the way towards the
bandstand.

'I vow I am green with envy, Lia. Where did you
buy that lovely thing? I have not seen ought to match
it.'

'The shops are full of such trifles, Cass. Try at
Hanningtons, if you can tear yourself away from the
muslins.'

Aurelia's face gave nothing away. She continued to
smile and chat to the others, but her mind was filled
with dread. Something must be sadly wrong for
Salterne to risk passing her a message in such a way.

In her preoccupation she was scarcely aware of the
music, but to her relief the end of the concert was
followed by yet another display of fireworks, and all
eyes were fixed on the sky. A burst of fiery stars
followed the flight of each rocket, lighting the faces
about her. She felt in her reticule for the fan, opened
it, and waited for the end of the display.

On this occasion the Prince had outdone himself.
He had ordered a representation of the eruption of
Mount Vesuvius as the *pièce de résistance*.

Aurelia glanced down at her lap. In the reddish
light which illuminated the grounds she could read the
message easily. It was brief, giving only a time and a
place.

She looked towards Salterne, to find his eyes upon
her. She nodded. Then she rose to her feet to accompany the others as they walked back to the Steyne.

CHAPTER TWELVE

'YOU may go to bed, Hannah. I shall not retire just yet. An hour with my book is what I need.'

'What you need, Miss Lia, is a rest.' With the licence permitted to one who had known her mistress from the cradle Hannah sniffed. 'Burning the candle at both ends. . .and after an inflammation of the lungs? I shouldn't wonder if you were carried off before the end of the month.'

'I did *not* have an inflammation of the lungs, and that will do, thank you.'

Hannah showed no inclination to be snubbed, and it took a great deal of wheedling and a promise to read but a single chapter before she could be persuaded to retire.

As her footsteps died away Aurelia sighed with exasperation. Hannah had insisted on helping her into her bedrobe and unpinning her hair. She could not dress it high without help so she tidied it as best she could. Old retainers could be so. . .so officious.

A search through her wardrobe revealed one of her old gowns. It was a round dress of grey cambric, high at the neck, and with long sleeves. And there should be an all-enveloping cloak, which she was used to wear at Marram. She threw it about her shoulders, drawing the hood close.

Then she opened her door the merest crack. The silence from below was reassuring. Thank heavens that Caro had elected to share her mother's room

223

since Ransome was away. Their candles had been snuffed, so she guessed that they were both asleep. She stole quietly down the narrow staircase to the hall.

The heavy iron bar across the door almost defeated her efforts to remove it, but she dared not leave the house by the passage to the stables. Matthew was a light sleeper, and devoted to his charges. At the least sound he would rouse the household, convinced that thieves were about to rob his mistress of her prized bloodstock.

Aurelia redoubled her efforts and at last the bar slid back. One glance at the deserted Steyne assured her that the coast was clear. She hurried across the road to the closed carriage waiting in the shadows.

The door opened at her approach. Then Salterne reached out for her hands and drew her in beside him.

'I had to warn you,' he said in a low tone. 'Matters are coming to a head and you are all at risk. I fear for your sister, in particular. Should she question Ransome. . .'

'I had thought of it. It was unfortunate that she should mention Ransome's supposed win before Sir Francis and his friend.'

'She could not know that he had lied. Sir Francis is discreet, but there were others in the company. Clare cannot fail to hear the gossip. He has informers everywhere.'

'But. . .but even if Ransome were to admit his treachery to her she cannot testify against him, as his wife.'

'She would not be given the opportunity to do so.'

Aurelia froze. 'You cannot mean. . .?'

Salterne gathered her trembling figure in his arms, and in her terror Aurelia clung to him.

'They would have no alternative but to silence her, my dear.'

'You cannot mean it!' Aurelia's blood turned to ice. Dear, foolish Cassie, with her passion for clothes and trinkets, and not a thought in her head of treachery.

'Clare would not harm her. He is a friend.' Her voice quavered as she tried to convince herself.

'He might be given no choice. There are others in high places who have even more to lose than he.'

'He has known my sister for an age.'

'He does not trust Ransome.'

'Then why did he include him in this. . .this plot?'

'Your brother-in-law has excellent connections on both sides of the Channel. You will forgive me for saying this, but he is known to have no qualms of conscience where money is concerned.'

'What you say is true, but Cassie. . .? Oh, what shall I do?'

'You must be prepared to leave Brighton at once should the need arise. Go to Salterne. There you will be safe. No one will follow you, but I will warn my people, just in case. . .'

'Then you think. . .you think. . .'

'I can only guess at the probable outcome of tonight's meeting at Newhaven. Ransome is already in disfavour. Clare warned him not to draw attention to himself, but the temptation to boasting and extravagance was too strong. He will be lucky to escape with a whole skin.'

'You cannot mean. . .?'

'Clare has already been taken to task for including

Ransome in the plot. To protect himself he will agree to the majority decision.'

'And if it goes against Ransome?'

'I do not know, but we must be prepared. Now give me your word. You will go at once if I ask it of you?'

'Of course.' Aurelia forced out the words through stiff lips. 'Yet suppose Ransome is able to convince the others that no harm has been done? He may return to Brighton.'

'That is my fear, Aurelia. Should he realise that he is under suspicion he may cut and run to save his own skin. It is more than likely that he would come to you.'

'He has no love for me,' she cried harshly. 'He knows that I should not protect him.'

'Not even for your sister?'

'She would be better off without him.'

'He knows that, my dear, but it would not be affection for his family that would draw him back to Brighton. You keep gold in the house, I imagine, and I have often admired your jewels. To a man on the run money is essential.'

'He need expect no help from me.'

Salterne took both her hands in his.

'My dearest girl, I know you better than that. At the first threat to Lady Ransome or to Caro you would give him all you had.'

The tenderness in his voice caused Aurelia to release her grip upon his coat, but she seemed to have no control over her shaking limbs.

'May we not go now. . .tonight? I must get them out of danger. If we leave within the hour. . .'

Salterne was silent for what felt like an eternity, and when he spoke it was with difficulty.

'Allow me to explain. Ransome may yet persuade the others that he is still of use to them. If he returns to find you gone he will sense that something is amiss. He may give the alarm. Then, if his fellow conspirators bolt, we shall lose them.'

'And they will continue to trade with France?'

'I fear so.' His voice was hoarse and almost unrecognisable. 'I should not ask this of any woman, but I must. Will you do it? Will you stay? The choice is yours, and my offer holds. You may leave for Salterne tonight if you wish. . .'

'No!' Aurelia had already made her decision. 'Cassie will never be safe as long as Ransome is at large. Should she learn the truth at any time he would fear that she might betray him. And apart from that. . .I cannot condone treachery.'

'What a jewel you are!' He drew her close and his lips were against her hair. 'I knew you could not fail me.'

Aurelia's heart was pounding, but now it was from another cause. She longed to reach up and lock her arms about his neck, drawing his face to hers. How dear he was! And how his nearness set her blood afire!

She disengaged herself from his embrace.

'I am so sorry,' she whispered. 'It can be no pleasant thing to learn that your betrothed is the daughter of a traitor.'

'Can it be that you have not yet understood?' Salterne sounded incredulous. 'I had to get close to Ransome in a way that would not arouse suspicion.'

'I. . .I have wondered. . .' Aurelia's heart leapt.

'As well you might. I thought I had made my feelings plain. Must I assure you that I have not the slightest interest in your niece?'

Aurelia's face grew warm. The conversation had taken an unexpected turn.

'She. . .she is very lovely.'

'She is indeed. Her beauty was the key to the whole. Even an ageing roué like myself might be so affected as to offer for her.'

'Suppose she had accepted you?' Aurelia gave him a demure look which was full of mischief.

'A child of that age confronted by a monster of iniquity? It was unlikely, and then, you see, I had made enquiries. Her heart, I knew, was given to another.'

'What a devious creature you are, my lord! And how you bamboozled us when you came to Marram with your horsewhip at the ready! You might have enjoyed success on the boards.'

She heard a low chuckle.

'I flatter myself it was a good performance. I might have enjoyed it more had Caro not been so distressed. Ransome ill-treated her sadly and I am sorry for it.'

'I shall not soon forgive him. . .for anything,' Aurelia promised fiercely.

'I am glad to hear it. Let it stiffen your resolve. You will need all your splendid courage, my dearest.'

The endearment made her feel shy.

'I must go,' she said quickly.

'Not yet.' He bent his head to hers and sought her lips. As the cool, firm mouth came down on hers Aurelia sensed that his need matched her own. As she had done before she found herself responding with all the fervour of a woman deep in love, in the throes of a dizzying passion.

'I adore you, my enchantress,' he murmured

huskily. 'Now go, while I still have the strength to allow it.'

Half dazed by his embrace, Aurelia slipped away into the darkness. All her fears had vanished, to be replaced by a sense of joy which threatened to overwhelm her. He loved her. . .he loved her. . . Had he not said so?

She had left a single candle burning in her room, but it was not until she slipped off her cloak that she noticed the motionless figure sitting in the corner, almost invisible in the shadows.

She raised a hand to her mouth to stifle a scream.

'Where have you been?' Cassie's voice was cold with anger. 'Are you so sunk beneath reproach that you must sneak out at night like any common trollop?'

A furious reply rose to Aurelia's lips, but she bit it back,

'You forget yourself, Cassie. I need not account to you for anything I choose to do.'

'This man? Is he so far beneath your touch that he cannot approach you with propriety, as a gentleman should?'

Aurelia did not reply. An explanation was out of the question.

'Pray do not tell me it is nothing of the sort,' Cassie continued. 'I should not believe you.'

'I do not intend to lie to you,' Aurelia said steadily. 'You may think what you wish.'

'Indeed! The creature is married, I suppose. I wish you joy of him, though doubtless the gossips will have the tale within the week.'

'Doubtless, but do not allow it to distress you.' Aurelia's tone was stiff. How could Cassie believe that she would allow herself to become entangled in some unsavoury liaison?

'Could you not have confided in me?' Cassie burst into tears, rocking to and fro in anguish. 'I know how unhappy you have been in these last few years, but this. . .this affair will bring you further grief. How I wish that we had not come to Brighton. Nothing has gone right since we arrived. . .and now Ransome has disappeared.'

'Ransome is used to come and go without explanation. Did you not tell me so yourself?' Aurelia put her arms about her sister and hugged her close.

'Something is amiss, I know it.' Cassie's sobs redoubled.

'You will feel better in the morning. You are over-tired, my dear.'

Cassie still looked heavy-eyed when they assembled for a late nuncheon on the following day, and Aurelia sighed. She too had had a troubled night. Her joy in the knowledge that Salterne loved her was already tinged with sadness.

Her own connection with Ransome meant that she herself was tainted with treachery. Anger threatened to choke her. The man sowed the seeds of ruin all about him. His behaviour had crushed any hope of happiness which she might cherish. Even should Salterne wish to marry her she could not accept in the knowlege that she would stain his name. The man she loved was as far out of reach as ever.

She looked up as Frederick was announced.

'Is your father come with you?' she asked in a curt tone.

'I have not seen him, ma'am.' Without a by-your-leave Frederick seated himself at the table and began to pile his plate with food.

'No need to stand on ceremony is there, Aunty? In Brighton, so I understand, we dispense with the conventions.' His sly grin persuaded Aurelia that he was in possession of information which boded no good for someone.

'Do you stay long in the town?' she asked. 'We did not see you at the races.'

'I was there. Here, there and everywhere, one might say. And sometimes in the most unexpected places.'

Aurelia's expression did not change. He was hinting at something, but what? She had been so careful. He could not have seen her leave the house. . . She waited for his explanation, but Frederick addressed himself to his plate.

'Must you always be making a mystery, brother? Cannot you say what you mean for once?' Caroline's voice was unexpectedly sharp, and Frederick turned to stare at her.

'So!' he sneered. 'The worm has turned at last. Is this due to Aunty's influence? You had best not let Father hear you.'

'Why not?' As the harsh voice reached them from the doorway Aurelia's blood turned to ice.

Ransome swung his riding crop impatiently against his boot as his gaze roved from one face to another. Aurelia hid her trembling hands beneath the table. She must have managed a few words of greeting, for he appeared to find nothing strange in her manner, but later she could not recall a word that she had spoken. Anyhow Ransome did not reply. It was clear that he was under an appalling strain. A muscle jerked incessantly in his temple, and his eyes were unnaturally bright as he regarded them with a fixed smile.

Aurelia looked around the table. As always in her father's presence Caroline's face wore a hunted look, but Cassie stared straight ahead. Only Frederick seemed at ease.

'No word of greeting for me, my love?' Ransome walked over to stand behind his wife's chair and rested his hands on her shoulders. She winced as the curved fingers dug into her flesh, and turned her head as if to make a sharp retort. Then she caught Aurelia's eye and muttered something unintelligible.

'I beg your pardon, my dear? I did not quite hear that, but I am prepared to believe that you are over joyed to see me.'

'Will you not join us, Ransome?' Aurelia gestured towards the food in an effort to draw his attention from her sister.

'I'll take some wine.' He flung himself into a chair, drumming his fingers on the polished surface of the table until Aurelia thought that she must scream. She cast about wildly in her mind for some topic of conversation which might lift the tension in the room.

'Are you not surprised to see Frederick?' she asked. 'We did not expect him, you know.'

Ransome looked at his son.

'How came you here?' he said abruptly. 'I thought you had not a feather to fly with. . .'

'I had good fortune at the tables, sir.'

The stem of Cassie's wine glass snapped in her hand. She looked down dully as a few bright drops of blood fell on the skirt of her gown but she did not move.

'Oh, my dear, I am so sorry. This is the second time

within a week that we have had such an accident. It is all my fault. I had doubts about the quality of the glass when I bought it.' Aurelia felt that she was babbling as she tried to staunch the flow of blood with her handkerchief.

Ransome's eye were fixed intently upon his wife's face.

'Come, Cass, the wound must be bathed at once. Hannah will find linen for a binding,' Aurelia urged.

'I will see to it.' Ransome seized Cassie by the wrist.

'There is no necessity for you——'

'You have some objection?'

Aurelia stared at him helplessly. She could think of nothing to say.

'Ma'am, Mr Robert Clare has called. He wishes to see Lord Ransome, if that is convenient.' Jacob stood in the doorway. 'I have shown him into the salon.'

'You had best go to him, Ransome.' Little as Aurelia wished to see Robert Clare, she blessed his opportune arrival. Ransome, she knew, would force the truth from Cassie at the earliest opportunity. Her sister was unable to dissemble, and he had known at once that something was wrong.

She left Cassie in Hannah's capable hands and made her way to the salon. As she neared the door she heard raised voices, but as she was about to enter Jacob admitted another visitor.

'I trust I see you well, Miss Carrington?' Salterne was immaculate in a dark blue coat of Bath superfine and buff pantaloons. His starched cravat fell in snowy folds, and he carried a clouded cane.

Aurelia hurried to him with shining eyes. He saw the relief in her face.

'Remember we are enemies,' he warned as he

looked beyond her. 'Caro, my dear, I felicitate you on that charming gown. How well it becomes you. I vow you will take the town by storm.'

He nodded to Frederick, who had accompanied his sister to the salon, and stood back to allow the ladies to precede him.

'Ransome, your servant. . .and yours, Clare. Such a pleasure to see you.' The underlying sarcasm in his tone brought a flush to Ransome's cheek, but Clare stepped forward with every sign of satisfaction.

'The pleasure is mutual, Your Grace. We are all, I see, unable to resist the charm of Miss Carrington and her family.'

'And Lady Ransome? She is well, I hope?' The question was casual, but Aurelia was quick to notice that the Duke's hand had tightened on his cane.

'My sister has suffered a slight accident,' she said at once. 'It is not serious. The stem of a wine glass broke and cut her skin. She will join us directly.'

'Let us hope so.' Salterne favoured the company with his most charming smile, and turned to Aurelia and Caro. 'I am charged with messages for you. The Dowager Duchess hopes that you will do her the honour of calling upon her. She is at home tomorrow.'

Caro joined Aurelia in thanking him.

'She much enjoyed your company at the races,' the Duke continued. 'I am very much afraid that she has another fund of scandalous stories for you.'

'We need not look far for scandal,' Frederick broke in. 'You might look to your household, Aunt Lia. Closed carriages and females slipping through the gate at night are not at all the thing.'

The cold hand of fear closed tight about Aurelia's heart but her expression did not change.

'What *can* you mean?' she said calmly.

'Exactly what I say.' His words were accompanied by a leer. 'I was too far away to catch the wench, but you may take my word for it.'

Salterne raised his quizzing-glass. Centuries of power, of wealth and of influence were behind his look and Frederick squirmed.

'Remarkable!' the Duke pronounced at last. 'Such concern for the morals of the lower classes! If only I might claim the same devotion to their welfare. Alas, I find the nocturnal activities of my servants of not the slightest interest to me.'

The snub was severe, and it silenced Frederick, who took his leave with the air of a man who had just survived an encounter with a striking snake.

'Do you attend the cricket match today?' His Grace turned to Clare with his customary affability. If he had seen the strange glitter in Ransome's eyes he affected not to notice. 'And you, my lord? Cricket is one of your many interests, is it not?'

He was interrupted as Cassie came into the room. Under cover of a chorus of greetings Aurelia moved aside, hoping to regain some semblance of composure. For Frederick's words had shaken her to the core. They had not gone unnoticed by either Ransome or Clare; that she knew. Ransome had betrayed himself with a sudden start, and though Clare had more self-control she had seen him stiffen. She was forced to admit that her worst fears had been realised. Salterne had done his best to dismiss the incident, but she doubted if either man believed him. A closed carriage for an assignation with a servant? The idea was incongruous.

She shot a look at Ransome from under lowered

lids. That heightened colour, his jerky movements and the tell-tale tic beside his eye told her that he was close to breaking-point. She could almost smell his fear.

Clare, on the other hand, betrayed no trace of anxiety, tl ugh his eyes did not leave her face. To her horror he strolled over to stand beside her.

'Do not take it so hard,' he advised kindly. 'One cannot forever be keeping an eye upon the servants. It was ill-advised of Frederick to mention the matter in public.'

'In private I should not have minded quite so much.' Aurelia hoped that her downcast eyes would convince him that her manner betokened embarrassment and nothing more.

Clare helped himself to a leisurely pinch of snuff.

'Perhaps it was fortunate that Frederick was too late in his pursuit of her,' he murmured smoothly.

'I should not care to be brought from my bed to deal with a hysterical girl.' Aurelia forced a smile.

'Of course not, though one cannot help but wonder. I doubt if your maid would have an assignation, and your cook, I believe, is no longer young.'

'It could have been one of the kitchen-maids,' Aurelia said with resolution.

'Ah, yes, to be sure. What beauties they must be to warrant a closed carriage. . .!'

'Forgive me.' Aurelia sent a plea for help in the Duke's direction. 'His Grace, I believe, is anxious to speak to me.'

'I am entirely at your disposal, Miss Carrington.' The Duke came to her at once. 'Shall you think me importunate if I mention that the match is due to start quite soon? I believe you ladies expressed a wish to see it from the beginning. That is, if Ransome has no objection. . .?'

Ransome gave his consent with barely concealed impatience. Aurelia gained the impression that he could not wait to be rid of them. Both men, she surmised, would wish to discuss the mysterious figure who had left the house the previous night. She felt an unwelcome lurching in the pit of her stomach. Not even the presence of the Duke could dispel the fear which consumed her.

'You will be ready to leave tonight if necessary?' Salterne had fallen behind the others, and his voice was low.

Aurelia's attempt at a smile was pitiful. She looked at him with terror in her eyes.

'My darling. . .don't. . . I cannot bear it. I want to take you in my arms and keep you safe for always. This is almost at an end. Will you be brave for just a little longer, my own true love?'

His presence steadied her. He was so large and so. . .so dependable. Had he not promised that she would be safe? She could refuse him nothing, whatever the cost.

'What has happened? Has Ransome convinced the others of his good faith?'

'They are under no illusions, but they have let him run. They need him for one more night. He does not know it, but the verdict went against him. He is to be. . .disposed of.'

Aurelia felt sick. She stumbled, but a firm hand held her upright.

'Does he suspect?'

'You have seen him, Aurelia. He goes in fear of his

life. Clare has been ordered to make sure he does not escape.'

'We cannot go back to the house,' she murmured in anguish. 'Do not ask it of me. Should he be cornered. . .'

'You must not distress yourself. You will not return until he has gone. There is little time left to him, and he must decide. . .'

'You do not know him as I do. If he should slip away from Clare he might return for Cassie.'

'He will not encumber himself with your sister. His enemies are implacable. . .on both sides of the law.'

'I wish that we might never see him again,' she burst out passionately. 'I do not hope for his death, but if he would go away and never return. . .'

For answer he relieved her of her frivolous little parasol, and appeared to struggle with the catch.

'Do not open it,' he warned. 'This is but a precaution, but you will feel safer if you have it by you. You know how to use a pistol?'

He returned it to her and she felt the added weight. Then he increased his pace to catch up with the others.

'Lady Ransome, the Prince was distressed to see the damage to your sister's fan. He begs that you ladies will accept these trifles. They are oriental curiosities.' He handed each of them a fan, smiling at their exclamations of delight. 'They are murderous objects, I fear. Let me show you.' A slight pressure of his fingers caused Aurelia's fan to fall apart, disclosing a sharp knife. 'They are known as dagger fans,' he said cheerfully. 'I do not suggest that you use them for their original purpose, but they make excellent paper knives.'

'The blade is very sharp,' Caroline said doubtfully.

'I should be afraid to cut myself, though it was kind of His Royal Highness to think of us.'

Aurelia suspected that nothing would surprise the Prince more than to be thanked for his gifts. She guessed that he knew nothing of the weapon which lay so innocently in her palm.

'Let me keep yours for you, Caro,' she suggested. 'See, I will put it in my reticule. Then you will not lose it. Cassie?'

Cassie shook her head.

'I will keep mine by me,' she muttered.

'Shall you come to the Prince's villa for cards this evening?' Salterne's question betrayed no more than casual interest. His eyes were fixed on the player at the stumps, but a slight pressure on her arm persuaded Aurelia to acquiesce. She was more frightened than she had ever been in her life, and the fact that Salterne had seen fit to offer her a pistol and a knife convinced her that they were all in grave danger.

'I. . .I believe we are promised to it,' she faltered. 'Cassie is fond of cards. Is that not so, my dear?'

Cassie stared at her with dull eyes. She made no reply.

'And Caro enjoys the parties,' Aurelia continued brightly. She looked at her niece, but Caro's thoughts were far away.

Aurelia turned to Salterne with a pitiful little smile, and something in her expression caused him to bend towards her with a look of such warmth that she could not mistake his regard.

'Do not look so,' he whispered softly. 'You try my resolution. You will come to no harm, I promise you. Nor will you be asked to defend yourselves. I thought merely that you would feel safer with a weapon.'

For the rest of the afternoon he appeared to be engrossed in the cricket match, and spoke of nothing but the merits of the players. Aurelia made a valiant effort to take an interest, but her nerves felt as tight as bowstrings, and she was filled with dread at the thought of returning to the house on the Steyne.

'May we not stay to watch the foot-races?' she begged when the match had ended. She would do anything to delay their return.

'As you wish.' His look was a caress, and she found herself recalling the way he had drawn her close the previous evening. She had thought that it was simply an attempt at comfort. He could not know how deeply she loved him, but she treasured those moments in the carriage when she had allowed herself to rest against that broad chest and had realised for the first time that he had no thought of marriage to Caroline. She had put her own soul into that single kiss, believing then that her affection was returned. Now, with every nerve a-quiver, she became a prey to uncertainty. Was he simply using her for his own ends?

He had offered for Caroline, knowing that he would never wed the girl. Excusable, perhaps, when the safety of his country was at stake, but it had shown that he would stop at nothing where duty was concerned.

Had duty led him to make love to her? He had seemed sincere in his profession of love, but then, he had proved times enough that he was a master of deception.

Her face burned. She could never marry him, but there was no need to trample on her heart in order to persuade her to give him the help he needed. She would have given it gladly even if he had not spoken of his feelings.

'Doubting me again?'

Aurelia looked up, startled by his perspicacity. What she saw in his eyes resolved her doubts once and for all, and she began to breathe quickly. Only a fool would mistake that expression for anything other than the love she craved.

'I trust you, my lord.' She spoke the words in all sincerity as his eyes held hers for a long moment. Then he transferred his gaze to a point beyond her shoulder, and she looked round, dreading what she might see. The only person close to them was a shabbily dressed man who scratched gently at his ear.

'You are in no danger,' Salterne murmured. 'Ransome has left the house.'

She was tempted to ask him how he could be so sure, but she decided to believe him. She turned to Cassie. 'We have little time to dine and change,' she said cheerfully. 'Let us go back at once. The Prince makes up his tables early, and we must not keep him waiting.'

They would be safe indoors. She took her leave of Salterne and followed Cassie into the house.

'Shall you wear your new apricot sarcenet with the black net overdress, Cass? The contrast is so striking. It is quite one of Madame Claudine's most successful gowns.'

Cassie stared at her without a word.

'Hannah shall dress you first,' Aurelia said briskly. 'Then you shall talk to me while she does my hair.'

She ached with pity, but there was little she could do to comfort Cassie.

She tossed aside her half-poke bonnet, and cast off

the dress spencer which she had worn for warmth over her sprigged muslin. A bathe in cold water helped to refresh her, and the knowledge that Ransome was no longer under her roof served to lift her spirits further. She slipped unaided into her gown of primrose lustring as she considered what jewels she might wear with it.

When she turned she caught sight of her reflection in the long dressing-glass, and was surprised. Somehow she looked different. The change could not be ascribed to the high-waisted robe, which set off her figure to perfection. She stepped closer and looked at her shining eyes. There was no mistaking their message. She might as well have announced her love for Salterne to the world, she thought ruefully. For the first time in years she felt truly alive, and it showed in her animated expression. She blushed and wondered if he was aware of it.

Her joy was short-lived as memory flooded back. Had she not told herself that her love could never be? There seemed to be no end to Ransome's destructive influence. She rued the day that Cassie had ever met him.

Pushing her vain regrets aside, she reached into the drawer for her jewel box. As she opened it she gasped.

The box was empty and the key to her money chest had vanished.

CHAPTER THIRTEEN

AURELIA reached into the bottom drawer of the tall-boy, moving a pile of clothing to one side. The small chest was still there, but she did not need the lack of weight to assure her that it was empty.

Doubtless the bag of gold which she kept locked in her writing desk would also have disappeared.

So Ransome had gone. She felt only an overwhelming sense of relief. The theft convinced her that he did not intend to return. If that was so he was more than welcome to her money and her jewels.

A knock at the door caused her to close the drawer. She turned to face Cassie with a smile.

'I was right,' she said cheerfully. 'That gown becomes you well.' She did not comment on her sister's lack of bracelets, earrings, necklace, or even a locket.

'Mama, I cannot find my pearls!' Caro hurried into the room in a state of high anxiety.

'My love, I forget to tell you. Had you not noticed that the clasp was loose? I sent them to the jeweller this morning. Are not the rosebuds ornament enough? Ought else would be too much, especially as you are wearing a wreath upon your curls.'

Caroline sat down upon the bed.

'Then you approve my gown, Aunt Lia?'

'It is altogether charming.' Aurelia's hasty explanation about the missing necklace had satisfied her niece, but Cassie remained silent.

'Will you wear your diamond drops, Miss Lia?' Hannah stood back to admire her mistress's toilette. As Monsieur Pierre had directed, Aurelia's fair locks were caught high with a length of primrose ribbon embroidered with silver thread.

Aurelia was careful to avoid Cassie's eye. She stood before her mirror, apparently considering whether or not she would wear the diamonds.

'I think not.' She picked up her scarf. 'Let us make haste, my dears. There is little time to dine before we go.'

Relieved though she was to think that Ransome had disappeared, possibly for good, she could not repress a feeling of deep unease. Her efforts at conversation met with no response from Cassie, and finally even Caro gave up the pretence that all was well with her mother.

Aurelia caught her niece's eye and shook her head. This was no time for questions. Cassie was close to breaking-point and an incautious word might snap her self-control at any moment.

Perhaps in the company of her friends her sister's mood might change. With this in mind Aurelia moved quickly through the crowds in the outer hall of the Prince's villa. She was searching for a familiar face. . . Lady Bellingham. . .or even the odious Mrs Ingleby—anyone who might capture Cassie's attention.

She led her sister into the gallery. It was a favourite lounge for the Prince's intimates, but though she stood on the first step of the ornate staircase to raise herself above the crowd the faces turned to hers were those of strangers.

For once the figures of the Chinese fishermen bearing their lamps aloft failed to charm her. The gilded carvings of dragons and serpents seemed to have taken on a strange life of their own. She shuddered. It was all so macabre. The atmosphere of the place had a subtle tinge of nightmare.

She pulled herself together at once. Tonight she was allowing her imagination to run riot. The shock of discovering the loss of her jewels and her gold had unnerved her. . .that was all. She must forget these fanciful notions.

Perhaps they should not have accepted the Prince's invitation for this evening, yet a last-minute refusal would have given offence to His Royal Highness. Taking Cassie's arm, she moved into the south drawing-room.

Sanity returned as she looked at the tables, already set out and awaiting the players. The tall figure of the Regent was easily recognisable. He was deep in conversation with a group of *émigrés*, moving from French to Italian and then to German with equal ease.

As she hesitated in the doorway he looked up and saw her. He came to her at once.

'Will you not join us?' His pleasant deep voice was confortingly familiar. 'We are indulging in a little frivolous chatter before we begin the serious business of the evening.' He gestured towards the tables.

Aurelia looked into the bright blue eyes. As always, in spite of his vast bulk, she could see traces of the handsome young man who had captured the affections of the townspeople some thirty years earlier.

'Melton is in form tonight,' he observed. 'I must ask him to tell you the story of Bullock's race.'

No stranger to depression, he had sensed at once that Cassie was not herself, and he exerted himself to cheer her.

'Bullock was not of the *ton*, Lady Ransome. I doubt if you have heard of him, but he was an unusual character, and of a vast size. Come, Melton, you have the tale at your fingertips. It will divert the ladies.'

Aurelia recognised Melton as the man who had stepped on her gown at the Old Ship Inn. He gave her an apologetic look. Then, encouraged by her smile, he launched into his story. It lost nothing in the telling and the Prince slapped his thigh with glee as Melton described Bullock's wager with Lord Barrymore.

'You must remember, ladies, that the man was hugely fat. When he offered to beat My Lord Barrymore in a foot-race for a purse of gold, His Lordship accepted at once. Being young and healthy, he agreed to Bullock's terms—the choice of time and place, and a thirty-five-yard start. The man was cunning, one must allow. He chose the narrowest passageway in the town, and Lord Barrymore could not pass him.'

A shout of laughter greeted the end of his story and Aurelia was happy to see that some of the colour had returned to Cassie's cheeks.

'Lady Ransome, do you care to take your place for the gaming?' The Prince glanced about him as the room began to fill. 'Allow me to seat you here. You know Lady Bellingham, I believe, and Broome and his wife will make up the number.'

At his bidding Cassie sat down, and the Regent turned to Aurelia.

'May I beg your indulgence, Miss Carrington?' he said in a low tone. 'The Dowager Duchess is here alone tonight. Salterne is called away, and I fear my old friend is inclined to over-tax her strength. You are a particular favourite of hers. Will you sit with her for

a time? She must not spend too long at the tables. . .
but perhaps later?'

Aurelia at once assured him of her willingness to
forgo the gaming.

He led her through to his private sitting-room,
excused himself, and left to rejoin his guests.

'Well, miss, and how do you go on?' The Duchess
was resplendent in a gown of oyster satin beneath a
heavily embroidered tunic in the same shade. A
matching turban, ornamented with plumes, sat atop
her thinning hair. As she looked up it slipped to one
side, and she gave it a tug of exasperation.

'Allow me, Your Grace.' Aurelia settled the head-
dress firmly in place.

'Much better, my dear, I thank you. But you do not
answer me. . .'

'I am well, ma'am, as you see.'

'But troubled still, I fancy. Well, Salterne has
warned me that I must not question you. . .though I
cannot abide a mystery, I will confess.'

Aurelia was silent. The news of Salterne's sudden
absence had left her feeling vulnerable and very much
alone.

'How is Charlotte, ma'am?' It was an effort to make
conversation when her thoughts were elsewhere, but
the Duchess answered her readily enough.

'The child is as mischievous as ever, my dear. At
present she has a passion for riding along the promenade in the goat-carts which are for hire. Now she
must tease Salterne for an animal of her own.'

A twinkle came into Aurelia's eye.

'He has agreed?'

'Not yet, but he is weakening. The child needs a

mother, Aurelia. My grandson is too easily swayed. . .'

'And you are not, dear ma'am?' The teasing note in her voice brought a sparkle to the old lady's eyes.

'Perhaps, my dear, but I could wish——'

She was interrupted at that point. The door opened to admit the Prince, accompanied by Salterne.

A flush of colour suffused Aurelia's face, and her heart began to pound. She was careful to avoid the Duke's eye as she pretended an interest in a bowl of roses close beside her.

'Now, Duchess, you shall come with me. Here is your grandson returned, and I have promised him that you do not play high tonight.' The Prince proffered an arm and was promptly taken to task.

'Stuff!' the Dowager said briskly. 'Do not listen to him, sire. I have no patience with his namby-pamby ways.'

This description of the formidable figure standing by her side caused Aurelia's lips to twitch, but the Regent preserved his countenance.

'Salterne is a sad case,' he agreed drily. 'But I am inclined to missishness myself, so you must bear with me.'

The old lady gave a crow of delight at this piece of impertinence and suffered herself to be led away.

Aurelia sat down suddenly. She felt that her legs would no longer support her. Salterne's grave manner had told her at once that he had news.

'Is it over?' she whispered faintly.

'The leaders are taken, Lia, but. . .'

'Something is wrong?' She had sensed his mood at once. 'Please tell me. . .'

'Ransome and Clare were not among them,' he said slowly.

'Is that all?' She felt light-hearted with relief. 'Pray do not concern yourself. Ransome is gone these several hours, and I cannot believe he will return.'

'What has made you so sure?' As he looked at her the implications of her lack of jewellery struck him at once. 'He took everything?' he asked grimly.

'It is not of the least importance.' Aurelia laid a placatory hand upon his arm. 'The loss is nothing if it means that we shall not see him again.'

'If only I could be sure. . .'

'Surely he would not dare to return? He will be far away by now.'

'And you have no idea of where he might have gone?'

'None! And I do not care to know. He has harmed my family for the last time.'

'I hope you may be right. Does Lady Ransome know of his departure?'

'She knows,' Aurelia said bitterly. 'Though she will not speak of it. I had not thought to see my sister so distressed. She has been used to give up her possessions to him, but now she fears disgrace, and worse. I am thankful that she does not know the whole.'

'It is doubly hard for you,' he murmured. 'I know how much you care for her.'

'I cannot bear to see her so changed.' Aurelia's voice shook with emotion. 'What is to become of her?' She buried her face in her hands.

A strong arm slipped about her waist and the Duke drew her close.

'Do not give way, my dearest. All may yet be well.'

Through the fine fabric of his shirt Aurelia could hear the thudding of his heart. She allowed her head to rest against his shoulder, wishing that the moment could last forever. Then she pulled away.

'Your kindness weakens my resolution,' she whispered. 'I am become a watering-pot and. . .and I do not mean to be so foolish. I beg you will forgive me.'

'You speak of kindness? Lia, look at me! Do you doubt my love for you? God knows, I have made it plain enough. You are all I want, my darling. Will you not say that you will become my wife?' He bent his head to hers and sought her lips, but she put up a hand to stop him.

'I cannot, my lord. You must know that. Oh, please, this is impossible. . . To continue can only cause pain. . . We must go. . . Someone is sure to come upon us.'

'In the Prince's private apartment? No, my dear. That will not serve.' He possessed himself of her hands and felt her quiver beneath his touch.

'Is marriage such a dreadful prospect?' he asked in a low voice. 'Your happiness will be my first consideration always. You have heard stories, Lia, but they are not true. Something of an evil reputation was needed for my purpose, but I am not the rake you may think me.'

Involuntarily she put up a hand to his lips to stop him.

'I do not think you a rake at all.' Aurelia's eyes were bright with unshed tears. 'I know you for the man you are.' Her fingers traced the long line of the white scar on his cheek. 'I. . .I have a high regard for you, Your Grace.'

He kissed her then, with infinite tenderness at first,

and then with growing hunger. Aurelia abandoned herself to the warmth of his lips until she felt herself drowning in a sea of passion. She made a despairing effort to struggle free of his embrace.

'I beg of you, do not try me further,' she whispered. 'You cannot offer me marriage. If you will not consider yourself you must think of Charlotte and the Duchess.'

'Aurelia, you will not tell me that my grandmother might disapprove of you? She has been scheming for this moment since we met. And Charlotte is still looking for her mermaid. . .' His eyes were filled with private laughter.

She could give him no answering smile.

'You have not considered, my lord. In future the taint of treachery must always be upon my family. I would not. . .could not allow your own to suffer.'

Salterne's face hardened.

'Will you let Ransome destroy you? I cannot believe it. I should want you for my wife had he been hanged at Tyburn.'

Aurelia shuddered.

'He might yet return. You hinted as much yourself. Think of what that would mean. . .for all of us.'

'My dearest, will you not think of yourself for once?' He made as if to seek her lips again, but she turned her head away, feeling as if her heart must break.

'Please go.' Her words were scarcely audible. 'This is too painful. . .for both of us.'

He did not reply and she turned to him at last with a question in her eyes.

'My lord?'

'I am waiting, Aurelia.'

'For what? I have explained. . .'

'I am waiting for you to tell me that you do not love me and that I may not hope. Say that and I will leave you.'

The room was so quiet that she could hear the ticking of the ornate clock which stood upon the mantelshelf. The scent of roses drifted towards her from the bowl beside her hand. It lent an added poignancy to the scene. Roses for love, she thought inconsequentially, and now, with her next few words, she must destroy any hope of future happiness. The constriction in her throat was choking her, and she felt that she could not breathe.

'Well?'

He would never know what it cost her to do so, but she forced herself to meet his eyes.

'You are mistaken, Your Grace. My regard for you is that of a friend. . .and nothing more. I am sorry if I have led you to believe otherwise.'

He looked as if she had struck him, and the colour drained from his face.

'I see,' he said abruptly. 'Do not blame yourself, Miss Carrington. It was wrong of me to force my attentions on you. I had imagined. . .Well, it does not signify. I should have realised that my case was hopeless from the start. You will not soon forget the deception I have practised on your family.'

'Oh, please!' An involuntary cry of protest broke from her lips. 'You had little choice, and the stakes were high. I honour you for the course you took. You must have found it repugnant.'

'Not all of it.' His twisted smile cut her to the heart. 'I found you, and from the first moment of our meeting I hoped that when this terrible business was done I could come to you and offer you my love.

What a fool I have been! Yet even now I can't believe——'

'We should not suit,' she told him firmly, but the tremor in her voice betrayed her.

'Lia, my love. . .' Again he attempted to take her in his arms, but she drew away.

'This is not kind in you, my lord. You must believe me. I do not feel those sentiments for you which would lead me to accept your offer, though I am honoured. . .'

'Good God! Will you send me away with words such as those? You might have learned them by rote. Are we nothing to each other?'

'Not. . .not in the way you would wish, but I shall always stand your friend.'

His face closed and when he spoke his voice was bitter.

'You surprise me, ma'am. For a female whose affection is not involved you gave an excellent performance.'

Her own hurt betrayed her into an angry retort. 'It could scarce rival your own, Your Grace.'

He laughed then, and it was not a pleasant sound.

'It is to be spinsterhood, then? The condition will not suit you, Miss Carrington, or else I am no judge.'

'Who better? Your experience of women is so wide, is it not?' His cruel reference to her own response to him incensed Aurelia.

Salterne's face paled, but the expression in the glittering eyes caused her to shrink back. Then he bowed. 'I shall not trouble you again.' He strode out of the room.

Aurelia sat motionless, exactly as he had left her. A ladybird crawled slowly up the stem of one of the roses and, unthinking, she followed the progress of the little insect. The heavy perfume of the flowers drifted towards her. She had always loved their scent, but now she found it cloying. It might have been a drug which had robbed her of all will to move. A sense of deadly inertia possessed her, and her brain refused to function. She knew that feeling must return in time, and with it an agony which she dared not contemplate.

He had looked so. . .so stricken. Her throat ached with unshed tears. How could she meet him again and continue to pretend that she did not care?

Salterne was angry now. . .and hurt. . .but when he had time to think he would guess that she was lying. She rose to her feet and began to pace the room. Her refusal had been so ridiculously formal, she thought wretchedly. She had acted like some simpering miss who wished to keep a suitor dangling. What must he think of her? She had sounded so unlike herself.

And there lay the danger. If he forgave her she would not be proof against a renewed appeal on his part. She must take herself far out of his reach. Not to Marram. He could find her there. She must think. . .but not of the love which she had so recently refused.

She would go to London. There she could see her bankers, replenish her funds, and seek refuge in some unfashionable quarter of the city while she considered her future plans.

Her sorrow was too deep for tears. Those plans could not include him. Above all, she must convince herself of that. And now, before she could change her mind, she must find Cassie and explain. . .

She came to an abrupt halt. Of course. . .Cassie

and Caro. She had not just herself to think about. Since Ransome had gone they were dependent upon her. And how could she explain to her sister that she was fleeing from the Duke's love?

She threw out her arms in a gesture of despair. She was trapped in a tangled web from which there could be no escape. She sat down suddenly, feeling that her legs would no longer support her, and buried her head in her hands.

'Lia, my dearest girl, what on earth has happened? Rollo stalked past me looking as if the world had come to an end. You have quarrelled?' The Dowager Duchess laid a sympathetic hand upon her shoulder.

Aurelia nodded, searching for her handkerchief.

'Take mine.' A scrap of lace-trimmed cambric was pressed into her hand. 'Do not distress yourself, my love. Rollo can be hasty, but he doesn't mean one half of what he says. His temper, you know. . .'

'He. . .It was not his fault, ma'am. I alone am to blame. I beg your pardon; I thought you were at the tables.'

'I pleaded exhaustion.' Aurelia heard a low chuckle. 'What a busybody I am! Yet I could not sit by when two people who are dear to me are at such odds with each other.'

'You guessed?'

'I know my grandson, Lia. I have not seen that look on his face before. . .at least, not since Elizabeth died.'

'Oh, do not say so! I cannot bear it. I have been so cruel.'

'He has offered for you?'

Another sob was her answer.

'Well, then, my dear, that is no cause for sadness. His love is not given lightly, I assure you.'

'I. . .I refused him.'

'You must have had cause, Aurelia, for you do return his love, I think?'

'I said that I did not. . .' The muffled words were almost inaudible.

'And he believed you? Great heavens! The man must be wandering in his wits, and so I shall tell him.'

'Oh, please do not! I cannot marry him, Your Grace. There are reasons, believe me. It is impossible. Forgive me, but I dare not say more.'

'Then the secret is not your own?'

Aurelia shook her head.

'Harrumph! My dear, I am an old woman. I have seen much unhappiness in this world and much of it was self-inflicted. Will you not reconsider?'

'I cannot.'

'Very well. I will say no more. Now you shall compose yourself and come with me to find Cassie and Caro. Ransome is not here tonight?'

'No.' The word was spoken with great violence, but though the Duchess looked up sharply she did not comment. Instead she took Aurelia's arm and, leaning heavily on her gold-topped cane, she walked towards the door. There she paused for a moment.

'This will pass, believe me. Now hold up your head and brave it out. Let us not set the gossips' tongues a-wagging.'

Together they walked slowly through the crowded rooms, pausing to greet an aquaintance here and there. The Duchess was careful to avoid lengthy conversations, pleading the lateness of the hour, but she contrived to draw attention from Aurelia with a few salty remarks in her usual style.

'What riff-raff the Prince draws about him in these days!' She remarked succinctly. 'And what airs they give themselves! Letty Lade, so I hear, complains of the admission of the wives of cits to the assembly. For a strumpet that is coming it too strong.'

She did not trouble to lower her voice, and heads turned in her direction, but recognition brought only indulgent smiles.

'Fools!' the Duchess said briskly. 'You will please to note, Aurelia, that to do and say as one pleases one must be very old or very rich. Fortunately I am both.'

In spite of her deep unhappiness the forthright words brought a faint smile to Aurelia's pallid lips. She felt a surge of affection for the Dowager, appreciating the way in which the old lady had protected her, covering up her distress until the blessed moment when she might call her carriage and return to the house on the Steyne.

'May I give you a word of advice, my dear?' The satin turban had slipped askew once more, but the eyes beneath it were wise. 'You have been under a strain. I don't know why, and I must not ask, but you are overwrought. Will you give yourself time to reconsider?' She did not wait for Aurelia's reply, but turned to greet the Prince. He came towards them swiftly, a frown marring his normally amiable countenance.

'Duchess, I am charged with a message for you. Salterne is called away. May I provide you with an escort to your home?'

He looked about him, and raised a finger to call Melton to his side.

'Pray do not trouble, Your Royal Highness. We are

leaving now, and shall be happy to accompany the Duchess. If you will allow me but a moment I will find my sister. . .'

'Then Melton shall summon your carriage, ma'am.' He stayed beside the Dowager, engaging her in conversation, as Aurelia excused herself and went in search of Cassie.

She was not much surprised to find that her sister had left the tables and was sitting on a sofa with Caro by her side. The set look was still about Cassie's mouth and Caro's attempts at conversation were falling on deaf ears. Aurelia forgot her own misery, and in her concern she did not notice her niece's heightened colour, nor her air of suppressed excitement.

'Come, my dears,' she said gently. 'We are to take the Duchess home.' She shepherded her party to the entrance hall and shook her head in a plea for silence as the Dowager glanced at Cassie's face.

Aurelia could not shake off a sense of foreboding which had nothing to do with her refusal of the Duke. Perhaps it was her imagination, but no one seemed quite themselves. The Prince's normally cheerful manner had vanished, and in his eyes she detected a curious mixture of anger and regret.

'Something is troubling Prince George.' As they settled themselves in the carriage the Duchess put Aurelia's thoughts into words.

'Ma'am?'

'No doubt it is his debts again. Still, if one is inspired to pay ninety guineas each for handkerchiefs trimmed with Brussels lace it cannot be wondered at.' The old lady gave a sniff of disapproval.

'Is that true, Your Grace?' Caroline's eyes were round with astonishment.

'It is perfectly true, I assure you. When the Prince is beset by his creditors he must needs spend more in order to raise his spirits.'

Caroline chuckled at the dry remark, and the Duchess continued to divert her, drawing her attention from the evident worries of her mother and her aunt.

Uncharacteristically, Cassie preserved an uncompromising silence, oblivious of the need to hide her feelings. She seemed incapable of speech.

Aurelia was deeply troubled. For the first time in her life she felt that Cassie was beyond her reach. Nothing she could say or do brought a spark of interest to her sister's eyes, or drew her thoughts back to the present. Cassie had retreated into a world of her own, and what her thoughts were Aurelia dreaded to imagine.

Her own dejection turned to icy rage as she thought of Ransome. She had prayed never to see him again, but now she longed for the chance to. . .to do what? Perhaps to crush him like the vile reptile he was. As handsome as Lucifer, she thought savagely, and just as evil.

She clenched her hands in a effort to control her fury. He should never be given the opportunity to harm Cassie again. She must be calm. If only she could think, but for that she needed a cool head. The Duchess had advised her to give herself time. It was excellent counsel, if only it might be obeyed.

Her thoughts returned to Salterne. It was unlike him to abandon the Dowager Duchess without a word. What could have drawn him away on such an urgent errand? When the answer came to her she began to tremble. It could only be Ransome or Clare. He must have had some message.

Hideous pictures formed in her mind, and try as she might she could not shut them out. The two conspirators were desperate men. If he had followed them alone he might be in deadly danger, even at this moment. She must not think of that, or what might follow.

If they had not quarrelled he might have taken her into his confidence. If only he had told her something to set her mind at rest. Perhaps he was accompanied by troops? It was a forlorn hope, and she knew him better. He would go alone, still hoping to find some way of protecting her sister and Caro from disgrace.

She roused herself to bid the Duchess farewell, but it was with a heavy heart that she sought her bed that night.

She was awakened by the sound of voices, but they seemed far away. Late revellers in the street, she thought drowsily.

Then a hand grasped her shoulder. She opened her eyes to find sunlight pouring through the half-opened curtains, and Hannah bending over her.

'Miss Lia, it's Lady Ransome! Will you come?'

'What is it? Is she ill?'

'I don't know, ma'am. She will not speak.'

Aurelia threw on her robe and ran to Cassie's room. On the threshold she stopped, appalled. She might have been facing a marble statue. Cassie stood motionless, holding a letter in one hand.

Aurelia drew it gently from the nerveless fingers and began to read. The content brought on such a wave of nausea that she felt faint. She threw her arms about Cassie's rigid form, but her sister did not respond.

'Warm blankets, quickly!' Aurelia ordered. 'And

bring me some hot, sweet tea. Lady Ransome is in a state of shock.'

She read the letter again. The words danced before her eyes, but the message could not be mistaken.

If you wish to see your daughter alive, come to the crossing at Ditchling on the Lewes Road. You will be met at noon. Tell no one. You are being watched. If you are followed the girl will die.

CHAPTER FOURTEEN

AURELIA heard a low moan. She turned to see Cassie
sliding to the ground.

'Lift her on to the bed.' She signed to Jacob and
Matthew who were standing in the doorway. 'What
o'clock is it?'

'It is eight, Miss Lia.'

'I shall want the phaeton and the greys at once.'

'But ma'am, there is no need. Matthew shall fetch
the doctor.'

'No!' Cassie's eyelids fluttered open. 'It is but the
effect of my sleeping draught. I felt a little dizzy.'

Jacob looked at Aurelia.

'You heard Lady Ransome. . .no doctor.' Aurelia
fixed him with a quelling eye. 'Now have the horses
put to.'

She turned to Hannah.

'There is no necessity to wake Miss Caro. Lady
Ransome will soon be well.' In her haste to reach
Cassie's side she had not thought to look in the cot in
her own room.

'Miss Caro ain't in the house, and well you know it,
ma'am. Did I not try to rouse her too?' Hannah's eyes
were full of suspicion. 'She's never run off again?'

'Hold your tongue, Hannah. I shall bring her back
before she is missed. Lay out my riding habit, please.'

Hannah tossed her head and left the room.

'Lia, I beg of you. . .you must not go.' Cassie's face

262

had aged in minutes. 'The letter was sent to me. I was to tell no one, else they will kill her.'

'Can you drive the phaeton?' Aurelia demanded. 'Don't be foolish! They will not fear a woman.'

'We cannot be sure of that.' Cassie wrung her hands. 'I don't know what to do. Salterne is most nearly concerned, apart from ourselves. Had we not best ask him?'

Aurelia hesitated. Cassie was right, but, though she longed for the Duke's protection, to involve him might place Caro's life in danger, and there was no time.

'He is gone away from Brighton. In any case, the instructions are clear. No one else is to be involved.'

'Then what can we do?'

'Not you, my love. I shall go alone.'

'No, you will not! Caro is my daughter. We shall go together.'

Aurelia looked at her in amazement. Cassie's colour had returned and she held her head high.

'I shall not hold you back,' the latter said firmly. 'But I must go with you.'

Aurelia wasted no words on further argument. She could only be thankful that Cassie's sanity had returned. At one time she had feared for her sister's reason.

They left the house together in the teeth of Hannah's furious reproaches and worried looks from Jacob and Matthew.

Aurelia gave her horses the office, and then she turned to Cassie.

'I heard nothing in the night, did you?'

'No. Caro must have been tricked into slipping out. She may have thought to meet Richard. . .' Cassie's lips trembled. 'I paid no attention to her, even when she came to bid me goodnight.'

'You were not yourself, my dear.'

'If only I had not taken the sleeping draught. . .I must have heard her leave.'

'You must not blame yourself.'

'But Lia, what can this mean? All the world knows that we have no money. Do they believe that I can pay to have my daughter returned to me?'

'We cannot know until we meet them.' Aurelia glanced at her watch. 'I had best spring the horses. Shall you mind?'

Cassie shook her head. 'I am sorry that Ransome took your jewels,' she said suddenly. 'The gold, too, is gone?'

'Everything, but it is no matter. We have more important concerns. . .'

Cassie was silent for some time. Then she said, 'Ransome must be involved in this. I am sure of it.'

'You must be dreaming, Cass. To take his own child? What can he gain by it? He does nothing, as you know, without advantage to himself.'

'We shall see.' The set look was back on Cassie's face, and Aurelia hastened to divert her attention.

'This is Ditchling,' she announced. 'And here is the turning for Lewes. Do you see anyone?'

'Not a soul. Have we misjudged the place?'

'Look!'

In the distance a solitary horseman was silhouetted against the skyline. As they watched he raised a beckoning arm.

Aurelia lost track of the twists and turns in the country lanes as she followed him in the phaeton. He was leading them far from the well-used roads.

'I should have come alone.' Cassie's face was ashen. 'There may be danger. I should not have allowed you to accompany me.'

'You couldn't have stopped me.' Aurelia felt in her pocket and her hand closed about the comforting solidity of her little pistol. She felt oddly elated. Better by far to confront the enemy openly than to struggle blindly in a web of intrigue and deceit.

They had entered the confines of a wood, and the path ahead was little more than a track. Overhead the trees leaned towards each other, blocking out the sun.

'How dark it is. Do you see anyone?' Cassie's voice was but a whisper.

'It's lighter up ahead. There's a clearing and a hovel.' Aurelia brought the phaeton to a halt. This must be their destination, for the path did not run beyond it. The place appeared to be deserted.

Cassie made as if to step down.

'Stay where you are,' Aurelia warned. 'Up here we have the advantage.'

'Quite so,' drawled a familiar voice. 'For that reason you would be wise to relinquish the reins, Miss Carrington. May I assist you?'

Aurelia looked into the smiling face of Robert Clare. Instinctively her hand tightened on her whip.

'I should not advise it,' he said smoothly. 'We have much to discuss. Let us preserve the niceties.'

Aurelia sprang down, ignoring his outstretched arm, and moved round the phaeton to help Cassie.

'Where is Caroline?' she asked coldly. 'And what is the meaning of this charade?'

'Where would your niece be but with her father?' Clare asked in mock-surprise. 'Shall we return her to her fond mama?'

As he looked towards the doorway of the hovel Ransome appeared, dragging Caroline by the hand. The girl was filthy and dishevelled, and a purple bruise had closed one eye.

'You beast!' Aurelia moved towards him so fast that Clare was unable to restrain her. She raised her whip and struck Ransome hard across the face.

With a curse he started for her, the blood running down his cheek, but Clare stepped between them before he could reach her.

'Please to control your temper, my dear,' he reproved. 'We must not let our passions run away with us. At least, not yet.'

Caroline was in her mother's arms, weeping incoherently, but Cassie looked beyond her to where Ransome stood. He was attempting to staunch the flow from the wound, and he did not meet her eye.

'What do you want of us?' Cassie spoke quietly, but her voice was so changed as to be unrecognisable.

'I hoped to restore you to your husband,' Clare said with great good humour.

'That you will never do. Come, Aurelia, let us go.'

'Not so fast! You do not fully understand, Lady Ransome. Your husband and I are in some little difficulty. Matters have not gone well for us of late. All might have been well had you not harboured a spy within your midst.'

'You are insane!' Cassie turned to help Caro into the phaeton.

It was then that Clare's composure vanished. He dragged Caro down again and thrust her roughly towards her mother.

'Take care!' he warned. 'Do not try me too far, or I

may be tempted to leave you to your husband's tender mercies. Would you prefer him to explain, or shall I?'

'Get on with it!' Aurelia flung the words at him through gritted teeth.

'It was stupid of you to leave the house at night, Miss Carrington, and the carriage was Salterne's, was it not? Oh, yes, you were recognised, but not by Frederick. He had only to describe your height and your slender build for me to guess.'

'What is that to you? Are you the guardian of my morals?'

'If it were only that! But you must not try to gammon me, my dear. Those who play a deep game must take the consequences. Doubtless you have informed your sister of Ransome's part in our plot.'

'She knows nothing. I was told not to speak of it to anyone.'

Her hand flew to her mouth. With those few words she had confirmed his suspicions.

'It does not signify. She cannot testify against her husband, but you. . .now, that is a different matter.'

'A plot?' Cassie stood perfectly still. Her eyes were fixed on Ransome's face.

'You really did not know? I have misjudged Miss Carrington. Your husband, dear Lady Ransome, has been assisting us. It was merely a matter of moving— er—currency to France.'

'Treachery?' Cassie stood very still.

'If you will have it so, but we are wasting time. The question is, what are we to do with Miss Carrington? She bears no love for either of us.'

'I told you what to do.' Ransome's chilling expression left Aurelia in no doubt as to his meaning.

'An extreme solution, my friend. You forget that I

have a *tendre* for the lady. If she will but consent to be my wife. . .'

Aurelia laughed in his face.

'Have you taken leave of your senses? Nothing would persuade me. . .'

'No?' Clare looked beyond her to the shrinking figure of Caroline. 'We have the girl and she lays no claim to fortitude. If you had but heard her screams when her father attempted to show her her duty. . .'

Aurelia heard a light click, and looked down to see the gleam of metal. Cassie had opened the dagger fan. In one swift movement she stepped behind her sister and lunged at Clare with the wicked-looking knife.

He brushed her aside with a gesture of disdain, and she fell heavily to the ground.

'Enough of this!' Clare's veneer of sophistication was wearing thin. He bent to retrieve the fan. 'You see our dilemma, Miss Carrington? But for Salterne we had been wealthy men. Now we shall be hunted from one end of the kingdom to the other.'

'You deserve far worse,' Aurelia cried hotly.

'Possibly, but that is a fate which we intend to avoid. You have a choice, my dear. Either marriage to me—in which case Ransome and I will make good use of your fortune—or the unfortunate course which Ransome does not cease to urge upon me. The result would be the same, as I understand that your sister will inherit.'

A silence fell upon the glade. Overhead the sun shone from a cloudless sky, the birds were singing, and a pair of squirrels chased each other around the bole of a tree.

This can't be happening, Aurelia thought in disbelief, but the smiling face before her was implacable.

Bereft of speech, she put out a hand to help Cassie to her feet.

'Have you no pity?' Cassie pleaded. 'I will go with Ransome gladly and I shall not speak of what has happened here, but please. . .I beg of you. . .Caro is but a child, and my sister will not harm you. Let them go. . . I will vouch for their silence.'

'How touching!' The sneer brought a flush to Cassie's cheeks. 'You have forgot the trifling matter of money. Now, Miss Carrington, must you have a demonstration of our determination?'

He picked up Aurelia's whip and beckoned to Caroline.

'Come here, my dear. I trust you are in good voice?'

'Stop! You shall not touch her.' Aurelia's voice was high with panic.

'Very well. Ransome, get the parson!'

Aurelia stood as if turned to stone as Ransome lurched towards the hovel. He was holding a pistol when he reappeared, but she was only half aware of the weapon. Her attention was fixed on the thin figure of a small man in clerical garb who walked towards her.

Her fingers closed about the gun in her pocket. When the parson was close enough to shield her from Ransome's line of fire she brought it out swiftly and took aim.

'Stand back!' she cried. 'Cassie, put Caro in the phaeton. You will manage the team as far as the road to Brighton.'

'No! Lia, you cannot. . . I shall not leave you here.' A sudden blow from her husband caught Cassie full across the mouth and sent her reeling.

For one vital moment Aurelia's attention was distracted. It was enough. She gave a cry of agony as Clare raised the whip and struck her hard on the wrist, knocking the pistol from her hand.

'No more tricks!' he warned. 'Ransome has been under a strain. His finger is over-light upon the trigger.'

Aurelia glanced about her wildly, praying that someone might come upon them—a swineherd or a charcoal burner—even a poacher—but there was no sound within the wood.

'Aunt Lia, you cannot. . . .' Caroline mumbled the words through bruised and swollen lips. The tears were streaming down her face.

'I agree, Miss Carrington; you cannot and you shall not.' Salterne's voice came from behind them.

With a sob of relief Aurelia swung round. He was strolling towards them with a wicked-looking pistol in each hand.

'God damn you!' Ransome fired once and the glade erupted in a haze of gunsmoke, flying metal and tattered flesh.

Aurelia looked down at the mangled, bloody figure at her feet and then she fainted.

She opened her eyes to find herself seated in her own phaeton, supported by a pair of massive arms. As memory flooded back she moaned and turned to bury her face against a comforting chest clad in a coat of Bath superfine.

'Don't dwell on it, my love,' the Duke said gently. 'Ransome did not suffer. His death was instantaneous.'

'What. . .what happened? When he fired I thought he must have killed you.'

'The gun exploded in his hand. It is not unheard of.'

Aurelia shuddered. The horror of the sight still filled her mind.

'Lia, you must believe that it was for the best. He will not now stand trial.'

'I know. . .but Cassie. . .'

'Your sister did not see it. When he struck her she was stunned.'

'And Caro? She was standing close to him.'

'She is unharmed, though she was dazed by the blast.' He looked across the glade to where Caro stood beneath the trees, locked in the arms of Richard Collinge.

'How came he here?' Aurelia said blankly.

'I made it my business to seek him out.' The dark face gazed at her fondly. 'You will recall the night that Caro met him in the Prince's stables?'

Aurelia nodded.

'I—er—accosted him as he left. I managed to convince him that he might serve both Caro and his country if he would lend me his assistance.'

'He is but a boy,' Aurelia said in wonder.

'There you are mistaken, my dearest. He is a man, and a sensible one. He was unknown to the conspirators, and could show himself where I could not. I have great hopes for him. There is an old head on those young shoulders.'

Aurelia sank back against his broad chest.

'Then you have forgiven both of them for deceiving you?'

'I can be magnanimous, my darling. I have even forgiven you for deceiving me.' His laughing face was very close to hers, but as she looked up at him she saw fresh lines of strain about his eyes.

'I confess that I was very glad to see you, my lord.'

'Well, that is something, I suppose. I must be thankful for the odd kind word.'

Aurelia sensed that his chaffing had a purpose behind it. The light, teasing words were intended to calm her and to prevent her from dwelling too much on Ransome's hideous death. She was thankful for his understanding, but panic still gripped her as she looked about the clearing. Ransome was gone, and she could not feel regret, yet there was another. A man who terrifed her far more than her wastrel of a brother-in-law.

'And Clare? Where is he? I pray to heaven that he was taken, for I shall not soon forget. . .' she looked about her fearfully.

'Clare escaped in the confusion. It is better so. The prince would not wish to have it known that one so close to him was an enemy of England. But I too shall not forget.' His face was grim.

'But. . .but if he should return. . .?'

'He will be shot on sight. He knows it. Whatever else, the man is not a fool. His greatest mistake lay in recruiting Ransome. You may be easy in your mind, my love. You will not see him again.'

Aurelia could not control her shaking limbs.

'It was so horrible,' she whispered. 'That dreadful parson! I. . .I thought he must be sure to marry us.'

'What a horror you have of parsons,' the Duke teased tenderly. 'I must hope to change your mind.' His arms tightened about her. 'The man was a dupe, Aurelia. He played no part in the smuggling. He agreed to Clare's plan for gain.'

The glade was full of men, most of them in military uniform. No one had so much as glanced in her direction, but now she noticed one or two grinning faces. Belatedly she remembered the proprieties and struggled free of the Duke's embrace.

'I must go to Cassie,' she murmured.

Salterne jumped down from the phaeton and held up his arms.

'Come,' he said. 'She is inside.' He gestured towards the hovel. 'We did not wish her to see. . .'

A wave of nausea threatened to overwhelm Aurelia as she looked towards the spot where she had last seen Ransome. The only evidence of the accident was a patch of scorched brown earth, and some darker stains where the grass looked wet and sticky.

She shuddered and averted her head. For the rest of her life she would carry with her the memory of that terrifying day.

Later she could remember nothing of the drive to Brighton. Her mind was filled with images of that dreadful scene in the clearing. She could not bring herself to think of the outcome had Salterne not arrived in time. Wearied to death, she closed her eyes.

When she opened them it was to find that the phaeton had drawn to a halt before the Duke's mansion.

'No, not here,' she demurred. 'I should like to rest. We must go back. . .'

A large hand covered her own.

'No one will trouble you, my love, and Hannah is waiting upstairs.'

Aurelia was too tired to argue further. She expressed no surprise to find her maid in the bedroom which was prepared for her. She suffered herself to be tucked between the silken sheets without a word.

It was dusk when she awoke. A candle was burning in one corner of the room, but a screen had been placed before it to shield her eyes.

For a moment she could not think where she was. Then Hannah crept over to the bed to look at her.

'Cassie? Where is Cassie?' Aurelia attempted to struggle to her feet.

'Lady Ransome is still asleep, and Miss Caro too. Now do you lie still, Miss Lia. His Grace has given orders that they are not to be disturbed.'

'His Grace does not give *me* orders,' Aurelia said with dignity.

'But, Miss Lia, he is right. You would not wish to wake them after what has happened. . . Is it not best that they should rest?'

'That may be so.' Aurelia hesitated. In her desire not to be beholden to the Duke she ran the risk of behaving foolishly, but to remain under his roof? That would never do.

'His Grace knows what is best,' Hannah said smugly.

Aurelia threw aside the coverlet, suffering a stab of pain as she was reminded of her injured wrist, now bathed and bandaged.

'I must see him,' she announced. 'We cannot stay here, and I must make arrangements. Help me with my hair, Hannah. I cannot go down to him like this. . .'

'You are not to go down at all. Your supper will be sent up here. His Grace says——'

'Hannah! The Duke has been most kind, but he does not rule me or my servants. That must be understood.'

'Then you had best tell Jacob and Matthew, ma'am.

The Duke has sent them to the Steyne to fetch your clothes.'

'They are here too? Great Heavens! I must speak to him at once. . .'

'His Grace is not at home.' Hannah's face wore a look of triumph. 'He was summoned to the Prince.'

'Then I will see the Dowager Duchess,' Aurelia said coldly.

It was clear that Hannah approved whole-heartedly of the Duke's high-handed ways, and it was time that she was disabused of such notions.

'Now, Miss Lia, don't you go flying into the boughs. His Grace means all for the best.'

'Hannah! How many times must I tell you? I will not be beholden. . .I mean. . .I am grateful, of course, and I will thank him. . .but he shall not dictate to me.'

Aurelia dressed quickly, pointedly ignoring the smile on Hannah's face.

'Where is the Duchess?' she asked.

'Waiting for you in the salon, ma'am.'

'Oh, sometimes I could slap you, Hannah! Why did you not tell me?'

'His Grace——' Hannah stopped at the expression on Aurelia's face.

'I'll wear the muslin, though it is badly crushed, but the Duchess will understand. . .'

'Very good, Miss Lia. When your other gowns arrive I'll hang them up at once.'

'Oh!' Aurelia gave a cry of exasperation and left the room.

She found the Duchess lying on a day-bed in the salon. As Aurelia entered the Dowager put her book aside.

'What a time you have had, my dear!' She held out both her hands. 'I am so sorry! Rollo was like a man possessed when Hannah came to say that you had gone.'

'Hannah?'

'Why, yes. Did she not tell you? Your man brought her to us before you had been gone five minutes. Rollo was in a rare state. He could not think why you did not ask for his help.'

'We were warned that the house was being watched,' Aurelia said simply. 'Cassie wished to tell His Grace, but I. . .I thought him gone away. . .'

'And that was the only reason?'

'We parted on the worst of terms, ma'am, as you know.' Aurelia looked down at her hands.

'My dear! A lovers' quarrel was enough to persuade you to risk your life. . .and Cassie's too?'

'I must explain. We did not know that Ransome was involved. Who could imagine that he might abduct his daughter?'

'You could scarce expect whoever took her to be other than a rogue, Aurelia.'

'You need not remind me that I have been foolish beyond belief, Your Grace, but we did not know what to do. I thought that if we followed their instructions. . .and if I offered to pay for her release. . .You see, they threatened to kill her.'

'I understand. . .but I doubt if you will convince Rollo. He thought he had lost you, Lia. I hope never to see him in such case again.'

Aurelia looked at her steadily.

'Nothing has changed, my dear ma'am. Ransome is dead, but he was yet a traitor. The stigma must always be there. I cannot marry your grandson.'

'So what are your plans, Aurelia?' The old lady had lowered her eyes, and appeared to be searching through her reticule.

'I shall go back to Marram, and take Cassie with me. I may be able to persuade her that Richard Collinge is a suitable match for Caro. . .'

'You think it likely?'

'The child has been constant in her love for him,' Aurelia said warmly. 'Not all the pleasures of Brighton, nor the beaux, have swayed her. She asks only to be his wife.'

'A laudable ambition!' The Duke's voice startled Aurelia and she blushed to the roots of her hair. He looked directly at his grandmother.

'Ma'am, may I beg your indulgence? I have much to say to Miss Carrington, and I believe you would not care to hear it.'

The Dowager's eyes snapped.

'Now, Rollo, do not get up in your high ropes, I beg of you. Miss Carrington will be no more pleased than I to be scolded and ordered about as you are used to do.'

'Indeed not, ma'am, I assure you.' The light of battle was in Aurelia's eye.

The Duke strode over to the door and opened it.

'You will grant me a word in private, if you please. Or do you stay here in the hope that my grandmother will protect you?'

The taunt was enough to bring Aurelia to her feet. With her head held high she swept past him and into the hall.

'In here.' He thrust her before him into the library and closed the door. With folded arms he leaned against it and regarded her with a steely gaze.

'You will please to give me an explanation of your folly,' he said without preamble.

Aurelia's anger rose to match his own.

'I beg your pardon, My Lord Duke,' she said crisply. 'You shall not take that tone with me.'

Even as she spoke she could understand the reason for the change in his manner towards her. The tenderness which had been so apparent when he'd first come to her rescue had given way to rage. She had known the same reaction herself when danger threatened Caro. A first surge of relief to know that the girl was safe had led at once to a need to vent her feelings in a furious outburst.

'I am under an obligation to you,' she went on more calmly. 'And I am more grateful than I can well express. I owe you my life, but I will not brook your ordering of it.'

'Indeed!' The grey eyes snapped. 'Please to go on, Miss Carrington. I'm sure that you have much more to say.'

She threw him a smouldering look.

'You have removed my staff to your home without my permission, and now you see fit to question my actions. You have ordered my maid to follow your instructions and. . .and you have even dispatched my men to fetch my. . .my. . . .'

'Baggage!' he supplied helpfully.

He was not referring to her trunks, as she well knew, but she ignored the gleam of amusement in his eyes.

'Perhaps I do owe you an explanation,' she continued. 'We had no choice but to follow Caroline.'

'It did not occur to you to seek my help?'

'I believed you to be away,' she said stiffly. 'And then. . .I thought. . .'

'You could not imagine that I might refuse? Oh, Lia! How little faith you have in me!'

'It was not exactly that,' she said in some confusion. 'The message was worded in such a way that we. . . I. . .felt we must go alone.'

'I read it.' His eyes never left her face. 'Hannah brought it to me. You dropped it in your haste.'

'So that was how you knew where to find us?' Her eyes fell before his. 'Cassie wished to send for you, you must know, but I would not hear of it.'

'Headstrong and wilful as always,' he observed. 'I am to understand that you receive a message which threatens murder and you plan to handle the matter yourself?'

'I. . .You gave me a pistol.'

'And much good it did you. I have always thought you sensible, my dear, but on this occasion your sister showed more judgement.'

Aurelia sat before him like a recalcitrant schoolgirl, gazing at her hands.

'Cassie suspected that Ransome was involved,' she said wretchedly. 'I would not hear of it. I. . .I could not believe that he would threaten to murder his own daughter.'

'Did you not assure me that he was capable of anything?'

'Anything but that! I. . .I thought it must be someone who saw the chance of gain. I believed myself to be the target.'

'And so you were, but to offer yourself as the sacrificial lamb. . .!'

'What else could I do? I. . .you. . .' Aurelia was on the verge of tears.

He came to her then and took her in his arms.

'I am out of reason ill-humoured, my dearest love, but I thought that I had lost you. You cannot know the torture of that journey. . . We mistook the way when we left the Lewes road, but thank God we were in time.'

'We?'

'The Prince called out the militia. Clare and Ransome had been seen twice on the previous night, but they escaped the net. It was when I read the note that we were certain of their whereabouts.'

'But how did you know that the message came from Clare and Ransome?'

'It was obvious.' Salterne's expression was grim. 'It could scarce be coincidence that the bait was offered so quickly.'

'And I took it like a gudgeon!'

'A beautiful gudgeon, my love.' He kissed the nape of her neck.

'Ah! Do not. . .I have not changed my mind, Your Grace.'

'Then I must try to change it for you.' He kissed each eyelid tenderly, and sought to find her lips.

Aurelia averted her head.

'I cannot forgive myself,' she said in a low voice. 'You have made it all too clear that I was the victim of my own failings. I have been obstinate and over-sure that I was right.'

'A sad character indeed! But I do not despair of you. In time you may learn to mend your ways.' The grey eyes were dancing.

'It is not kind in you to mock,' she cried indignantly.

'The thought did not enter my head. Though when one is perfect, as I am myself, it is hard to understand the vagaries of others.'

A gurgle of laughter escaped Aurelia's lips, but the Duke frowned in mock-reproof.

'It is not at all flattering to think that my claim to all the virtues is greeted with such merriment.' He shook her gently. 'Let us be done with the sackcloth and ashes, Lia. It is not in your style.'

He cupped a hand beneath her chin, and as his lips found hers she was swept away into a dizzying vortex. Her head was spinning when he released her.

'Darling, maddening Lia! How I fought against my love for you. You were the threat to all our plans. Had Ransome guessed. . .'

'He accused me of—er—attempting to attach your interest.' Aurelia coloured and rested her burning cheek against his coat.

'He was cleverer than I. You were always so cool and distant in my company. . .'

'Not always, my lord.' Her blush deepened.

'That's true!' His eyes were filled with private laughter. 'I might have ruined all that night at Lady Bellingham's, when my resolution failed me. I had vowed to wait until I might approach you with propriety, but I was sorely tried. . .I longed to hold you in my arms, and when you stumbled I was lost.'

'The night conspired against us,' Aurelia said in a dreamy tone.

'Thank heavens it did! I had welcomed our growing friendship, and hoped that you were losing your contempt for me. . .'

'Never that!' she said softly. 'I found you arrogant, and I could not understand your wish to marry

Caroline, but I soon discovered that I was mistaken in my judgement of your character.'

'How well you concealed your change of heart! I suffered a number of sharp set-downs, my love, and lost much ground when you found me in conversation with Harriet Wilson.'

'I was jealous.' Aurelia hung her head. 'That was when I first discovered. . .well. . .it is no matter. I was not kind to you.'

'A masterpiece of understatement,' he said drily.

'I wished to discourage your. . .your unseemly behaviour, sir. Not only were you a shocking tease, but you appeared to lose no opportunity to—er——'

'Behave like a man in love?'

'I did not know that at the time. I found you over-familiar in your manner.'

'But you are irresistible, my enchantress. . .and a challenge to any man.'

'My lord, I wish you will not say such things. They are quite untrue.'

'Are they, my dearest?' His eyes grew serious as he cupped her face in his hands and forced her to look at him. 'I cannot think so.' He bent his head to hers as if to kiss her again.

'Papa, are you pretending to be the prince?'

Blue eyes and grey stared at Charlotte in confusion as she stood before them clutching a battered doll.

Salterne sighed.

'Which prince is that, my puss?'

'I mean the one who wakened the princess with a kiss.'

'Er. . .something like that.'

To Aurelia's amusement the Duke looked almost shy in the face of Charlotte's interested expression.

'Did it work?'

'You must ask Miss Carrington.' A slight flush darkened his tanned skin.

Aurelia gave him a reproachful look. It was unfair of him to enlist the services of the child she loved so much in an effort to overcome her scruples.

'Did it waken you, Aunt Lia?' Charlotte scrambled on to her lap. 'Grandmama said that I must be very quiet this morning because you were asleep.'

'Well, now, as you see, I am awake.'

'It works! It works!' Charlotte slid to the ground and began to dance about the room. 'Papa always said it did, though Grandmama and I did not believe him.'

Salterne grasped his daughter firmly by the shoulders.

'You will find your great-grandmama in the salon,' he announced. 'I believe she wishes to speak to you.'

'Oh, yes. Now I shall be able to tell her. . .' Charlotte assumed an expression of great importance as she ran towards the door. Then she stopped.

'And you will marry the prince, Aunt Lia, won't you?'

'Shoo! Away with you.' Salterne flapped his hands at her.

'Oh, dear, I hope that she does not. . .' Aurelia felt acutely uncomfortable.

The Duke reached out and drew her close. Her heart began to pound as she was enclosed once more in that dear and familiar embrace.

'Aurelia, you are the most chivalrous and the most generous person I know. You are also the most honest. I will ask you again. Do you love me?'

'I love you so much that I cannot agree to harm you. We spoke once of friendship. Will not that serve?'

'Like this, you mean? And this?' He pressed his lips against the inside of her arm, and then into the hollow of her neck.

A delicious warmth began to pervade her body. Instinctively she began to stroke his dark head as she murmured inarticulate endearments. It was only when he raised his eyes and gave her a quizzical look that she answered him.

'You know I have no thought of marriage,' she protested faintly. It was a last despairing effort to withstand him.

The Duke's shoulders began to shake.

'You shock me deeply, Lia. Only consider the scandal!'

'Oh, how can you? You know that I did not mean what. . .what you are suggesting.'

'I am suggesting that you become my wife. Had you not best consider it? Your judgement is at fault again, I fear.'

'I suppose it is,' she agreed breathlessly.

A lingering kiss destroyed the last vestiges of her resistance. Dizzy with joy, she clung to him. Then he looked into her eyes.

'We are no strangers to affection, you and I. We have both loved before, but you, my darling. . .You are my last enchantment.'

And after that there was no need for words.

"All it takes is one letter to trigger a romance"

Sealed with a Kiss—don't miss this exciting new mini-series every month.

All the stories involve a relationship which develops as a result of a letter being written—we know you'll love these new heart-warming romances.

And to make them easier to identify, all the covers in this series are a passionate pink!

Available now   **Price: £1.99**

MILLS & BOON

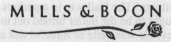

LEGACY *of* LOVE

Coming next month

A DANGEROUS UNDERTAKING
Mary Nichols
East Anglia 1746/47

Hoping to live with her great-uncle Henry Capitain, Margaret Donnington found him a reprobate and took refuge at Winterford Manor. It seemed Roland, Lord Pargeter, was in need of a wife, and he offered Margaret a marriage of convenience for one year. She thought she had strayed into a madhouse but, with little money and no chance of a job, she had to accept.

Only after the marriage did Margaret learn of the family curse, and how dangerous it would be for her...

DEAR LADY DISDAIN
Paula Marshall
London/York 1818

Running Blanchard's Bank after her father's death was fulfilling for Anastasia but, even so, she felt there was something missing from her life. Problems with the branch in York decided Stacy. She would go herself. But the November weather turned severe and, with her retinue, she sought refuge at Pontisford Hall.

It was a nightmare! The Hall was in a parlous state, and the man she thought to be the butler turned out to be Matthew, Lord Radley. He was quite as forceful and autocratic as herself, and the sparks that flew during their enforced stay had repercussions that quite appalled her...

LEGACY*of*LOVE

Coming next month

MY LORD BEAUMONT
Madris Dupree
Carolina 1742

Danielle Cooper had no prospects and no hope, until she
escaped from London's gutters and stowed away on a boat to
the Carolinas, dressed as a boy. Discovery brought Lord
Adrian Beaumont to the rescue, who bought 'him' as his
indentured servant for five years—until, in the privacy of his
cabin, Adrian uncovered Danny's disguise…

THE CYGNET
Marianne Willman
England, late 1500s

Dark-visaged and demanding, Giles, Lord of Rathborne,
faced being sent to the Tower. The only one who could save
him from ruin was a young girl of ethereal beauty who called
herself Vera, claiming she had no other name.

Vera knew only that Giles already had her heart, for the lord
of the manor had awakened in her a passion to rival any of
the intrigue to be found at Elizabeth's glittering court.
Revealing her real identity could wreck everything…